THE FALL
OF EDEN

THE FALL OF EDEN

RICHARD MICHAELS

BERKLEY BOOKS, NEW YORK

THE BERKLEY PUBLISHING GROUP
Published by the Penguin Group
Penguin Group (USA) Inc.
375 Hudson Street, New York, New York 10014, USA
Penguin Group (Canada), 90 Eglinton Avenue East, Suite 700, Toronto, Ontario M4P 2Y3, Canada
(a division of Pearson Penguin Canada Inc.)
Penguin Books Ltd., 80 Strand, London WC2R 0RL, England
Penguin Group Ireland, 25 St. Stephen's Green, Dublin 2, Ireland (a division of Penguin Books Ltd.)
Penguin Group (Australia), 250 Camberwell Road, Camberwell, Victoria 3124, Australia
(a division of Pearson Australia Group Pty. Ltd.)
Penguin Books India Pvt. Ltd., 11 Community Centre, Panchsheel Park, New Delhi—110 017, India
Penguin Group (NZ), 67 Apollo Drive, Rosedale, North Shore 0632, New Zealand
(a division of Pearson New Zealand Ltd.)
Penguin Books (South Africa) (Pty.) Ltd., 24 Sturdee Avenue, Rosebank, Johannesburg 2196,
South Africa

Penguin Books Ltd., Registered Offices: 80 Strand, London WC2R 0RL, England

This book is an original publication of The Berkley Publishing Group.

This is a work of fiction. Names, characters, places, and incidents either are the product of the author's imagination or are used fictitiously, and any resemblance to actual persons, living or dead, business establishments, events, or locales is entirely coincidental. The publisher does not have any control over and does not assume any responsibility for author or third-party websites or their content.

PRINTING HISTORY
Berkley trade paperback edition / November 2009

Library of Congress Cataloging-in-Publication Data

Michaels, Richard, 1965–
    The fall of Eden / Richard Michaels.—Berkley trade paperback ed.
        p. cm.
    ISBN 978-0-425-22994-1
    1. Family vacations—Fiction.   2. Caribbean Area—Fiction.   3. Terrorism—United
States—Fiction.   I. Title.
    PS3570.E447F35 2009
    813'.6—dc22

                                                                    2009029835

PRINTED IN THE UNITED STATES OF AMERICA

10   9   8   7   6   5   4   3   2   1

ACKNOWLEDGMENTS

The author would like to thank Mr. Michael Ovitz, Mr. Richard Prince, Mr. Chris George, Mr. Tom Colgan, and Mr. Eric Main for their significant contributions to the conception of this manuscript. Without their vision, this book would not have been possible.

In addition, the author must thank Mr. James Ide of The Villages, Florida, who labored over every page and whose own contributions to the writing of this book were significant and invaluable.

Nancy, Lauren, and Kendall Telep provided the motivation and encouragement to forge on despite the challenges of the research and sometimes grim subject matter.

Finally, the author would like to thank the management and staff of the Eden Rock Hotel for their kind assistance and public relations documents detailing their remarkable accommodations and services.

The royal throne of kings, this scepter'd isle,
This earth of majesty, this seat of Mars,
This other Eden, demi-paradise,
This fortress built by Nature for herself
Against infection and the hand of war;
This happy breed of men, this little world,
This precious stone set in the silver sea.

—William Shakespeare, *King Richard II*, Act 2 Scene 1

ONE

ST. BARTHÉLEMY emerged from the Caribbean Sea where those turquoise waters met the darker waves of the western Atlantic Ocean. As I stared out the port-side window of the Twin Otter, I wondered how many planes had crashed and sank to the bottom of that sea, their smooth metal fuselages joining the ancient timbers of French galleons whose cannons shone up from the bottom like the eyes of giant squids. My thoughts were morbid, decidedly so. My father was dying, but he had chosen at eighty-one to lose his mind first, professing that he would join his old friend Luc Vacher down in St. Barts to hunt modern-day pirates. My brother Dan and I were headed to the island to bring the old man home, before he hurt himself or others. Originally, Dan and I had planned to go together, leaving his fiancée and my wife and children back home, but it had been Dan who had convinced me to take everyone along. That I had protested his change of heart still haunts me to this day.

We continued our descent toward the island, an eight-square-mile piece of *fei-ts'ui* jade in the open bracelet of the Lesser Antilles. Part of me did, in fact, acknowledge the island's beauty, but there was no shuddering off the deep sense of dread that left me cold for most of the ride from St. Martin. You could not fly directly into St. Barts; you had to land at Juliana Airport on the much larger island of St. Martin and catch a ride on a sea shuttle (a foil-assisted catamaran) or fly over in a smaller plane like the Twin Otter to reach the Aéroport de St. Jean and its precarious airstrip that required special training for pilots. Thus, with lumps in our throats we had taken off, the morning crisp and clear, with excellent visibility and with Christmas looming just four days ahead.

Vanessa had gone to Chamberlin's and bought some all-natural hair dye before the trip, and I missed the gray more than I thought I would. Admittedly, I was worried that college-aged men like my students would begin referring to her as a MILF, an acronym that I had only recently discovered on Google, one that made me cringe. She'd just turned fifty like me, but she was having a much harder time accepting it, in part because her business was holistic healing, essential oils, and other natural health care products designed to make her clients look and feel younger. Men grow regal; women grow old, so they say, but I told her *they* are shallow dolts, and *they* would never see the beauty in those ornate brushstrokes of silver that shimmered above her dark blue eyes. She said only an out-of-touch English professor would call someone a "shallow dolt" when "asshole" would suffice. Point taken.

I glanced back at Chloe, who, despite being a lovely and polite nineteen-year-old with only her ears pierced, spent more time commiserating with her portable electronic devices than she did actually talking in person to real human beings. She argued, of course, that human beings were on the other end of those communications, but that was of no consequence to me. A few days ago, after she'd returned home from her very first semester at the University of South Florida, I posed as a Republican and violated her privacy. I got into her laptop, read a few of her emails, thinking this might be the only way I'd ever know my daughter. Be careful what you wish for. I learned Chloe was more frightened than I could ever have imagined. Her world was a cruel and merciless place, not the Long Island of my youth, a world so dark and deep that the pressure threatened to crush her every waking moment. She didn't know who she was or how she fit in. We all felt that. But her closest colleagues deeply troubled me. One was a cutter who bled to feel anything, and the other had twice tried to commit suicide after she'd been raped by her stepfather. They wrote of these traumas with the remarkable candor of memoirists praying to be selected for Oprah's Book Club. They were young and self-destructive and these were my daughter's peers, hallelujah.

Chloe looked up at me, removed one of her earbuds, and said, "What?"

"Look down there," I said, raising my voice against the plane engine's reverberating drone. "You can see it now."

She rolled her eyes and returned to her iPod.

I pursed my lips and shifted my gaze to James. His forehead rested on the window as he stared transfixed at the boomerang-shaped island and the clay-colored tin roofs of "case" houses puzzled into the lush green mountains. The roofs, I had read, were designed with elaborate gutter systems to collect rainwater, a precious commodity on a piece of rock with few natural resources beyond iguanas, chic shops, and nightclubs.

Of all of us, James was arguably the most excited. He'd been saving his money for years to backpack across Europe once he graduated from Columbia in the spring, so any chance to travel abroad left the poor boy shaking with anticipation. He raked fingers through his sandy blond hair and caught me staring.

"You see the size of that runway?" he asked, pointing down to the narrow strip positioned just northwest of our hotel.

"I see it." I lifted my chin toward the pilot and copilot speaking in French into their headsets. "Think they can do it?"

He wriggled his brows. "We'll find out."

James had inherited a sense of risk taking from Vanessa that repeatedly left me in awe. He didn't just go out for crew at Columbia; he made captain of the team. He didn't just apply to law schools; he applied to Harvard and was accepted. He had an amazing future ahead of him. Remarkable. He was not his father's child.

Ten others had boarded with us: honeymooners, retired folks, and a trio of heavily tattooed young men no older than James who were heading down to party. Vanessa had tried to convince me that we should make the best of it and turn the outing into a family vacation while still dealing with Dad. The trouble was, I hadn't seen my father in the last few years, and although I spoke to my brother once or twice a month, we'd never been very close. I didn't fit the Spencer mold, Dad used to say. Cub Scouts, Boy Scouts, United States Marine Corps, hooah! Men should be men. Work out, juice up, arm wrestle, get into bar fights, sleep with as many women as possible, and never, ever, let down your guard. Might makes right. There is no problem that cannot be solved with a sufficient supply of explosives. Become a sniper. Take aim. Hold your breath. Wait for it. Understand the forces of wind and gravity. Understand the bullet drop. Kill people without remorse. It is your job.

I'd made it as far as the Boy Scouts before I lost myself in books and realized that I didn't need a mask of power to prove I was worth something. My father, the retired Marine Corps lieutenant colonel beloved by all his devil dogs, had been devastated. He'd left the service to become a successful civil engineer in Pennsylvania and had been forced to turn over the firm to his younger son, not the older one—and there was something sacrilegious about that. He'd told me I'd been a fool for going into the liberal arts, into education. I should have gone to Drexel, majored in engineering, and taken command of the company, with my younger brother at my side. Although Dad never said it, it was clear he had no respect for me or the choices I'd made in my life. Now he had an inoperable primary tumor in his occipital lobe. The tumor had already blinded him in his left eye—an omen of the inevitable seizures to follow. I'd asked Dan if the tumor had mellowed him; on the contrary, Dad had become even more ill-tempered and stubborn.

As the pilots banked hard and came around to align us with the airstrip, my thoughts returned to those sunken galleons. I floated down into the shadows and was consumed by the murky depths where I was free of all stress. Vanessa nudged me and said, "Can you hold my hand?"

We took deep breaths and stared down at the sloops, catboats, ketches, schooners, and catamarans, along with the colossal yachts, and a trio of cruise ships anchored near Gustavia, the island's capital, with houses clambering over hillsides overlooking the rectangular harbor. I'd seen the photographs and been told that St. Barts was the home of the "glitterati," and that reality finally hit home. I spotted one yacht that had a helipad on its aft deck, like something out of a James Bond movie. On another yacht a half dozen bikini models were doing a photo shoot. It was Oz for the terribly rich and pretentious, a secret land where underpaid educators faced the reality of their career decisions. I wanted to do what I love, teaching, and make what they made without screwing people over. My anger is almost humorous now. Almost.

A throng of tourists had positioned themselves along the mountain road running perpendicular to the airstrip. From there they would watch and take pictures of aircraft that came within fifteen feet of their heads. I was shocked at our proximity to them as Vanessa squeezed my hand and the wheels finally touched ground with an appreciable thud.

"That was awesome," grunted James. "Awesome."

I turned back to Chloe, who managed to glance up from her screen and actually take in her surroundings. Her expression said, *Big deal.* I sighed.

Chatter rose in the cockpit, and my French was poor, which was to say nonexistent, but James frowned and looked at me. "There's something going on."

"What?"

"I didn't catch it all. Some kind of communication problem with the cell phone towers, maybe."

"Well, I'm sure they'll fix it. God forbid these millionaires can't call their lawyers and traders."

We taxied toward a row of single-story buildings (there was no gate), where I spotted Dan and his fiancée Hannah waiting for us. Dan hadn't changed a bit: salt-and-pepper crew cut and permanent scowl etched on his face, the antithesis of my unkempt long hair and paunch. He was the action figure Dad wanted him to be. Hannah, whom I had never met, could've been one of my students. She was achingly young, no more than twenty-five or -six, while Dan was about to turn forty-eight. The marriage proposal, I knew, was a charade to keep her on the leash. Fast talk, fast cars, and a big house bought Dan women like Hannah, blond receptionists with community college degrees who worked to support their shopping and salon addictions while spending nights online searching the ads of computer dating services. They were, in a word, vacuous, but Dan had a penchant for sweet smiles and boob jobs, and in Hannah, he'd found both.

"You see Uncle Dan's fiancée?" asked James.

"Don't stare," warned Vanessa.

"Something's definitely wrong with them," said Chloe. "She looks like she's going to cry."

"I'm sure your uncle hurt her feelings," I said.

The copilot stood and worked the door with attached stairs, lowering it carefully until the support lines pulled taut. We stood and slowly deplaned while attendants outside pulled their carts around to unload our luggage.

I issued a halfhearted wave to Dan, who trotted over, his eyes widening as he left his fiancée standing there, as though at the altar. "Charles!" he cried, his tone curiously urgent.

The other folks who'd been waiting for their friends to deplane were working their cell phones, some shaking their heads. One older woman knuckled a tear from her eye.

"What's going on?" I asked Dan. "And why'd you leave her standing there?"

"We have to get your stuff, get a car, and get right back to the hotel."

"Uncle Danny, what's wrong?" asked James.

Dan pulled me aside and lowered his voice. "There's been a missile attack on the U.S. Everything's gone down back home."

"Bad joke."

"I'm not kidding. I don't want Vanessa and the kids to freak out."

"Yeah, right? You think this is funny? Come on, man, I'm not in the mood. It's taken us forever to get here."

"Look at me, Charles."

I did. "Jesus . . ."

"Just calm down."

"Hey, everyone, come here." I turned back to the others and repeated what Dan had told me. They deserved to know immediately. Dan, of course, in his infinite alpha-male wisdom, assumed they were too weak to handle it, but I knew my family.

"Oh my God," Vanessa gasped.

"It's worse," Dan added. "They say Europe might be involved. So far there's no one talking in the northern hemisphere."

James started cursing, and I raised my voice. "All right, everybody, calm down. We don't know anything for sure. Let's go get our bags and our car. Then we'll see what's going on."

"If the nukes flew, the EMP wave would've wiped out all electronics," James said. "But I guess it didn't reach us down here."

"What are you talking about, idiot? No one's stupid enough to launch nukes," said Chloe. "Probably some terrorist stuff or some accident or hoax."

"Or aliens," James said, smirking at her.

"Hi, everyone. I'm Hannah."

We hadn't realized she'd walked up, and we all looked at her in a moment as awkward as asking after a person who's died. She frowned, her improbable cleavage glistening in the sun. I winced and said, "Nice to meet you, Hannah."

She forced a smile, and we walked back toward the car rental building.

Though painful to admit, I thought if something terrible had happened like a terrorist attack, my father and I would be distracted enough not to focus so closely on the fault line between us. I welcomed the diversion, and as ridiculous and illogical as it sounds, feared my father more than nuclear holocaust.

However, in the days that followed, my feelings on the matter would be placed into extraordinary perspective as we began living at the mercy of the wind.

TWO

"I'M Charles Spencer. We should have a reservation," I told the agent at Turbe Car Rental after we'd cleared customs and immigration. Dan had arrived the day before us and had already rented a Jeep Wrangler; we picked up a Suzuki Jimmy. The small four-wheel-drive affair whined in protest as we pulled away from the lot and rode up to the Eden Rock Hotel, following Dan, who sped across the narrow, winding road.

The hotel was built on a rocky promontory rising into the northeast trade wind. Pristine beaches and the wandering dark shadows of coral lay in the sapphire-colored waters of St. Jean Bay, also home to three small islets standing like sentinels out there, the largest to the west, the others descending to the east. Much farther to the northwest rose the camel back of an even larger islet, and beside it a smaller one seemed to be on its knees paying homage to its larger brother. Several yachts were already motoring out of the bay, but oddly, a host of sunbathers were lying on blankets or teak loungers or strolling along at the water's edge, seemingly oblivious to current events. In fact, the entire land-scape suggested anything but world war. A uniformed attendant even carried drinks out to one couple. Perhaps they hadn't heard or didn't believe it was possible or were determined not to have their vacations ruined by the inconvenience of a catastrophe.

My brother had emailed me the hotel press kit, and I'd read that Eden Rock had evolved from a private house built by Rémey de Haenen, an eccentric Dutch adventurer and aviator who had named the place and who was the first mayor of the island. He had once fired his pistol in town hall to reestablish order when a town council meeting got out of hand. Greta Garbo, Howard Hughes, Robert Mitchum, and dozens more American and Euro-pean celebrities were close friends, and his thirst for adventure inspired the architecture of those early buildings.

Decades later the hotel had grown into beach houses, diamond suites, premium suites, cottages, and six-star villas as large as six-teen thousand square feet. I was not surprised that our father and his French buddy had chosen the place. They both had money, time, and taste in spades, and Eden Rock did not disappoint. Dad had booked himself in the Howard Hughes Loft Suite, one of the diamond suites situated above the main building atop the rock.

When we arrived, Dan told the valets to leave his Jeep idling at the entrance. I asked why, but he ignored me. We all headed up to see my father and his friend. Dan assumed that our father had not heard anything and wanted to tell him. I wanted the kids to say hello to their grandfather, yet I dreaded that awkward moment when we both faced each other like old enemies with derringers on a cool morning in an open field.

My legs felt heavy as we climbed the stairs and reached the suite. A trio of sun terraces offered a panoramic view of the bay with pelicans wheeling overhead. Hardwood floors swept out across the main bedroom with its contemporary furnishings. Vanessa and James gasped over the utterly chic accommodations, while Chloe shrugged and repeatedly speed-dialed her friends back home to no avail.

Dad had parked his six-foot, four-inch frame on a lounger facing the bay, his sagging chest and gut covered in gray hair, his head shaven, with rivulets of sweat already forming around his temples. He wore a pair of Ray-Ban aviator-style sunglasses and lifted a cigar to his lips. Most people did not believe he was eighty-one. Sixty-five maybe, but never that old. He'd lost at least twenty pounds since the last time we'd spoken in person, and I wasn't sure if the tumor or some new diet was to blame.

Beside him on another lounger sat Luc Vacher, a lean French-man with a shock of gray hair and broken capillaries on his nose and cheeks from a lifetime on the wind-blown sea. Vacher was a kid at seventy-four and a retired major (equal to a U.S. sergeant major) from the *Escouade de contre-terrorisme et de libération d'otages* or ECTLO—France's maritime counterterrorist and hostage res-cue squad. Vacher's bony frame barely tented up a floral print shirt complemented by a puka-shell necklace he had probably picked up on one of his adventures to Hawaii or the Philippines. Seem-ingly glued to his head were a pair of those oversized, wraparound sunglasses that made old people resemble aliens in science fiction films. He was just lowering his own cigar when we approached.

"James, Chloe, say hello to your grandfather and give him a kiss," I said.

James ambled up and thrust out his hand. "Hey, Grandpa."

"Well, well, well, Jimmy boy, nice to see you," my father cried. He groaned, sat up, and accepted James's hand. "I'd like to see you cut that hair."

My son looked at me and grinned.

"Hi, Grandpa," Chloe said. Though her tone betrayed the act as a chore, she managed to lean over and plant one on my father's cheek.

Vanessa kissed my father as well, then shook hands with Vacher, whom we'd known for over twenty years. My parents had met Vacher and his wife on an Alaskan cruise and they became fast friends, traveling a lot together. When Mom died, Vacher spoke at the funeral. When Vacher's wife died, Dad did likewise. They say women outlive their husbands, but Dad and Vacher had beat the odds, although you could tell that when they spoke of their spouses they would have rather gone first. Both women had been fiercely loyal to them, if not independent themselves. They'd come from another generation, some said the greatest generation. At least my mother had been exceedingly happy as a military wife. She'd always told me she'd known from the get-go what she'd signed on for, and she loved being Dad's wife. She was proud of him, of the life they'd made together. I certainly respected and admired her for putting up with Dad's battering ram of a temper and suffocating ego for all those years.

I caught my father's gaze for a moment, waiting for him to say hello, but he averted his eyes, faced the bay, and said, "How's it going, Charles? Must be nice to take a break from all those faggots, dykes, and liberal commie pinkos you work with, huh? Come down here to visit your old man. Good boy."

Every muscle in my body hardened like stainless steel. I opened my mouth, flicked a glance to Vanessa, who hoisted her brows, then I glanced down and sighed. Attacking my job and embarrassing me in front of my wife and children was just the beginning, the bowl of Wheaties that Dad ate to start his day.

Thankfully, my brother hunkered down next to Dad and began speaking quickly in his ear.

"Is something wrong?" Vacher asked, his English excellent but still hinting of a French accent.

I shifted over and told him what we knew. He rattled off something in French that might have been a string of epithets.

My father scratched at the gray stubble on his chin, then leaned over to his friend and said, "I didn't think we'd live long enough to see this day—if it's true."

Vacher nodded. "Let's put on the TV. Maybe they know something."

My brother lifted his voice. "All right, Dad, you and Luc just lay low. And I want the rest of you to stay here, too. Don't even worry about checking in yet, Charles. I need you to come with me."

"Where are we going?"

"Come on, I'll tell you on the way."

"Dad?"

"James, take it easy, all right?"

My son made a face. I turned and hurried after Dan, who bolted down to his waiting Jeep as though he were being chased by thugs. I was barely in my seat and wholly out of breath when he roared out of the parking lot.

"Jesus Christ," I gasped.

"This is it, Charles. I'm telling you. This is it!"

"Where we going? What're you talking about?"

"You'll see."

"Dan, slow down, man! Slow down." We raced along a two-lane road that began running west and parallel to the landing strip, with densely forested hillsides to the south.

"Charles, some people will be ready for this. Most won't."

"Ready for what? We don't even know what really happened."

He downshifted and barreled into the oncoming traffic lane

to pass a Mini Moke in front of us, the obese bald guy at the wheel and his female passenger taking in the view from the open-air, golf-cart-like contraption.

The fat man waved a fist at us, and Dan flipped him the bird.

I shook my head. "What're you doing? I'm telling you to slow down."

"Charles, I know you don't believe in God, being a nerd and all, but I do. I believe Jesus Christ almighty has already decided who lives and who dies. And he wouldn't have put us on this island at this time, on this day, if he wasn't sure about us. I mean about us helping ourselves."

My eyes were beginning to tear from the wind, and I gripped the roll bars even tighter. "You're going to kill us before we help ourselves."

We eventually reached a traffic circle where our road met four others. Dan cut the wheel hard, and we nearly caromed off the rocky curb as we reached the southernmost exit, where stood the statue of a young Arawak with a spear in one hand, a conch to his lips, and an iguana at his ankle as he blew the conch to warn his tribe. I stared long and hard at the statue as we rumbled away, heading toward Gustavia.

"Dan, do you know something I don't? One of your military buddies give you a call or something?"

"My military buddies are dead. So are all your friends. Everyone back at school? All dead. Or about to die. Real soon . . . Everyone you ever knew, except us."

"You don't know that. You don't know anything."

"How many lives would be saved if people reacted from a worst-case scenario instead of living in denial, waiting for the official report, which always comes in too late. You think your government is going to tell you what really happened?"

"I don't know what to think. At least I'm acting rationally. Where the hell are we going?"

"You'll see."

And I did. Within five minutes Gustavia harbor appeared directly ahead, many of the big yachts forming a line out of the harbor.

"See that? They're already evacuating."

"To where?"

"St. Thomas. Nearest American military bases. Those yacht captains want to know what's going on."

"Why don't they just ask you?"

"Don't be a wiseass, Charles. And don't think we've got time to sit around at a committee table and debate this like you do up in Rochester."

"Debate what?"

"Survival, man."

I bit my lip. I had no idea what my brother was about to do, and I had no idea that later on I would, with burning eyes, deeply respect him for it.

We reached the harbor and sped along a road adjacent to the docks. Suddenly, Dan pulled over and hopped out. "That's Vacher's yacht right there," he hollered.

Vacher was the proud owner of a three-cabin version of the Jeanneau Prestige 50 S motor yacht, with a top speed of twenty-eight knots, cruising speed of twenty-two. The boat ran dual Volvo 575-horsepower engines and was fifty feet of pure luxury. This was the platform from which those crazy old men had intended to thwart the drug and gun runners and other assorted pirates. At the time I knew little about yachts and only later would I fully appreciate the craft and its million-and-a-half-dollar price tag. No, Vacher had not acquired such a toy on his military salary.

After retirement, he'd become a "consultant," where he'd made his real money.

I followed Dan across the dock and up onto the aft deck, which housed a garage containing a Zodiac. Three quick steps up put us on the spacious deck saloon. Dan fished around in his pocket and produced a set of keys, gaining us entry past a hatch beside the cockpit. He eased down some ornate wooden steps and into the main saloon, a nest of reflective wood, supple leather cushions, and a double-sink galley.

"All right, Frenchy, where'd you hide 'em?" Dan asked aloud.

"What are we looking for?"

"Jesus, Charles, are you a complete idiot?"

Dan stormed over to a curving row of seat cushions and tore them away like a burglar rifling through someone's drawers. Beneath the cushions were a series of locked compartments, and Dan immediately fingered through the key ring, found one, opened the lock, then raised the door.

"Bingo."

"Aw, no," I said as he withdrew a pistol (single-action, French made, I would later learn). "You're kidding me."

Dan removed the pistol's magazine, checked it, then reinserted and retracted the slide, chambering the first round. He tossed the gun to me, and I nearly dropped it.

As I stood there, beginning to tremble with this piece of deadly metal in my hands, he slapped palms on my shoulders and said, "Charles, listen to me very carefully. Vacher's got this boat armed for bear—pistols, shotguns, rifles, the whole nine. We're bringing it all back to the hotel."

"We're stealing his guns? Why do we need them? Why don't we just ask him? And why does he have all this stuff in the first place?"

"He's ex-military. Like he needs an excuse? Besides, he was serious about hunting pirates or drug runners or whatever. He bragged about all this ordnance last night over dinner, like God wanted me to hear that, so now I know what to do."

"No, we can't do this. I won't. The old man might get pissed and press charges."

"Press charges? Get with the program, big brother. It's the end of the world."

"What evidence do you have to support that assertion? Fragmented reports from South America?"

"Get off your high horse. What do you want to do—wait around and find out? You know if you would've joined the Corps we wouldn't be having this conversation. You wouldn't be throwing that mumbo jumbo at me."

"But I didn't join the Marine Corps. I joined the club of rational thinkers."

He grinned sarcastically. "You mean all those dead guys up in New York?" He held up another pistol. "You think I'm jumping the gun here?"

"Oh, that's funny. This is really the time to joke around."

My brother closed his eyes, took a deep breath, then suddenly seized me by the throat. "Just do what I say. I'm going to keep us all alive. This place is going to go nuts, and when it does, the people with the guns will control what's left. We might wind up stuck on this rock, and if that happens, we'll be in control, not someone else. Do you read me, Charles?"

I tried to nod. I'd never seen my brother like this; for a few seconds, I wondered if he might kill me.

But then his grip went slack, and I rubbed my sore neck. I tossed the gun onto one of the seat cushions and headed toward the steps.

"Charles, where you going? I need your help."

"I'm not subscribing to this. Not any of it."

I headed up onto the deck and started for the dock, where a group of people, about six in all, thundered down the planks, screaming and crying. They leapt onto a nearby yacht and rushed around, preparing to launch.

I was rapt just watching, listening, feeling the vibration of their motors work its way up into the fiberglass of Vacher's boat. Several more boats were pulling out, creating large wakes and damning harbor rules to hell.

Across the road, a small sedan raced at high speed, tires squealing as it took a corner. I swallowed. The ocean's tang was on my lips now. Yes, it was hard to comprehend events of the outside world while in a place as remote and unscathed as the island. I wondered if the birds, the other animals, sensed anything. I searched the sky for some portents. Nothing. Picturesque. Yet out in the harbor, the scene was chaos as two yachts, vying for the next position in line, collided with each other, their crews hollering.

Dan arrived behind me. "Charles. I found the rest of the guns. We can't waste any more time."

I faced him and began to choke up. "You really think they did it. You really do."

He hesitated. "I'm sorry, Charles. But yeah, I do."

"What about Vanessa? My kids? What now? Chloe just started college. James was going backpacking across Europe. I was up for a big grant. The dog's still at the kennel."

He took a long breath. "I don't know about that. I know we have to get those guns and ammo back to the hotel. Are you with me?"

I wasn't sure. Was I still a professor, still a citizen of the

United States of America? I couldn't speak. But I couldn't leave my brother either, as unbalanced as he was. So I followed him back toward the cockpit, and we got to work loading the guns, and when we were finished, Dan took a moment to stare out across the harbor and then, quite suddenly, he screamed at the top of his lungs, cursing the well-dressed leaders of the modern world who sat sipping coffee in their bunkers while perusing intelligence reports of the devastation.

THREE

WHEN Dan and I were just kids, maybe ten or so years old, we built a tree fort in the woods across the street from our house. We gathered old pieces of water-damaged plywood and two-by-fours we'd found in the garbage bins of construction sites. We stole nails from Dad's toolboxes, borrowed his hammers and saws, and enlisted one of the neighborhood kids, Ricky, to steal some rope from his father's boat so we could string up a ladder. We spent the better part of the summer building our fortress in the sky, painting Keep Out! signs, and hoisting up rocks and dirt bombs to defend ourselves against attacks.

When we were finished, we dug a series of two-foot-deep holes that fanned out around the tree house, filled the bottoms of those holes with dog crap, then gathered dozens of long twigs that we positioned over the gaps to form grilles of wood stable enough to support a camouflage bed of leaves. These booby traps would, we believed, make trespassers from the next block over think twice about raiding our fort when we weren't there, after all, their sneakers would be full of shit.

Inside the tree house were a number of prized possessions: baseball cards and gloves, tennis balls, a few bats, a slew of G.I. Joes with kung fu grips, and the ultimate triumph, the Holy Grail of finds that we kept inside a tackle box secured by a small wire bicycle lock.

Every once in a while, we'd hold a meeting with our most trusted confidants, open the box, and let them have a brief look that would leave them slack jawed and asking where the hell we'd gotten it. Dan liked to brag about how he'd secured it from Dad's closet, smuggled it out right under the old man's nose, and been able to keep a straight face when he'd been interrogated by the colonel himself.

But the kids weren't as impressed with Dan's story as they were with Miss July's breasts. Most of them had never seen a *Playboy* magazine before, and we were the heroes of Avenue B, the boys who had introduced all those shallow-breathed kids to the world of centerfolds.

Our glory days did not last long. We arrived at the fort one Saturday morning to find the place trashed, the tackle box gone, our G.I. Joes missing their heads. We heard that the older brother of one of our friends had told some teenagers we had a *Playboy*, and they had planned and executed a nighttime raid. We did take small consolation in that at least one of the bastards had dropped into our poop trap. And so with heavy hearts and mind's eyes still trying to conjure up Miss July's ample bosom, we abandoned our fort and moved on to other interests.

Indeed, we'd had something to protect in our fort, and so as I drove with Dan back to the hotel, I realized we weren't just going to hole up in our room with guns. We were going to do a lot more, and I still wasn't sure I could go through with it. I looked at him breathing steadily as he maintained a white-knuckled grip on the wheel. Somewhere in the distance, a police siren wailed. There were two planes on the ground at the airport, but nothing else coming in. We rode along the bay, and the sunbathers I'd seen earlier were gone, not a soul on the beach, the sun directly overhead.

Back at the hotel, the valets were gone. We realized that many of the guests were at the front desk or inside standing like zombies before the flat-screen TVs, watching news reports coming in from South America.

"Perfect," Dan said. "Let's get going."

We had a decent cache of weapons: seven Ruger Model 77 stainless rifles with plastic stocks, along with ten boxes of ammo, twenty rounds per box; five Mossberg military and police ten-shot pump-action, single-barrel shotguns with twenty-five boxes of ammo; five Colt Commander .45 caliber stainless automatics with fifteen boxes of ammo, fifty rounds per box; two Beretta 9 mm pistols, with fifteen boxes of ammo, fifty rounds per box; one Beretta .380 (9 mm short) pistol with the same amount of ammo; and, finally, one .50 caliber Barrett semiautomatic with bipod and fifty rounds.

At the time they were all just a bunch of pistols and rifles to me, but I had an aching feeling that I would become much more familiar with all of them. And I did.

We had taken some blankets from the boat and now used them to wrap up the rifles and shotguns. We loaded the pistols into a pair of pillowcases. It would take two trips to get all the guns and boxes of ammo up to Dad's suite. I got on my Blackberry to have James come down and help us, but the call wouldn't go through.

Inside the suite, Vanessa came toward me, her eyes swollen

with tears. "I turned off the TV. It was all in Spanish or Portuguese or whatever, but they showed missile strikes in the U.S. and Europe."

"Video?"

"No, computer animation."

"Then they're just speculating."

"Vacher went down and talked to one of his yacht buddies. They're all saying the same thing. Nuclear strikes in Europe and the U.S. No one knows who started it, what happened, nothing— just that major cities all over the northern hemisphere are gone. One of the news stations said it just got video from an eyewitness somewhere in the Midwest that shows the missiles launching from the U.S."

I tensed, clinging to gossamers of hope that maybe, just maybe, we were all wrong. "When I see it, I'll believe it."

"God damn it, Charles, it's happened. It's happened." She clenched her teeth and buried her head in my chest. "How could they do this to us?"

"James, come with me," said Dan.

I craned my head. "No, I'm coming back down."

Dan cocked a brow. "Let him help me."

"Come on, Dad."

"All right, we all go." I gently released Vanessa and brushed a tear from her cheek.

"What do you got in those blankets?" asked Vacher, who'd fixed himself a drink, something stiff no doubt. "Or should I avoid such questions."

Dan removed the pistol from the back of his belt and showed it to the Frenchman. "Look familiar?"

Vacher drew back his head. "You went down to my yacht?" He rushed across the room to his fanny pack sitting on the coffee table.

"Don't bother. I have your keys."

"You've taken all my weapons? Are you insane?"

"Calm down, old man. I'm going to keep you alive. I'll keep all of us alive."

"Or you'll draw the violence to us, because we already have guns," I said. "I know what you're going to do, Dan, and it's too soon. Let's just wait till we have more information."

Hannah, who'd been standing silently on the terrace as though she were an extra in the movie of her life, came forward. "Dan, I'm scared . . ."

He crossed the room, went out and gave her a hug, then whispered in her ear.

"This is ridiculous!" shouted Chloe as she bolted up from the sofa. She reared back and threw her cell phone into the cushions. "I can't get anyone!"

Vanessa went to Chloe, but she wrenched away from her mother's grip.

Dan returned from the terrace and lifted his chin toward the door. James and I followed him out, and he double-timed down to the Jeep. When we returned with the rest of the weapons and ammo, we were met by Vacher holding a shotgun to Dan's face. "Nice try, Daniel, but you won't use my weapons like this. Not like this."

"I thought you might have a problem," snapped Dan. "That's why I stole them. I thought, he's a military guy, he'll be on board with the plan. Then I thought, oh, yeah, he's a Frenchman, and it's all about ego."

Vacher began speaking in French through his teeth.

James and I set down our guns and rose, lifting our hands.

"Oh my God, what's going on now?" asked Vanessa, drifting back from the television. "Luc, what are you doing?"

My father finally swung his legs off his lounger and got unsteadily to his feet. He removed his sunglasses, revealing his blind eye. "Luc, my boy knows what he's doing. Put down that goddamned shotgun. He'll save us all."

"What are your plans?" Vacher asked Dan.

"We don't have any plans yet," I said, answering before Dan could. "This is just a precaution. We'll go down to the desk and see if they know anything else. Otherwise, we should all just relax. We need to check in; then maybe we'll go down to the restaurant and get some lunch."

Even as the words left my mouth I realized how pathetic I sounded. I was a man trying desperately to comfort his family when he already saw them bald and coughing up blood as they crawled across the beach.

Dan moved over to Vacher and motioned with his hand for the man to lower the weapon.

"Okay, but whatever you do, I come with you," said the Frenchman.

"Agreed."

Vacher sighed and tipped his barrel.

My brother turned to me. "We're not going down there to get some lunch. We're going down to recruit an army. We'll explain it to them. We'll take over this hotel. Hole up here. We'll do it early. We'll do it now. And because of that, when things really go south, we'll be way ahead of the game."

I snorted. "The game? Is that what this is? You're getting off on this now, aren't you?"

"Guys, let's not argue," pleaded Vanessa. "Dan, I don't think it's smart for you to go down there waving guns. I saw the security guards."

"Puppy patrol." Dan took a step back and lifted his voice. "All of you. Listen to me. Listen carefully. This is not the time for wait and see."

"So it's the time to kill 'em all and let God sort 'em out later?" I asked.

"Charles, will you shut up and let your brother talk?" Dad cried.

I glowered at my father, who began shaking his head at me. Of course he wanted Dan to go down there with guns blazing. He probably wanted to join him.

"Dad, please, Uncle Danny might be right," James said, pursing his lips.

"Let's get ahold of the kitchen staff, the chefs, the waiters. Let's get them armed and on our team. We form a little company, get some rifle squads put together, seize the supplies, and form a perimeter, just like the good old days in Kuwait. These locals will go for it."

"It's too soon for that," I said. "We still don't know the extent of what happened."

"Charles, turn around. Look at your wife. Your children. *They're going to die!* Do you understand that?"

"We're all going to die. The question is how soon. You're being impetuous."

"Don't throw your fifty-cent words at me. Vacher, you coming? James?"

"I'm with you, Uncle Danny."

I glared at my son. "Oh no you're not."

"I'm twenty-two. Sorry, Dad."

I searched the room for some support, finding it in my wife's gaze, but then even she gave a half shrug.

I groaned through a sigh. "Dan, look, I'll play along. But let's go down there quietly. We slip down and talk to these guys, feel them out first. You can't go down there and shove guns in people's faces, then tell them we're buddies."

"I'll go that far. We'll conceal our weapons. We'll talk, and if it falls apart, then you know what's coming. Dad, I want you to stay here. Vacher, get rid of that shotgun."

The Frenchman nodded and went over to the cache to find himself a pistol.

"James, you ever fire a gun before?"

"Only a BB gun."

"Come here, I'm going to show you."

I stood there, feeling as though a plane engine had just dropped from the sky and crushed me. My brother was corrupting my son, and all I could do was stand there and watch. I turned my attention to Chloe, my angel, who'd gone out to the terrace and was leaning on the railing, her head lowered. I went out there and draped an arm around her shoulder. "You all right?"

She faced me, her lower lip quivering. "Is everybody really dead? I mean everybody back home. They're dead?"

"We don't know."

"Don't bullshit me, Dad."

"Don't talk to me like that."

She wrenched away and started back into the living room. "Uncle Danny? I want a gun. I want to come, too."

"She can't come," said James, incredulous.

"Because I'm a woman?"

"No, because you're an idiot."

"Chloe, you're staying with me," said Vanessa with a wink that said she had something else planned.

"Don't go anywhere," I warned my wife. Then I pushed past them, took one of the pistols, and asked Dan if he was ready.

I hadn't fired a weapon since I was a teenager and could have used a little instruction myself, not that I would've admitted that to my brother.

We left the suite and went down to the Sand Bar, a little breakfast and lunch place on the beach. The On-The-Rocks, the hotel's main restaurant located below Dad's villa, wasn't open yet, but the cooks and other employees were inside, preparing the evening's specialties.

We neared the Sand Bar, and Dan confronted one young olive-skinned man behind the counter whose name badge read Alexandre. "Alex, do you speak English?"

"Yes, sir, but not perfect. I study a lot and practice here at work."

"Good. You heard about the missile attack?"

"We're not supposed to talk about it. Not with the guests. It's not a very happy thing."

"No, it's not. You know what's going to happen, right? The people who are left here, right? You know what's going to happen."

"I think so."

"Well, let me make it clear. The fuel that supplies the generators will stop coming. The power will go down. All the food in the refrigerators will spoil. And then, whatever's left everyone's going to fight over. It's not going to be happy at all here."

"Yes, sir."

"I want you to talk to your buddies back there. We want you to join us. We've got guns. We're going to take over the hotel and control the supplies. We're going up there. You come with us right now. I know you want to live, right? Because you know how bad it'll get. Everything's changed."

"Yes, sir." The kid took a deep breath, a sheen of indecision coming into his eyes.

"Alex, I'm not lying to you, man."

He nodded. "Please, wait a moment." He left the counter and headed toward a back room.

"He's going to call security. He's going to call the police, and this is all going to be over," I muttered to James. "They're going to arrest us."

"No, they're not," said Vacher. "We'll take 'em out first."

I regarded Vacher, swore under my breath, then added, "Are you nuts, old man?"

"Sir? Sir?"

It was Alexandre, calling to us from the side of the place and waving for us to come around back. We did and there stood the rest of the employees, five in all, staring at us anxiously.

"You have guns?" asked Alexandre. "We want to see them."

Dan removed his, and the rest of us did likewise. I felt like an overage gangbanger huddling in a back alley on a rainy night somewhere in Detroit. The only thing missing were the small bags of funny white powder.

"See?" Dan asked. "We mean business. We need to control these supplies. We need to control this entire hotel. Do you all understand? Because if we don't, you're going to die much sooner than you want to. Much sooner."

Suddenly, a woman in her twenties in the back began speaking rapidly, her language not exactly Spanish—Portuguese perhaps.

"What's she saying?" asked James.

"Margot says we're fools if we going along with you. She's says we should all leave the island."

"And go where?" Dan asked. "It's going to be the same wherever you go. St. Martin will be even worse because it's more populated. The food will go even faster. These people with their yachts? They'll eventually run out of supplies, too. Some of them will wind up right back here."

"Maybe she's right," I said. "Maybe we need to get the hell out. The assumption that we should stay could be completely wrong. Wind patterns could shift. If there's fallout, it could reach down here."

"Charles, you should've stayed with Dad."

"No, this plan needs a conscience, and it'll be me."

My brother smirked. "Always with the smart remark. Nothing changes. Alex, come on, let's go up to the restaurant. We can make this happen nice and quiet. Do you know any of the security guards here?"

"Yes."

"We need to get them on board, too."

Alexandre nodded, thought a moment, then frowned. "Sir, who are you?"

"I'm Dan Spencer. This is my brother, Charles, his son James, and our friend Luc Vacher."

"No, I mean are you from the United States government?"

"Not exactly. Used to be a soldier. Now I'm just a guy who wants to live."

The kid looked at me. "And you?"

I opened my mouth, but Dan spoke for me. "He's just an English professor from New York. You guys ready?"

James looked at me, shaking his head and warning me to remain silent.

Just an English professor from New York. He'd made it sound as though I wore a reflective vest and picked up trash from the side of the road.

As they started off, I remained behind, staring up at the

cluster of buildings glistening in the sun atop that outcropping of rock, with the surf lapping below. It seemed the most improbable place in the world for a coup orchestrated by the guests. I wondered if the Sand Bar crew was about to lead us into a little trap, and I wondered what Dan would do if confronted by security. I wouldn't put it past my brother to shoot them, and did I want my son bearing witness to that?

"James?" I waved him back.

"What? Come on."

"Just . . . stay close to me, all right?"

"Don't worry, Dad. Uncle Danny knows what he's doing."

"That's what I'm afraid of . . ."

FOUR

DESPITE being an academic, my doomsday education consisted primarily of the postapocalyptic novels and films I'd encountered over the years. There's an entire subgenre of science fiction dedicated to such tales. Consequently, I knew barely more than the average Joe about fallout being carried on the wind, about warheads and air bursts versus ground detonations, and about the effects of radiation on the human body. As an undergraduate I did take an elective course called Nuclear War and the Arms Race, and we had studied in great detail the nearly incomprehensible damage caused by these weapons. Ironically, I forgot most of the material but remembered the class because of the lithe blond who'd sat next to me so she could cheat during the exams. She washed her hair with a honey-scented shampoo, and when she tossed it, I grew weak-kneed and dizzy.

After all these years, I'd never considered what I would do in the event of a nuclear disaster. It's not something we average Joes ask ourselves when we get up in the morning. People who build bomb shelters in their houses or go out to the woods to establish survivalist compounds are considered eccentric, paranoid nuts—until the fateful day arrives. What would you do? You hear about the missiles in the air because everybody's got a camera and You-Tube, but you don't have any bomb shelter, so you huddle under the staircase as the sun becomes a sheet of blinding light moments before you and your crying children are vaporized—and that's if you're lucky. Then there's the slow death, the kind we might suffer up in Rochester, the brutal, merciless death that forces you to watch your loved ones be consumed, even as you are.

Yes, considering what you'd do is difficult. Considering what you would tell your children is beyond gut-wrenching. *Are we going to die?* they would ask. *Yes, but not now. Soon? I don't know. My hair is falling out. I know. It hurts to breathe. I know.*

It would take me months to finally reconcile with this, to finally sit down and talk to James and Chloe about what our lives would be and where we might be headed. I realized that even though they were adults, discussing the matter was no easier, no less painful. Chloe asked me the same question a thousand times: what can we hope for now?

Yet on that first day, it was all too much to process. One minute I was half accepting what had happened, the next refusing to believe it, and this tug and pull would soon tear me into a breakdown. Still, my reason to live was the same one I'd used the day before—that I was a father, a husband, and a teacher, and people needed me. I brought joy into people's lives. I taught people how to see the world in new ways. Deep down I thought that if I accepted what had happened, everything I was, everything I had struggled to achieve during my entire life would be gone. And I hated my brother for so quickly accepting his fate, adapting, and moving on. The military had taught him to survive, and

I'm unsure what would've happened to us had he been a different man, a man more like me . . .

Alexandre had a key to the On-The-Rocks, but before he opened the door, Dan asked him how many people we should expect to find inside. "Master Chef Jean Claude Dayreis has many employees. I think he is up to thirty now, but I think there may be only six or seven."

"The others come later?"

"Yes, about the time they open. There are eight or nine waiters in the evening."

Dan nodded. I checked my watch. It was nearly one in the afternoon. I was starving, and when the door opened, my stomach growled over the heavenly scents emanating from the unseen kitchen. I thought I smelled veal, spinach, and something else, a sauce of some kind. There were three levels of dining, with an open-air terrace. The views were spectacular, and I couldn't believe we would turn this ornate dining room into a bunker.

"I'll bring them all out here," said Alexandre.

"You're putting a lot of trust in these guys," Vacher told Dan.

"I think they'll get it," Dan said.

Vacher snickered. "Or they'll come out with their own guns."

Abruptly, Alexandre returned to the main dining room, trailing a short man with dark, wavy hair, thick brows, and wearing a pristine white chef's uniform, sans the hat. He was wiping his hands off on a towel and frowning at us. "What is the meaning of this?" he asked, his English heavily accented. "What are you doing in my restaurant? We're not open yet. You'll have to come back."

Alexandre spoke quickly in French, then regarded Dan. "This is Chef Dayreis."

"Uh, he looks pissed," James muttered to me.

"Uh-huh."

"Talk to him, Dan. Tell him it's the end of the world and we're taking over," said Vacher, sounding as enthusiastic about Dan's plan as I was.

Dan gave the Frenchman a look, then introduced himself and the rest of us, and finally proffered his hand to Dayreis, who held up his palm. "I don't shake until I know why you are here."

Three members of Dayreis's kitchen staff gathered behind him, glancing quizzically at the group from the Sand Bar.

"Don't tell me you haven't heard the news."

"There's been an attack. I know about it. But until my bosses tell me to stop cooking, life goes on here—otherwise the terrorists win."

"You think it was a terror attack?" asked Dan.

"I think so. Only cowards would start something like this."

"Who are your bosses?"

"William and Jane Mortimer," Vacher answered for him. "They're a British couple who bought the hotel some years ago."

"And they flew out just after the attack to see what's happening," said Dayreis. "They will call us from Guadalupe and let us know what to do. Until then, I have work. Now then, you'll have to leave."

"I'm afraid not," said Dan. "Is this everybody? I want everyone out front. Call them."

Dayreis shifted his head slightly and spotted the pistol tucked into the back of my shirt. "My God, you have guns?"

Dan raised his hands. "Look, the food and water are the most important things right now. We need to make a deal because we need each other."

The chef shouted to a couple of his people, and one darted back to the kitchen.

"If you're calling security, don't bother. We already called them here. They need to join our team."

"Our team?"

Dan stepped up to Dayreis and got in his face, Marine Corps style. "It's all going to hell, but we'll be ready, not like the others who will sit around in denial or party themselves into a stupor. We're going to put an army together, you and me, and we'll survive."

"You're crazy. People like you will force the island into anarchy. That's what this is. The French government is still in charge."

"Oh yeah? Turn on the TV. See what's coming out of South America. London, Paris, Moscow? They're all gone. Your French government is gone. We're all the government you got. We'll arm your staff, teach 'em how to shoot, and protect this place. We'll ration the food, go out and get more, see how long we can last. It's time to dig in, if you plan on seeing tomorrow."

Dayreis's face twisted into a knot. "This is preposterous. Get out. Get out now!"

"James, let's go," I said, ready to exit before Dan launched into psycho Marine mode, his canines already glistening with drool, his eyes beginning to ignite with the light of a madman.

But then, quite remarkably, my brother faced me, and his expression softened. Then he turned back to the chef and said, "Monsieur Dayreis? Here . . ." Dan removed his Beretta, rolled it around, and handed it to the chef. "Join us. We have the weapons you need to protect this place. You need to think about what's going to happen in the days ahead. We're offering security."

Dayreis glanced down at the pistol, then appraised Dan with his gaze.

As if on cue, two members of the Sand Bar staff came in with a pair of hotel security guards in ivory-colored uniforms. They had radios but no weapons. The men were assumedly South Americans, tall and lean, in their mid- to late twenties, and looked more like a couple of sailors than guards. The taller of the two had a name badge that read Marcos; the shorter one was Bento.

Marcos saw Dayreis with the pistol and cried, "Chef Dayreis? What's happening here?"

"It's okay, it's okay!" said Dan, waving his hands. "We're all okay!"

Marcos frowned at my brother. "Are you the man who wants to take over the hotel?"

"Yes."

"Very good. We want to join you."

Dan recoiled. "Are you kidding me?"

"No, sir. We know the mayor and the constable have already left the island."

"Where did they go?" Dayreis demanded.

"We don't know." Marcos turned back to Dan. "There are six policemen and thirteen gendarmes here. We know them all. There are fights breaking out in the other hotels. They won't be able to control it. They will either leave or do as you would like— take over a hotel."

Dan sighed and nodded, then whirled to face the chef. "It's already happening, monsieur. You need to make a decision, right here, right now. Marcos and his buddy have already done the right thing."

Dayreis narrowed his gaze on the guards. "Marcos, are you and Bento really going to join these men?"

The young man shrugged. "What else are we supposed to do

but our jobs? That's what they want, am I right? They want to protect the hotel."

"Absolutely," said Dan.

"Every man for himself, huh?" asked Dayreis.

Dan waved a hand. "No, we work together. That's the only way."

Four more of Dayreis's staff joined him in the dining room, and over a dozen people had gathered now, all gazes riveted on Dayreis, who closed his eyes, massaged them, then snapped his head up to lock eyes with Dan. "You have more guns?"

"Oh, we have a lot," Vacher said.

"Maybe I'm going to go to jail for this. Or maybe you are right, Mr. Daniel Spencer. Bring up your guns. Let's get started."

"You're doing the right thing. And I have a lot more questions, starting with a list of everyone who works here."

"Okay."

Dan started away from the chef and faced me wearing a broad grin. "I still would've come in with guns drawn, but I guess you learn something new every day. Thanks, brother."

"You did it the right way."

He dropped a heavy hand on my shoulder as he passed. "The right way, huh? Don't get too hung up on that because it won't last long."

I stood there as he passed, summoning up nightmare images of starvation and cannibalism and death. James came up to me with a reassuring nod. "Dad, it's all right. Uncle Danny will get these guys organized. We'll be okay."

"No, James. We won't. Not any of us."

"You can't be negative."

I swore under my breath. "I know. I'm sorry."

"Don't apologize."

"Why not?"

He averted his gaze. "Because it makes you sound weak."

"Is that what you think? You worried I'm not up for this? You think my brother can handle it but I can't?"

"Dad, I didn't say that."

"You didn't have to. Come on."

As we left the restaurant, a renewed sense of urgency seemed to infect everyone but me.

I was just a fifty-year-old professor, soft, *weak*, entirely out of my element, and unable to inspire confidence even in my own son. My father would shake his head and say, *I told you so. I tried to raise you right, raise you like a man, but you ignored everything I taught you.*

Now you're here with your own son and feeling like a failure because you are not a man. You are a little boy throwing dirt bombs at a nuclear warhead.

FIVE

WE brought some of the weapons back down to the restaurant, and Dan and Vacher started up their little gun school. I wanted to ask Dan what he'd do if one of the staff members turned traitor. After all, he was arming the whole crew. They could organize their own rebellion behind his back. Then again, I didn't want to burden my brother with more doubts; I had enough for the both of us. For the time being, the restaurant staff seemed to respect Dan's knowledge and leadership. He barked orders and people listened.

During the next hour, Dan recruited James and I to haul the big .50 caliber up to the hotel roof, where we'd begin constructing a sandbagged gunner's nest. I thought it would take a week to do that, but Dan said we could have it finished in a few days with the help of Alexandre and his friends. What Vacher had intended to do with the weapon was beyond me. I assumed he just kept it as a conversation piece.

I left James and the others to begin work on the nest while

I helped Vanessa and Chloe move our luggage up into Dad's suite, where we decided we'd stay despite Dad's presence. Since the suite was above the restaurant, it would be the most heavily defended, and a much better location than the one we had originally reserved down on the beach. I did my best to ignore my father until his complaints about food finally ignited me. I told him to shut up. We were going to eat soon.

"That's right," he said. "Toss the old man out like a piece of garbage. Forget about him—even though if he didn't come down here, we'd all be dead. I don't even get a thank-you for saving your life."

"Dad, I'll take you downstairs in a minute."

"Forget it."

I called Vanessa into the master suite and asked her to handle my father before I murdered him.

"Charles, take a deep breath. Now listen to me. I was talking to him while you were out. He's getting a little confused. He didn't remember where we were. What do we do when his meds run out?"

"I don't know."

"This is . . . I don't even . . . I can't . . ."

She collapsed into my chest, and I held her. "I know, but we have to be strong."

"It's going to get worse, not better."

"We don't know that."

"Yes, we do."

I stiffened, remembering my son's words. "We can't let James and Chloe think we're weak. We can't."

"But it's hard."

"Tell me about it. Who the hell knew we'd wake up to this nightmare?"

"I'm trying not to cry. I keep telling myself it's okay, that it didn't happen. Then I say, it did happen, but maybe it's not as bad as we think. Maybe most of our friends died instantly, you know? They won't suffer. And that's supposed to make me feel better. I spend my whole life trying to help people live healthier lives, and for what? Look what it all comes to. I don't have an oil or a crystal or a prayer that can fix this. I feel like my whole life was a waste of time because this is how it's going to end. We're going to run out of food and die."

"We just got here. We don't even know how much food is left, and you've already got us dead. Uh, excuse me, but last time I checked, there was a whole ocean full of fish. They can't all be contaminated."

I cradled her even more tightly in my arms and shuddered over the fact that she was feeling the same things I was and that I was a fool for not talking to her. After twenty-five years of marriage, you'd think I would've figured that out, but some men are as dense as desert ironwood and even fewer are willing to admit that.

"Let's make a promise," I began. "Let's make a promise that no matter what we won't stop talking to each other. Okay?"

"Okay. I just don't want any lies. I don't want to keep saying it'll be okay."

"We need to say something else, then."

She took in a long breath. "We need a reason to live. And the only one I have now is that I'm too scared to die."

"Maybe that's a start. Maybe we don't need to be religious or philosophical about this. Dying is scary. We don't like it. So we're staying alive to help each other."

Chloe tapped lightly on the door, and we faced her.

"Uh, I think Grandpa left."

"He what?" I asked.

"He left. I can't find him. He's not here."

MY father was wandering along the beach, barefoot, cigar in one hand, glass of scotch in the other. He still wore his bathing suit, and when he looked back at me stomping toward him, he shook his head and forged on, even after I called to him. I wished it was just the sand that put a wobble in his gait, but I knew he'd walk likewise on hard pavement. He was losing his equilibrium, tottering along like a drunk though he was only on his first glass of scotch.

Nearly out of breath, I crossed in front, blocking his path. "I thought you were hungry."

"I'd be dead in my box if I had to wait for you."

"Let's go. I'll get you something to eat. You shouldn't be out here alone."

"This is a good job for you."

"What is?"

"Being my nurse." He eyed the beach and twisted his lip. "Where the hell is everybody? I wanted to see some boobs down here. I got nothing. I come all the way down here, spend all this money, and I got nothing."

"Dad, people are leaving. Or they're hiding in their rooms. Or maybe they're out looting the island, who knows. But we need to get back."

"Why the hell are they doing that?"

I hesitated, unsure if his memory had failed yet again. "Uh, they're just crazy, Dad."

"Thank God for your brother. He'll get this place under control."

I didn't realize I'd balled my hands into fists until my nails were digging into my palms. "Can I ask you something?"

"Don't get all emotional on me. I can hear it already. And don't give me any of your sympathy. You know I don't want it. I had a good run. I came down here to have some fun and then die in peace. But you guys wouldn't let that happen, busting my balls till the end. And I know why you're here, but nothing's changed. I talked to Luc. We're still going out on his yacht. Soon as I know you guys are all right here, we're gone."

"What?"

"There's nothing you can do to stop us."

"Dad, you don't seem to understand. There was a nuclear exchange. There aren't any more pirates. There's nowhere to go. Nowhere."

He glanced up at the sky. "Oh yeah?"

"Don't do this, Dad."

"Charlie, you're the last one in the world I'd be taking orders from."

"I'm just asking. Let's go back to the restaurant."

"They'd better have a good steak. That's all I'm saying."

I was about to tell him that the food would be rationed when a shot rang out from the hotel.

As my jaw dropped, Dad responded in a deadpan, "Well, that sounds like your brother."

A crowd of about twenty people, most well-dressed hotel guests, stood outside the restaurant, and Dan had climbed onto a chair to address them with a pistol in his hand and with the security guards, Marcos and Bento, flanking him. The shot, it seemed, had been a warning round to get their attention.

"All right, listen up, and listen real good. I don't know what the hotel managers have told you, but the restaurant is closed indefinitely. So is the Sand Bar. You need to leave."

"And go where?" shouted one older woman, her face nearly immobile from one too many Botox injections, her one-piece bathing suit veiled by a black diaphanous wrap. My students would've referred to her as a "cougar." "We paid good money to stay here, and I demand to eat. Where is the manager?"

"Ma'am, it doesn't matter where the manager is. The restaurant is closed. Period."

Epithets echoed through the crowd amid the murmurs that guests had, in fact, taken over the place.

"Hold on, everybody, hold on."

I had to blink hard because I thought I was imagining him, thought I was suddenly watching a movie and not real life unfolding before my eyes.

But there he was in the well tanned, well waxed, and utterly manicured flesh: Mr. William Rousseau, thirty-year-old Hollywood A-list actor/Scientology leader who'd risen to superstardom over the past decade. His films had made more money than anyone, ever, and he could afford to buy the entire island from France if he wanted. With sapphire eyes, thick, jet-black hair, and a swimmer's physique, he looked every bit the movie star; it was no surprise that he was accompanied by a harem of supermodels, probably the ones I'd seen being photographed in the morning. Several other members of his entourage, including a barrel-chested bodyguard with gold teeth, stood by. Rousseau wore a white silk shirt, matching shorts, and when he lifted his arms, the Rolex on one wrist and the gold-and-diamond bracelet on the other glinted in the sun. "All right, listen to me. You all know who I am. And I came down here to St. Barts like I do every year to spend Christmas with my friends. And that's what's going to happen. And we're all going inside that restaurant to have an early dinner and pray for all those back home."

I glanced across the crowd at my brother, who was already baring his teeth. I didn't see this coming, and I was a fool for not expecting it. I remembered that episode of the classic *Twilight Zone* TV series where the one neighbor had the bomb shelter and all the other neighbors were banging on the door, crying and begging to get in. Who decides who lives and who dies? Who is worthy to play God?

Dan didn't see it that way. He saw survival as an objective, part of his Target Intelligence Package, part of his mission. There was only getting from point A to point B. There were no hotel guests involved. And somehow, he could live with himself. I wish I knew how he did that.

"Hey, Rousseau," cried Dan. "Don't get these people all riled up. The restaurant is closed. To everyone. I know somebody like you isn't used to hearing the word 'no.' Well listen carefully. *No, you are not getting in!*"

"And just who the hell are you, punk?"

Dan hopped down from the chair, even as I shouted to him, but it was already too late. He shouldered his way through the crowd, reached the movie star, and shoved one pistol into his forehead, a second one into the forehead of Rousseau's bodyguard, who appeared more stunned than the actor.

"Who am I?" Dan hollered. "I'm just the man in charge, the man with the guns. And I'm telling you the restaurant is closed, indefinitely."

Rousseau smirked and released a string of curses.

"Do not test me, young man. I don't care who you are. And as a matter of fact, who you are doesn't mean a goddamned thing anymore. Not here. Not now." Suddenly, Dan yelled at the top of his lungs, ever the Marine, *"Are we clear on all of this, Mr. Rousseau?"*

The movie star turned up his smirk a notch, nodded, then whirled around, draping his arms over two of his girlfriends. "We'll be back, old man. You can count on that. Everybody, follow me. I'll get us something to eat. We don't need to waste our time with these bastards."

Like peasants seeking a miracle from Jesus Christ himself, the crowd of guests fell into Rousseau's wake, even as the man's bodyguard cursed at Dan. Where they were headed I didn't know, but that wouldn't be the last time we crossed paths with them . . . or him.

"You believe these idiots?" Dan asked, chuckling over the whole thing. "That asshole thinks he's still got clout. What he's got is an attitude that'll get him killed."

"It hasn't sunk in yet. Not for everyone, really."

"Except for me, huh?"

I rolled my eyes, looked around for my father, and groaned. I'd lost him yet again. But then, out of the corner of my eye, I spotted him trailing Rousseau's group like a lost puppy. I ran down the sidewalk, caught up with the old man, and grabbed him by the shoulder. "Dad, where you going?"

"With him. He'll get us something to eat. If I have to wait for you—"

"Dad, you're not going with him. Not ever."

"All right. I never liked his movies anyway. He's too skinny. What ever happened to Audie Murphy?"

"I don't know, Dad. I don't know."

My gaze swept out to the bay, where a yacht motored along

the horizon. I imagined that dozens of sailboats and kayaks would be cutting across the waves were this a typical day, but there was no such thing anymore.

We went inside the restaurant, and Dad got his steak all right, a piece about two inches square, along with some asparagus and a potato dish that I could not pronounce. He asked, "That it? That's all I'm getting?" at least ten times.

During the entire meal, Vanessa and I stared at each other, wondering just how long this would last. Dan came out of the kitchen with Dayreis, and given the eight of us and the sixteen employees who'd joined our group, they estimated we had about three to four months of food if we rationed. But the real problem was water. And that, Dan said, we had to address right away, building as large a supply as we could, because there were no natural sources on the island, save for rainwater collected by the gutter systems. The hotel imported most of its water, and the supply ships were no longer coming. While we'd secured what was left of our supply from others who might try to steal it, we still needed more, a whole lot more, and we'd have to do some raiding ourselves. We had no choice.

Vacher raised the debate of leaving, presumably because he and Dad already had plans, though I didn't tip my hand to Vacher that I knew. My brother said we had to assume the same things were happening on all the other islands and that we'd be fools not to dig in first and collect everything we could on St. Barts. Vacher said he would maintain contact with a few of his buddies, one of whom had gone up to St. Thomas. He also said that the undersea fiber-optic cable running from the island to Guadalupe and Puerto Rico was still working and that we could try to find out what was happening in those places.

Meanwhile, it was clear that we needed to divide and conquer. One force would maintain security around the hotel, while the other would need to venture out and forage for supplies.

Dan formed the waiters into a trio of four-man squads. Armed with rifles and pistols, two would head out to Gustavia with a long list of items they might secure. He charged the third group with filling jugs of tap water drawn from the restaurant. He was intent on securing every drop we could from the hotel's reserves, even as he sent another group out to the island's main water tower to see if they could begin filling some jugs. Also, Vacher pointed out that while most of the villas throughout the island had access to city water, most also had their own cisterns, so they, too, could be drained—especially if their owners weren't around to put up a fight.

My brother referred to all of this as "digging in for the long haul."

I finally spoke up, asking Vacher if he knew whether or not the island had a library. The question drew a deep frown from my brother. "In your world, guns are power, but in mine, knowledge is, and we need to learn more about radiation and wind patterns and anything else we might need. We can assume that the fallout travels east of the explosions and that most of it will be limited to the northern hemisphere. But that might not be the case. The Internet's gone, but maybe there's something, even an old book on the subject, that we can use."

Dan shrugged.

Vacher nodded and said, "Most of the hotels have little librar-ies. We've got one here, and you can start with that. I don't know if there's a public library. Maybe near the town hall in Gustavia. There are also a few small bookstores, but I don't think you'll find much there."

"Maybe the hospital, too. I want to go there. Can we set that up?" I asked Dan.

"Yeah." He raised his chin at my daughter. "Chloe, you want to go?"

"Definitely."

"Dan, I'd rather she—"

"I know what you'd rather, but she needs to come."

"Oh, yeah, why's that?"

"Because everybody's got a job to do. There are no floaters here. And she needs to learn how to handle a weapon. Hannah? You're coming, too."

I had a fork in my hand. In my mind's eye, I stabbed my brother in the neck.

"Uncle Danny? I'd like to go, too," said James.

"I'll need you here, buddy. You'll get your chance to run a little recon, don't worry."

"All right."

I raised my palms. "You know, on second thought, I'll just take Alexandre, and the two of us will go up there."

"No go, Charles. There might be looters. I think you got a good idea, and we need to make sure we get what we can out of there. So let's finish up, and we'll get moving. We'll be in and out before nightfall. No more discussion."

Dan gave me a look, one I had seen more times than I cared to remember, a look that took me back to the night I dropped out of Boy Scouts, the night my father had called me a failure and my brother had told me how embarrassed he was because his older brother was a quitter. I just hated the other boys, couldn't relate to them, and the fathers were all like Dad, wanting to raise pit bulls instead of people. In a fit of hollering and tears, I called them all Nazis, ran to my room, slammed the door, and accidently broke the knob.

I think that was the night my younger brother no longer looked up to me. It was the night he assumed my role, the night my father turned most of his attention to him. My mother and I became stronger allies that night, and she understood what I was feeling. Days later, I overhead my father telling her he thought I might be "a queer" and that if I wasn't a queer I was turning into a wimp. She argued with him, said I was just a sensitive young man and that he wasn't giving me a fair shake. Not all boys were meant to be grunts; some were intellects. He said that as the son of a Marine I should know better. I should be painfully familiar with what his expectations were for me and that I should, at the very least, fake it in order to respect him and the Spencer family name. After all, British philosopher and economist Herbert Spencer had coined the phrase "survival of the fittest," and my father fervently believed (though he had never proven) that we were related to the man.

I don't remember what my mother said, but I never forgot Dad's words. I had a father who wanted me to fake my life to make him feel better. Remarkably, I didn't kill myself or wind up in lifelong therapy. As a matter of fact, I've never been to a therapist. I retreated into books, found my solace, and did not have to return until our trip to St. Barthélemy.

Indeed, the darkness and violence in my father and brother were also in me; however, while they released the pressure, I had a lifetime's worth of red-hot magma shuddering against my gut, threatening to erupt.

SIX

I was at the wheel of our Suzuki, with Alexandre riding beside me and Dan, Hannah, and Chloe jammed into the backseat. I told Dan that Alexandre should drive since he knew the island better than any of us, but Dan pulled me aside and said he didn't trust the kid enough for that. All right, I took the wheel, but I still thought it ridiculous that he insisted upon bringing Hannah and Chloe, and if we were confronted and Chloe was endangered, my brother and I would have it out like we'd never had it before. The heat was already spreading across my face as I turned another corner, heading up a narrow street toward the Hôpital de Bruyn, located about a half kilometer north of Gustavia. Eerily enough, we saw no other cars on the road.

Alexandre was feeding me the directions and explaining that the island wasn't the best place to have a medical emergency. There were only about seven or eight resident doctors and a dozen or so specialists, though many traveled and couldn't be reached for months at a time. It was not uncommon for vacationing doctors to be called to the hospital to assist with emergencies, and most serious cases were flown out to St. Martin, Martinique, or even Miami. During the "high" season, which we were in, the staff was larger; still, we weren't sure what to expect when we arrived.

The young waiter also suggested that after we hit the hospital, we should visit the laboratories and the X-ray lab located nearby. We could also stop at the Pharmacie de Saint-Barth in Gustavia, the one at the La Savane Commercial Center, and the one in St. Jean near La Villa Creole, if we still had daylight.

I made another sharp turn, dropping into a lower gear, and the engine groaned as we headed uphill, following a placard attached to a brick wall, along with another sign that Alexandre explained had to do with the hospital's ongoing renovation.

When we pulled in front, my heart sank. The facility wasn't third world or anything—no lean-tos caving in upon themselves or flies buzzing about malnourished kids being photographed by American news magazine crews, but it wasn't much more than a ramshackle collection of tin-roofed buildings with a yellow and blue sign out front and blue crosses on either side of the hospital's name. No other cars were parked out front.

"I take point," Dan said.

"What does that mean?" Hannah asked innocently.

"It means he goes first," said Chloe.

Dan and Alexandre started inside, and we followed past a pair of open screen doors. My brother and the waiter nearly knocked over a blond woman with thick glasses who was about forty. She had her hair pulled into a tight bun, revealing her streaks of gray, and she wore a deep frown. She carried several heavy leather bags, and Alexandre spoke quickly to her in French, but she answered in English. "I'm sorry, but the hospital is closed. Everyone's left."

"Who are you?" my brother asked.

She raised her brows. "Who are you?"

"I'm Dan Spencer." He went on to introduce the rest of us, then ordered Alexandre back outside to guard our vehicle.

"And you always walk around with pistols?" she asked.

"For our protection. You understand."

"So you haven't come to loot the hospital?"

My brother sighed. "We need supplies."

She shook her head in disgust. "I can't stop you from taking what you want. No one can, I guess. It's all happened so fast."

"You alone here?"

"I'm the last one. The others took off in their boats. I'm not sure if they're coming back."

Dan nodded, then tipped his head toward a long hallway. "Chloe? Hannah? Go down there. Get us anything and everything you can—bandages, disinfectant, you name it."

They pushed ahead of the woman, toward the dark hallway.

"What's your name?" I asked the blond.

"I'm Dr. Nicole Fanjeaux."

"Doctor?"

"Yes, general practice."

My tone grew more intense. "Where are you going?"

"My friend has a villa. I'm going to stay there until we figure out what to do."

"Is your friend a doctor, too?"

"No. He's, uh, actually my boyfriend. Now, unless you try to stop me, I'm going to leave."

She started past me, but Dan raised his pistol.

"What are you doing?" I asked him.

"We need a doctor—especially for Dad."

"So now we're adding kidnapping to our stolen weapons charges?"

"We're the law now, Charles. And we need her."

The doctor shrugged. "I don't care what you need. I'm leaving, unless you shoot me right here." She shoved her way past Dan and out the front door.

"You're making a big mistake," he called after her. "We have more food and water than your boyfriend. You'll die in his villa."

I ran out the door as she hurried away. "We're at the Eden Rock Hotel, if you change your mind!" I cried.

She shook her head and turned the corner, vanishing around the building.

I went back in, and Dan just looked at me as Chloe and Hannah came out of the hallway with bulging pillowcases.

"We got a lot of stuff," my daughter said.

Dan nodded, then faced me, his expression darkening. "We shouldn't have let her go."

"We didn't have room for her anyway. She either comes willingly or not at all. I won't kidnap someone."

"You'll learn soon enough."

"You talking about the doctor," Hannah asked. "She's crazy if she doesn't come with us. Where is she?"

"She left," I said.

"Wow, bummer for her."

"Yeah," I said through a snicker. "Bummer."

"All right, let's start loading up," ordered Dan.

While they did that, I went back through the examination rooms, looking for anything Hannah and Chloe might have missed. The hospital's supplies were meager, but I managed to bundle up a few slings and splints, more big trauma bandages, and another pillowcase full of syringes and tape and even some tongue depressors (maybe we could use them for something).

Alexandre eagerly accepted our supplies and jammed them into the tight confines of the Suzuki's cargo compartment. He even called out to the women, asking them to look for mosquito repellent if they could find it. He said sometimes after a very rainy season people on the island got dengue fever from mosquito bites. You got sick for about a week with headaches, rapid pulse, dizziness, a rash, and loss of appetite, among the most common symptoms.

He also said that from now on we should always post someone with the vehicle (Dan, Mr. Marine, had done so as an afterthought). He said we all needed to learn to be much more careful. For a young man, he was, indeed, wise beyond his years, and it seemed quite fateful that he was one of the first people we had asked for help.

My gaze caught a row of trees from which hung clusters of small, oval-shaped fruit that resembled limes. I asked Alexandre about them. They were "quenettes" and had yellowish pink pulp that tasted similar to lychee nuts. He said people made jams and syrups from them. I asked what other kinds of fruit or nuts grew on the island. He said he knew about almonds, tamarind, sea grapes, cherries, little apples, and some passion fruit. You had to know where to look. We grabbed a few quenettes and peeled back the skin. They were juicy all right.

Dan saw what we were doing and put Hannah and Chloe on fruit-picking duty. We grabbed as many of the quenettes as we could, filling more pillowcases and little plastic haz-mat bags we'd found in the rooms.

Once we finished at the hospital, we drove up to the labs, where inside the X-ray facilities I found something I suspected might be there: an alpha/beta/gamma detector, basically a radiation detector. This one was a Canberra France Model AN/PDR-77 battery-operated unit with its various handheld probes. The probes were dusty, but the batteries still worked. Readings were normal. I had once dated an X-ray lab tech while in college, and she'd told me about a guy from a nuclear power plant who'd come into the hospital after accidental exposure. She'd explained to me how they'd "run the Geiger counter" over him. That story reminded me of the fact that even a small hospital like the one on St. Barts might have such a unit. I was impressed they did, Dan even more so that I'd known to look for one.

We drove out to the pharmacies, but had no luck there. Armed crews from several yachts were already raiding them, and one man came out to our car and told us to leave if we didn't want any trouble.

"The police are on their way," I said to the cocky young man.

"Yeah, right."

Dan glanced over at me and said, "We'll come back." Then he suggested we hit the gas station at the airport, one of only two stations on the entire island. The other one was in Lorient, on the north side.

I was getting more used to the winding mountain roads and their unnerving lack of guardrails. I kept to the forty-five-kilometer-per-hour speed limit. Still, on two occasions I came preciously close to the edge, sending rocks and dirt toppling over as Alexandre lifted his voice to cry, "Careful!"

"And you were worried about Chloe," said Dan. "Your driving will get us killed."

I frowned and continued on, and as we reached the airport, a line of cars extending from the gas pumps snaked into view. Alexandre said the station was only open from two to seven now, but there was an all-night pump; however, you had to buy gas cards at the station in order to use it. There was also an electronics shop next door that we should check out.

As we neared the place, we spotted three gendarmes directing traffic, guns drawn. "So much for that idea," said Dan. "Let's get out of here. Screw the gas and the electronics for now. I don't want them seeing our weapons. We'll send out a crew tonight to start siphoning tanks and raid the stores."

"Uncle Danny, why can't we just ride bikes or something?" asked Chloe. "It's not like the island's that huge."

"We won't be using the gas for cars, at least not for long. When the power goes down, we'll need to start fires. We'll need it for light, and for cooking when the natural gas tanks run out."

"So this is the camping trip from hell that never ends," she said with a huff.

"Come on, sweetheart. It ain't so bad. Spencers never complain, right? And your dad didn't raise no princess. We need you hanging tough now."

"Yeah, whatever."

My gaze lifted to the rearview mirror. Chloe folded her arms over her chest and glanced absently out the side window. My heart ached because I had no words to comfort my child. I had nothing, save for a deep breath as we drove past the gas line, heading east toward the hotel. I repeatedly stole glances at her, wanted to tell her how proud I was, how much I loved her and was sorry for what had happened. But I was so drawn, so emotionally exhausted, that when we got back, I collapsed onto a sofa in Dad's suite, and the world, or what was left of it, faded into cool obsidian.

VANESSA woke me for dinner. I was disoriented and hadn't realized that the sun had already set on our first day. I'd had a dream that I'd taken James fishing and our boat had sunk and he and I were floating alone in the ocean, trying to stay afloat without life jackets, worried about sharks and about being found and about whether or not we should have gone in the first place when everyone else told us it was foolish because there was still enough food for a while at the hotel. But I had insisted that we go out, and Vanessa had warned me that trying to prove something to my brother was ridiculous and that I'd wind up getting James and myself killed. I kept hearing Vanessa curse at me as I watched my son swallow seawater and disappear beneath the waves.

I shuddered and asked, "Where are the kids?"

"Down in the restaurant already."

"Oh." I massaged my eyes. "I guess it all caught up to me."

"To all of us."

"So I guess we go eat."

"Charles, while you were sleeping, Dan came to me. He wants you to give a speech after dinner."

"What?"

"Yeah, he says he's not much of a talker. He wants you to rally the troops, he says."

"He's got to be kidding."

She shook her head.

"Well, what do you think?"

"I think you should do it."

My face screwed up into a knot. "Do it? And say what? That we'll all be fine until the food and water finally run out and the fallout drifts down here and we all wind up coughing blood and dying on the beach?"

She put on a huge, fake grin. "Exactly."

I closed my eyes. "There's nothing to say."

"Just do it for yourself. I know what's going on with you. Just get up there and use that smart brain of yours and give these people some hope. They're just as scared as we are."

"Why don't you do it?"

"Because Dan wants you. And I want you. This is what you need right now. You need to talk yourself into this because we're too scared to die, right?"

"Are we? Really?"

"What do you mean?"

"I mean, do we want to live long enough to see it get really bad?"

"Let's not go there. Let's think about the here and now. Each day will be a gift."

"I thought you said you didn't want any lies."

She wriggled her brows. "I lied."

I took a long breath. "I'm hungry. Let's go. I'm not promising any speeches. We'll see."

SEVEN

CHEF Dayreis would, I supposed, maintain his dignity to the very end. If he had to serve us stale crackers, he would make sure that he had some exotic butter or caviar to complement them. And despite the small portions, his chicken breast and sweet potatoes salad flavored with a curry vinaigrette was quite remarkable. Alas, I couldn't enjoy it, not really, knowing that kind of dining would not last long. Others at the various tables were chewing slowly, savoring every bite, the "mm" sounds of good food rising and fading like the breakers. No one scrutinized his tablemate's plate. Not yet anyway. In the months to come, were someone to get a single extra green bean, a fight could break out. It was too early for any of that, but I already caught myself weighing each piece of chicken with my fork and considering how much nutrition it would provide.

Reports had come in from Dan's four-man squads. The eight men who'd gone to Gustavia had returned with all kinds of items, even toilet paper and cleaning supplies and clothes looted from the designer shops. Vanessa and Chloe couldn't believe some of the names on them. Vanessa told me there was a dress in the pile worth over five thousand dollars, a meaningless number now. The teams reported that the local markets were under siege by other tourists and that they had witnessed a shooting outside. They were heading back in the morning to raid whatever boats were left in the harbor and find currently uninhabited villas that they would map and from which they would attempt to secure more water. Remarkably, no one had been injured. They had been confronted by other locals and tourists but were met by shouting and swearing rather than the business end of rifles. They'd seen several gendarmes looting as well.

The second group filling the water jugs had long since run out of containers and had gone off to search for more. They picked up anything they could find: pitchers, vases, bottles of wine, anything, but they reported that they would need more. A large area at the back of the lower-level dining room had been set up as a water supply station. Concurrently, all the supplies from the Sand Bar down on the beach had been transferred back up to On-The-Rocks, adding about forty percent to our stores.

While I'd been sleeping, a television had been moved into the upstairs dining area overlooking the bay, and when everyone was done eating, we watched a news program from Brazil on REDETV. Long-faced, dark-haired news anchors spoke quickly in Portuguese (anyone not speaking English is speaking quickly to me), and the female news anchor bore an uncanny resemblance to the actress who played Nova in the original *Planet of the Apes* film—or perhaps I was wanting to see her that way, since my world, too, had just been turned upside down. Alexandre was kind enough to translate for us, saying that they expected to show video taken from a news crew who'd gone up to Miami, once that crew arrived.

In the mean time, they continued to show crudely designed computer animation of bombs flashing over nearly every major city in the United States and in Europe. I kept shaking my head, asking myself, *How can they confirm this?*

The planet had become so wired into and dependent upon information that the total lack thereof was, at least for me, incomprehensible and led to the inevitable speculation conducted (unfortunately) by Dad's dear friend Vacher:

"No offense to those present, but I don't think it is possible for terrorists to have triggered something as complex and strategic as this, no. If you are a student of world news, as I am, you understand how oil and global economics have, in recent years, turned politicians into desperate men, threatening men, men who will, when their backs are against the wall, unleash hell because they will survive it. They will rebuild. And the political gains of such a restoration might be more attractive to them than trying to fix a broken machine."

"So you're saying the U.S. did it?" asked James. "Is that right? And we did it to wipe the slate clean?"

"I believe your president knew what was coming: yet another economic collapse and government bailout, along with an invasion by combined forces from Russia and China. I think he created a situation that would allow him the excuse."

"Luc, we're friends," said my father, who was seated on the far end of the table, "but if you think our president started all this, well, you've obviously had too much wine, rationed or not. As you began to point out, it's all about the oil, my friend. Make no mistake. But even if you're right, I'm sure our president took great delight in bombing Paris, if that's what happened." My father laughed over his joke; he was the only one laughing.

"Yeah, well we can all sit around and cavalierly chat about

nuclear war, but for the people who are up there right now, the ones who survived the attack—for now—I don't think they'll be making any jokes any time soon."

"And what makes you say that, Charles?" my father asked. "Don't you know that when people can't handle a situation they use humor to get through it? Haven't you ever watched a rerun of *MASH*?"

"What's *MASH*?" asked Chloe.

Vanessa put her fingers to her lips. Chloe rolled her eyes, then got up and walked over to the windows.

Dan was suddenly at my ear as Dad began muttering something to Vacher. "I want you to say a few words. Add in some quotes or something. You know, be like King what's-his-name in that Shakespeare play you used to talk about all the time."

"King Henry?"

"Yeah. Something big."

"You're making a mistake here."

"No, I'm not. All right, everyone," Dan said, raising his voice. "Now that dinner is winding down, I want my brother to say a few words."

I rose from my chair and gazed around the restaurant at the former employees, now part of the Spencer "tribe" as it were, though I knew Dan would prefer "unit" or "company" or some other such military term. It had all happened so fast, the blink of an eye, the flash of splitting atoms. I felt like a passenger on a doomed ocean liner or a guy floating in a space capsule watching his air run out. And I was supposed to get up and make happy talk. Looking back, I do regret what I said. I think I could have spoken more like my, ahem, father. Maybe I could've gotten drunk. Something.

"All right, ladies and gentlemen. Again, I'm Charles Spencer, Dan's brother." I paused after each sentence, allowing Alexandre to translate into Portuguese. "Dan wanted me to reassure you that we're going to be all right. We're doing a great job securing more provisions and protecting this place, because in the days to come, things will get worse. I don't know how many people are left on the island. Maybe four thousand? Maybe less. That's half the normal population. But even with half, the food and water will run out. Those who can't fish or have access to rainwater will die. We're going to watch that. And we're going to turn people away who beg for our help. But you know what the saddest part is? Even after all that—even after sacrificing everything we can to stay alive— each and every one of us will die much sooner than we'd thought. We're delaying the inevitable and making ourselves comfortable until the final hour. And we're doing this because we're too scared to die. Those bastards blew up our world, and that's still hard to comprehend. And maybe now all we've got is this. I came down to St. Barts to get my father. I had no intention of spending the rest of my life here. And I had no intention of telling you anything tonight but the truth. We're all just waiting to die. You don't beat this. The fallout will spread across the planet. The food supply will dwindle. The human race will become extinct."

I grinned sarcastically and took a seat.

"Wow, inspiring, Dad," Chloe said from the window.

Vanessa's look of disapproval was one of the sharpest I'd ever seen.

And if my brother's eyes weren't attached to his skull, they would've dropped. His face had darkened two shades, and he seemed quickly out of breath. Hey, I'd told him he was making a mistake.

My father, on the other hand, was already struggling to his feet, and every chair squeak, slight groan, and curse uttered under his breath carried across the silent dining room.

"Everyone, I'm Charles senior, and now that we've heard from the pessimist, I want to give you the United States Marine Corps' stance on this subject. When old Chesty Puller was surrounded by the enemy in Korea, you know what he said? He said, 'That's good—we got more of them to shoot now!' He didn't sit there and whine about dying, whine about the end of the human race. He got off his ass and made a difference. We're not going to have a pity party here. We're going to live every day to the fullest. That's right. You see, I'm blind in this eye because I got a brain tumor. The docs told me I'm on borrowed time. And I hate to say it, but I think it's poetic justice that now the entire world knows what it feels like to be me. It sucks, doesn't it? But you don't see me standing up here feeling sorry for myself or looking for sympathy. I've had a good run. You've had a good run. Let's make the best of it right here. We can live out the rest of our lives feeling sorry for ourselves, or we can come to terms with this and move on. There's work to be done. Concentrate on that. And ask yourself every day, 'What did I do to help someone else?' And if you did something, then that day's a victory. The rest is all bullshit. And that, my friends, you can take to the bank."

Alexandre finished translating, and the restaurant staff, led by Dayreis, began applauding, slowly at first, then loudly, accompanied by hoots and guffaws as I sat there and my brother glowered at me and my wife found great interest in her empty plate. James applauded loudly for his grandfather, who raised a glass and toasted the crowd. The old man was in his glory, and it seemed I'd done him a favor, at the expense of my own credibility. So be it. I just couldn't bring myself to put on a happy face.

I remained there for a long time, as the conversations returned around me. I burned, called them all fools, just wasting their time with pathetic diversions and long lists of denial. Then I told myself I was just being depressed, that I needed to go on for my family. They needed me, and I couldn't be weak, couldn't let them down, even though I had succumbed to my true feelings and embarrassed all of them.

Vanessa took my hand and led me to the far corner of the dining room, where we stood, staring out the windows at the starlit bay. "I would've been okay with the lies."

"I'm sorry."

"I'm proud of you."

"What?"

"I'm proud that you, I don't know, didn't give in. You spoke the truth, as you said. It was uncomfortable. We didn't want to hear it. But it's okay. Somehow it's okay."

"I have no idea what you're talking about."

"I'm trying to say I love you."

I held her tighter. "You have bad taste."

"So do you."

Then I thought a moment about tomorrow, about the libraries I wanted to visit, about how much longer we should all stay outside. I needed to talk to my brother about that. I thought it might be best to get what we could in the next few days, then stay indoors for a month while using the radiation detector to check outside. I assumed the fallout would follow the jet stream, moving from west to east. Anyone downwind of a major detonation had little hope in the coming weeks. We might be far enough south to avoid the worst of it.

And there I was, in one breath acknowledging and accepting doomsday, while in the back of my mind pretending it was all just a nightmare. When the hell would the alarm clock ring?

I glanced across the room at Dan, who was also near the windows, hugging Hannah and grabbing her ass in front of everyone, the crude bastard. They would hump like bunnies in the wee hours. Call it reckless abandonment. Inhibitions gone by the wayside. Drinks are on the house. All-you-can-eat buffet. Party like there's no tomorrow because there isn't.

Chloe ambled over to us, blowing an errant wisp of hair out of her eyes. "What're we supposed to do now?"

"What do you mean, honey?" asked Vanessa.

"I mean not now. I mean in general. Do we just keep driving around and collecting stuff or what?"

"I don't know," I said. "For now, yeah. But only for another day or so. We'll need to stay inside for a while."

"Then what?"

"I don't know."

"Dad, don't you get it? 'I don't know' is not an answer. I'm nineteen years old, and my whole life is ruined. You guys are old farts. You got to live your lives. What about me? What do I have now? Is this fair?"

"No, it's not."

"Chloe, listen to me," Vanessa began. "Your life's not over. It's still just beginning. God didn't want us to die, so he put us down here—"

"To prolong our suffering."

"No, for a reason. You need to believe that. Think about the odds. If they'd dropped the bombs one day earlier, we'd be gone. Just one day earlier."

"This is supposed to make me feel better?"

I put a hand on her shoulder. "You can be as pissed off as you want. You get a pillow tonight and beat the crap out of it, because it's not fair. And you need to get mad about that, okay?"

"Hell yeah, I am."

"Chloe?" called Alexandre, his brows lifted.

"I have to go," she said.

We watched her drift off toward the waiter.

"At least she's got people her age," Vanessa said. "But I don't think all of them speak English as well as Alexandre."

"He's a smart kid."

"Oh no, here we go," Vanessa muttered, her gaze lifting over my shoulder.

Dan had finally left Hannah to a conversation with Vacher and marched over like a middle manager, full of petty power and about to quote company policy, slap me on the wrist, and send me home early to think about what a bad boy I'd been.

"Charles," he began slowly. "You were right and I was wrong, and I'm man enough to admit that. I should never have asked you to speak, you depressing bastard. What the hell were you thinking?"

"I was thinking how much of a depressing bastard I am, and I thought I'd share that."

"Well, thank God for Dad. And you're out of the loop now. You just follow orders, and you'll be fine."

"Follow orders. You're God now, huh?"

"Don't be an idiot. I'm going to keep us alive, despite you."

"Have fun."

"Charles, maybe I was crazy, but I expected more from you. I wanted you as my right hand, but I'm going to take James. He's ready. You're certainly not. You'll undermine everything we do with that attitude." He regarded Vanessa with a frown. "Maybe you can straighten him out. God knows Dad and I have tried." He whirled and called out to James, who was chatting with Hannah and Vacher.

"Your brother is an ass," said Vanessa. "Can I say that?"

"Nice guys finish last. And my brother always wants to win."

She nodded, then lowered her voice. "I hid a bottle of wine in our room. Let's go upstairs, lock the door, and finish it."

"I'm right behind you."

EIGHT

CHLOE took aim across St. Jean Bay with one of the pistols Dan had given her. Vanessa did likewise, and Alexandre stood nearby, rifle in hand, his gaze sweeping over the beach for any one who might approach. My wife and daughter would each fire a practice round, then continue to get a feel for the trigger with empty magazines so as to conserve ammo. I was up in the res- taurant, finishing my single slice of toast and six ounces of coffee and watching through the windows. It was about ten a.m., nine up in New York, and I'd been thinking all morning about my colleagues at Monroe Community College in Rochester. That's right, I was a community college professor, not some glorious scribe at an Ivy League school. I'd been thumbing through the contacts on my useless Blackberry, reading the names, wondering who might still be alive. I calculated who was slower, more over- weight, more apt to succumb, like Margaret, our chairperson in English/Philosophy. She had already lost a foot to diabetes. Then there was Joseph, who'd just had bypass surgery, but Aaron, the fisherman, was the kind of guy who carried a Leatherman multitool, wore a diver's watch, and sported a beard more unkempt than mine. He'd go hiking, kayaking, and mountain biking, and that was just on any given Saturday. If he made it, I figured he'd be like Dan, doing the organizing and trying to make people feel better. He was the academic version of my dear brother, the best of both worlds if you will, and I thought a lot about him as the days wore on.

We finished gathering about as much as we could during the first week, limiting our outdoor exposure to no more than an hour or two at the most, despite the low readings on the detector. Better to be safe than sorry, Dan told the others a thousand times. We elected not to celebrate the Christmas holiday; there was far too much bitterness in our souls, so we pretended it was just another day. The gift cards we'd brought on the plane remained in their envelopes.

Dan sent a team to the island's generator facility, where they'd encountered a lone employee, an engineer who swore he would not leave his post no matter what happened. The man hadn't eaten in a few days, and our guys gave him some bread and crackers. We learned the island had a sixty-day fuel supply, thirty days' worth in the main tanks and thirty in the reserves. In two months, without a tanker refill, the power would go down, so we had seven weeks, according to the engineer. While we opted to ration the power, turning on the lights and other appliances only between six p.m. and midnight, we had no control of the rest of the island; nevertheless, we'd do our part to get as much out of the reserves as we could.

That news crew from REDETV finally reached Miami and captured images that left tears in our eyes. Jagged, blackened teeth rose from the shoreline where once stood million-dollar homes. Storms of ash billowed overhead, the sky gunmetal gray, the water ink black and speckled with flotsam and jetsam. Yachts and other watercraft drifted aimlessly, some having been ripped from their moorings. The small flat screen hardly conveyed the enormity of the disaster, worse than any hurricane the state had ever seen. Even the debris appeared scorched, blackened, as though the world were now printed indelibly negative—and we with our crisp linens, mosquito nets, and freshly cut flowers gaped at the alien landscape.

The reporter said they had unconfirmed news that the King's Bay, Georgia, submarine base had been hit, the military installations in Tampa had been targeted, and that the naval air station at Boca Chica in the Florida Keys had been obliterated. The crew sailed all around the Miami and Homestead areas, recording their passage, literally weeping as they reported and struggled with their maps to identify now unrecognizable terrain. In doing so, all of them were exposed to fallout and were already growing sick by the time they returned. Why they had not taken any protection I did not know (perhaps they didn't have any suits?), but I understood their willingness to go, the way reporters will stand in the middle of a typhoon to report on the weather, regardless of the danger. And the debate rages as to whether they were story whores or dedicated reporters. I felt as much sorrow for them as I did for myself and my family, perhaps even more because they had given their lives to confirm to me, beyond a shadow of a doubt, that our homes were lost forever. There was no more denial, only wondering who was suffering and who'd been spared by dying instantly in the explosions.

The hotel's library offered nothing in the category of nuclear survival texts—go figure. I rifled through travel guides, a few dog-eared copies of popular novels, nearly all of which had been made into films, and a host of magazines like *Forbes*, *Newsweek*, and *Le Nouvel Observateur* among others to which the Eden Rock subscribed. I figured the other hotels' collections would be the same and didn't bother with them. Maybe I'd hit the smaller bookstores, but I shouldn't expect to find much, as Vacher had said. I considered returning to the hospital or police station or fire station to see if they had any pertinent literature, but we had more important trips to make.

Dan had managed to convince my father and Vacher to postpone their pirate mission for a few more weeks, citing the possibility of fallout and our dire need of their help at the hotel. It was a good BS story, one only Dan could put forth; had I made the same argument, they would have ignored me. I was keen to avoid my father when I could, but the old man had decided to have his toast and coffee at the exact same time as I did, and there he was, right behind me, nursing his mug and staring out the window at my wife and daughter, as Vanessa's gun rang out.

My father cleared his throat. "I'm going to take a swim, Charles. Why don't you join me?"

"No, thank you."

"I'm not worried about radiation, and neither should you be. Vanessa and Chloe are out there."

"Not for long."

"Charles, I'm sorry your life didn't turn out the way you wanted it."

I faced him. "What are you talking about?"

"I always got the impression you wanted to be in the Marines, but there was something that stopped you. I don't know what."

Though ready to give him an earful, I just finished my coffee and headed off, down the stairs and all the way out on to the beach, where Chloe was clicking her empty pistol and gritting her teeth, aiming for one of the islets across the bay. The intensity in her eyes was unnerving.

"All right, are you guys done here? Better to move back inside."

"Yeah, we're done," said Dan. "I think they can shoot better than you, Charles."

"I wouldn't doubt it."

"Hey, Dad? Remember when we used to play cards?"

I smiled at my daughter. When she was eight or nine we'd spend an hour or so before bed playing card games, not the go-fish stuff mind you, but twenty-one, poker, the good stuff, and the little demon would double her allowance through my losses. "I remember."

"Well, we got plenty of time now. Alexandre and a few of the other guys are putting together a nightly game. You want to join us?"

"We'll see. Go on up and get something to eat."

She nodded, returned the pistol to Dan, then headed off with Alexandre at her side.

"He likes her," said Vanessa.

"I know. And does it matter if we approve or not? Does any of this matter?"

She opened her mouth, thought better of it, then padded on ahead of me. I craned my head to Dan, who came up and said, "We're not too bad for a first week."

"Where's James?"

He raised his chin to the hotel roof, where my son was manning the .50 caliber machine gun.

"You think he'll fire that thing if it comes down to it?"

"Oh yeah. And he knows exactly what to do. In fact, he can't wait to fire it. He's chomping at the bit."

"You're proud of turning him into a warmonger. And you did it in just seven days."

"Not a warmonger, a survivalist. And if you don't get with the program, the program will leave you behind."

"There is no program. There is no survival. There's us, running around here like ants until it all runs out—fuel, food, water, us."

"You know, you're the only one walking around here whining. When are you going to step up to the plate? If you don't do it for yourself, do it for your family."

"I'm trying to be realistic here."

"So am I. Now is the time for all good men to come to the aid of their country."

I laughed. "Famous quote from your typing class? That's a persuasive argument—to which I reply, what country?"

"Our country. The one we're making right here."

"With King Dan at the throne."

"God, what'll it take for you to come around?"

"I don't know."

He marched ahead of me, and I dragged my feet through the sand, catching a pelican soaring overhead from the corner of my eye. I thought we should watch the birds and other animals for signs of radiation poisoning. For now, though, the pelican would remain blithely unaware as it dove toward the waves.

I won't lie. My depression deepened, hanging off my shoulders like a damp woolen coat. I began spending more and more time in bed, sleeping twelve hours, spending another two just staring at the ceiling. I skipped meals and allowed Chloe and James to eat my portion.

At the end of the second week, for some odd reason I woke up very early, just before sunrise, and I went down to the beach and stood there and thought about my life, the one that had been hijacked from me. I envisioned the president of the United States holding a gun to my head while I was trying to fill up my SUV. I handed him my money. "I don't want your money," he cried. "I want your life!"

I was a teacher, but what use was learning about writing and literature now? Who cared about putting a comma between two independent clauses? Who cared about aesthetics? Who cared about the influence of music in the plays of William Shakespeare or the study of rhyme and meter in poetry or the minimalist movement in fiction? I felt as though all culture had been forsaken, that we would soon become Cro-Magnon, writing on hotel walls and communicating through grunts and waves of the club. I was just feeling sorry for myself, yet again, throwing a poorly catered pity party with watered down alcohol and finger sandwiches made with warm lunch meat and stale bread.

And then I spotted them, down on the beach, just silhouettes at first until I started over, and the more distinct they became, the faster I moved. I actually broke into a full-out run, my pulse rising for the first time in days.

I stopped breathless before them and grimaced.

They had spread themselves out on a blanket and had, it appeared, been staring at the stars, a Montague and a Capulet alone against a merciless universe. I recognized the boy; he'd been on our airplane, one of the young partygoers I had noted. The girl was unfamiliar, barely older than Chloe, and both were heavily pierced and tattooed, their "art" rising up from the plains of their ashen skin. I nudged the girl's arm with my toe. I wondered if that were a smile nicking the corners of the boy's mouth. I saw no evidence of gunshot wounds, so I searched around the blanket and found the bottles.

I'd thought it would take a lot longer for something like this to happen. After only two weeks, these kids had shut down and checked out. I began trembling violently, unable to control myself, and then, without warning, the dry heaves clutched my cheeks and throat.

The former security guard Bento, who was on duty along the beach, came jogging over after seeing me drop to my knees. When he saw the bodies, he slowed down and began shaking his head, muttering in Portuguese.

"They're dead," I said, shaking my head vigorously.

He made a face. His English was not good. He uttered something else in Portuguese, then added, "Terrible. Very terrible."

Still trembling, I rose, and I didn't realize until later that I'd been so overcome by the sight not because it was the first time I'd ever seen a corpse (I'd been to quite a few funerals), but because in those dead faces I had seen Chloe and James. That night, I dreamed of my children on that beach, and Chloe, her face gaunt and pallid, snapped up from the blanket and cried, "You did this to us! You made us so depressed and now we're dead! Are you happy?"

I understood exactly what she said, but her words came out in Portuguese, and I wanted to ask her why she was speaking another language—

But I shuddered violently awake. I'd soaked the sheets, and Vanessa rose and brought me a towel and tried to comfort me. As I lay there, I thought about the dream, about how my subconscious had been trying to work out the problems of my life, and if I had any sense at all, I would listen.

* * *

THE next morning, I called as many as I could into the dining room and made an announcement: I was going to begin teaching an English class to anyone who wanted to learn. I would have two one-hour classes, morning and evening, so that even the guards could participate.

Chloe, with a renewed gleam in her eye, smiled at me and said, "Dad, that's a great idea."

Vanessa looked at me as though I were Charlton Heston come down from the mountain with white dye in my hair. "So when did this epiphany take hold? It doesn't have something to do with those kids—"

"No," I lied. "Figured I'd make myself useful. And getting all these guys to speak better English can only help us, right?"

"Yeah. I'm sure Alexandre is pretty tired of translating everything for them."

I told everyone the first class would start in one hour, then headed down to the lower dining room to get prepared. The nervous excitement I always felt at the start of a new semester took hold; it was an addictive feeling that kept the job fresh. Every year there were new students and new challenges, and I was always thrilled to enter my classroom on that very first day, save for the one time when I'd failed to zip up my fly and that oversight was brought to my horrified attention by a cherubic-faced young man seated in the back row. Still, you don't remain a passionate teacher for over twenty-five years without feeling something, I always said, wardrobe malfunctions notwithstanding.

Teaching English to international students began during my days as an undergraduate English tutor working with my peers. I'd been hired by a writing center, and the majority of the students who came in were from places like South Korea, China, Brazil, Portugal, Russia, Spain, France, and many of the Caribbean islands. I'd learned the difficulties students had and why they often spoke the way they did. I used to have great fun teaching them idiomatic expressions and slang phrases. I remember one South Korean kid wanted me to teach him how to pick up women. He said it was more important to have a girlfriend than to speak English. I found that as amusing as it was true. I'd asked him to tell me what he might say when meeting a potential suitor: "Uh, hello, my name is Lee, and I find you to be most charming lady and want to have talking with you and some drink." Obviously, we'd had a lot of work to do.

With those memories close at hand, I nervously gathered up some supplies: notepads, pens, and a dry-erase board loaned to me from the kitchen. Vanessa helped me line up a few tables, the students filed in, and just as I was about to begin, a commotion came from the entrance behind us.

I strode over there to find Marcos arguing with a familiar woman at the entrance. It was Nicole, the doctor we'd met up at the hospital.

"Charles, she keeps yelling," said Marcos.

"It's all right." I pursed my lips and regarded Nicole. "How are you? Are you okay?"

"How do I look?"

Her eyes were swollen behind dusty glasses, her silvery blond hair was astray, and her shorts and top were as wrinkled as old leather.

"You look fine."

She cursed and adjusted her grip on the knapsack tugging at her shoulder. Then she started crying.

"All right, I'm sorry, what's wrong?"

"He left two days ago to find more food. We ran out of everything. He hasn't come back. I don't know where he is. I'm afraid to go look."

"You mean your boyfriend?"

She nodded.

"Do you want to stay with us?"

"No, I want to be with him. But I'm afraid to be there alone. I heard them going through the villas last night, tearing them up. They haven't gotten to ours yet, but they will."

"Do you know who?"

"No."

"All right, come on in."

Marcos blocked her path, and I gave him a sharp look. "It's okay. She's a doctor, and she's been invited here."

"We need to check with Mr. Dan."

"No, we don't."

"I'm sorry, Charles, we have to check with him first."

If I had a pistol on me, I would've shoved it into Marcos's head for the unwelcome reminder of my brother's all-powerful influence over these people.

"Okay, I'll wait here. You go get Mr. Dan," I said sarcastically.

Nicole backhanded the tears from her cheeks. "What was your name again?"

"Charles Spencer."

"Okay. Thank you, Charles. Thank you for helping me. But if I wasn't a doctor, would you still be doing this?"

I took in a long, unsteady breath. "Right now, yes. A month from now, I don't know."

NINE

TWO weeks after Nicole arrived, she told Dan and I in private that based upon our father's failing memory and more recent hallucinations and seizures that he probably didn't have much time left. Dan wanted a more exact estimate, but she could not provide one. She was not a specialist but had seen patients with brain tumors before, during her residency, and the signs and symptoms were all too familiar. Dad had finally taken the last of his meds, since he'd only brought down a one-month supply and had intended to have the rest shipped to him. All we could do now was try to keep him comfortable—and out of trouble. He was hardly bedridden and prone to wander. At least Vacher was with him most of the time and tried his best to remind Dad of where they were and what was happening. It was heartbreaking to listen to him do that, and a sharp edge had begun to creep into the old Frenchman's voice, even as he smuggled wine to my father to keep him more docile.

After a particularly trying day with Dad, I pulled Vacher aside and thanked him for his help.

"He is my friend and your father. Would a true friend do any less?"

"I guess not."

"What about a son?"

I sighed deeply. "What're you saying?"

"Make peace with your father."

"Make peace with him? Come on, Luc. He's always been a man of war. Dad's way or the highway. I took the highway, and I never looked back."

"Maybe. But those days are over. Do the right thing."

"For him? Or me?"

"No, for me. Ha! Because when you are not around, he talks about you. He wished things had been different, but he will never tell you this. I want him to start talking about something else. He's driving me crazy. He wants to make peace with you before he dies."

"I'll think about it."

"Don't think too long."

As the old man left, I wondered if Dad had said those things or if the Frenchman was trying to mend wounds by telling us both the same story. He was a clever bastard, I'd give him that, and I wouldn't put such a maneuver past him, given his own military background and experience passing along misinformation to the enemy. The best reconciliation I could make with my father was that we'd agree to disagree, and I knew I would agonize over any conversation. Just seeing him again had nearly killed me. I didn't know if I could watch him die while repressing the guilt. Indeed, I already felt relieved that soon he'd be gone. I imagined the same situation occurring between James and me and imagined how I would feel were my own son to wish my death. And that softened

THE FALL OF EDEN

me, made me realize that, yes, I probably would talk to the old man before we ran out of time. And all we would have to do, I'd tell him, was agree to disagree.

The English classes were, as the Brits might say, moving along quite swimmingly, although James and Chloe were undermining my efforts by teaching my students slang beyond what I had intended for them. Bento approached me after class one evening and said, "'Sup, my homey. Let's kick out the jams and see what's dropping tonight for me and my crew."

Yes, he'd gone on to explain that Chloe and James had taught him those words, and he was concerned why I'd made such an odd face as he'd spoken. Then he asked me if I was "tight," and I was unsure how to respond, though I was certainly under some duress. Tight, he said, was good, so I told him I was.

A few days later, I was up in my room after dinner, trying to recover from a migraine headache I'd had all day. Vanessa, who carried along her collection of essential oils wherever we traveled, was rubbing peppermint oil on my temples. I sighed with relief as Dan and James knocked on the open door and entered.

"We haven't gathered much intel," said Dan. "Just those few stragglers from the La Banane and the Tropical, but there was a guy who showed up yesterday who said there's about a hundred people over at the Carl Gustaf, and Mr. Hollywood Rousseau has taken charge. We had a look last night. Tonight we're heading out for a little combo recon and raid."

I sat up sharply and moved Vanessa's hand away. "A raid? What're you talking about?"

"I'm talking about getting some of their supplies before they burn through them all."

"You've got two teams out on the fishing boats every day. You saw the dorado that Lefort and his men brought in yesterday. There's more coming. The radiation levels are still nothing. Why do we need to do this? All you're going to do is piss off Rousseau, and then he'll send his cronies over here to make trouble. We don't need that."

"But we need water."

"Excuse me?"

"The tap's run dry at the hotel. Rest is in the tower, but someone's cut off the supply. We need to seize the tower, and we need to fill up a whole lot of bottles. The Gustaf's got one of the biggest wine cellars on the island. We're going to get in there and rip them off big time. I want the wine, and I want the bottles when we're done drinking."

"You plan to walk in and ask nicely?"

"You'll see."

"This is bad, Dan. I'm telling you, you rip off that guy, you'll start a war. I'll bet he's already got 'em thinking the mother ship's coming down to rescue them from the apocalypse."

"I could care less what he's saying. He'll never know what hit him. Trust me."

"You're wrong. You want to go out there and rip him off and have some fun, but you don't know what he's about, what's really going on over there. You could be walking into a nightmare."

"That's what Marines do. So get up. Get changed. We're leaving in ten minutes."

"James, you're sitting this one out," I said.

"No he's not," snapped Dan. "But you can stay close to him. You'll need him to protect you."

Even James had to frown over that. "Sorry, Dad. But come on, let's get moving."

"Maybe I'm not coming."

"You're coming."

"Why?"

"Because I need everyone else where they are, and I need a strong pair of hands. And because I won't let you lie here on your ass while we risk our lives to help the group. Do you read me, dear brother?"

"All right, let's go get shot," I said, bounding to my feet and glaring at him.

He crinkled his nose. "You smell like a candy cane."

THE Carl Gustaf Hotel was a pristine collection of pale white villas rising from thick foliage on the southwest side of the island. The hotel overlooked the harbor and offered breathtaking views from nearly every suite. The travel brochures described it much more eloquently, which was why I taught English at a community college and didn't write travel brochures. The extensive wine cellar Dan had mentioned was located inside the main restaurant, high up in the bluffs and accessed by a maze of winding, intersecting roads so narrow you could high-five the driver of an oncoming car.

We had two vehicles—James, Dan, and I in my Suzuki, and Marcos and Bento in Dan's Jeep, following. Dan thought it worth the gasoline because were we successful, we'd need the vehicles to transport the heavy cases of wine back to the Eden Rock. I checked my watch: ten p.m. As we neared the Gustaf, we would switch off our lights and drive by the moon.

"We need NVGs, damn it," Dan muttered.

"Another military acronym?" I asked.

"Night-vision goggles. We drive with lights out, but our driver can always see."

"When the time comes, I think I'll be all right. So what's the plan? And do you know if these guys are armed?"

"They are."

"We talking a few guns or—"

"They're armed. Period. One weapon is enough to give us pause."

"For how long? A second?" I asked.

"Just relax."

"Uh, I was only kidding when I said let's go get shot."

"Don't worry. They won't be shooting at us."

"And you know that for a fact."

"Yep. And we won't be hitting them for a few more hours. Marcos and Bento know what to do. And Alexandre is already in position. He's our eyes and ears."

I snorted. "You got this all figured out."

"We practice, we plan, then we do it all over again."

"Why wasn't I invited to the practicing and planning?"

"Not much you need to know. You follow us and help load, that's it."

"So you just needed an extra monkey."

"What do you want me to say? We're so thankful you decided to come along? Sorry that I couldn't make you mission commander, but you were too busy whining about the end of the world?"

"Actually, that would work."

"Don't kid yourself, Charles. You're going to start pulling your weight around here. The English lessons are good, but it'll get hairy, and you need to be ready to do what's necessary. Whatever it takes. I mean that."

We sat in silence for a few moments, then Dan broke the quiet with a laugh. "You know, I haven't pulled off a raid in a long time. Just like riding a bike, I guess."

"If you say so."

He lifted a walkie-talkie, one used by Marcos and Bento and other hotel security guards. Apparently the battery was still good. "Alexandre, you there?"

"Yes, Dan."

"How we looking?"

"Two men behind the restaurant in the alley. The same two. Three more out front, and two more along by the villas on the south side. Same as last night. That's it."

"Great. We're almost there. Just sit tight."

"Should we be worried?"

"Take it easy, Dad. We won't have to deal with any of those guys," said James.

"All right, lights off," said Dan.

The road grew ominously dark and seemed to wash out to either side. We drove higher into the foothills, then Dan told me to pull off at the edge of a long driveway that wound up and away, into the shadows. I killed the engine. The wind whistled as it ripped in off the harbor, and the night felt cool and damp. To our left, the fronds swayed with an underwater slowness. I took a deep breath as Marcos and Bento turned at a fork in the road below us.

"Where are they going?"

"On the other side of the hotel."

"Now what?"

Dan drew his pistol. "Follow me."

I gave James a look, and he nodded sharply and chambered a round.

"Hey," I said, putting a hand on his shoulder. "The most powerful weapon you got is right between your ears. Don't you forget that."

"Okay, Dad."

Admittedly, my adrenaline rose, and my pulse began drumming hard and fast, my breath ragged. And, oh God, I liked it. I was eleven and hiding in the woods, waiting to burst out and throw a snowball at the next car that passed. I hadn't felt a rush like that in years. Suddenly, I was guilt stricken because my son was along for the ride and I should be focused on protecting him.

We skulked our way toward a cross street, then hugged the shadows of a crumbling stone wall leading up to the back alley behind the restaurant.

Ironically, even Dan acknowledged the moment. We paused, just breathing, and he looked at me and said, "Pretty cool, huh?" He flashed a rare smile.

I rolled my eyes but secretly wanted to tell him, yeah, pretty cool. James appeared far too serious, and I warned him, "Hey, calm down."

He swallowed. "Okay."

Dan waved us on, and we rounded the corner and dashed up the next street, minding the racket of our footfalls, the sidewalk rising at nearly thirty degrees. My legs burned by the time we reached the next intersecting alley, where once more we crouched down and Dan peered around the corner. "There they are. Just wait."

I nodded, panting like a dog, electricity now coursing through my veins.

The canopy of fronds continued rustling overhead, and through that latticework I glimpsed the band of the Milky Way. I had never seen a sky as clear, and I knew that once the power went down, the views would be even more spectacular. My renewed interest in astronomy might have had something to do with soul-searching, with wondering if there really was a God despite my Protestant indoctrination. I wasn't sure. Maybe I was just groping for symmetry, order, and beauty. I hadn't reached the point of blaming God. I was still pointing fingers at the world's politicians. But I remember on that night, as we'd sat there along the corner, with our hearts racing and never feeling more alive, that I, for the first time since the attacks, liked my life, my new life. We remained there for nearly an hour, until Alexandre called over the radio to say that most of the lights in the larger villas had gone out.

"Good," Dan replied. "One more hour to go."

"One more hour?" I asked.

"Yeah, we want it nice and quiet."

"So we're going to slip in while the guards are sleeping?"

"What do you think this is, Charles, a movie?"

"You're not going to kill them, are you?"

He shrugged. "We'll try to avoid that."

"Avoid it? This isn't fun anymore."

"I said it was pretty cool. Fun it is not."

AT some point I had pressed my head against the wall and had dozed off. A hand rested heavily on my shoulder, and I snapped awake, a rush of blood to my head. "What?" James's face came into focus.

"It's time to move, Dad."

"Where we going?" I asked, still disoriented.

"To get some stuff."

Suddenly, a cacophony of small explosions resounded in the distance. Was that gunfire? No, the booms were too small, too closely packed together. Fireworks?

"All right, that's our boys down below, and there go the guards," said Dan. "Come on!"

We sprinted up the alley, toward a staircase, bounded up it, and reached a pair of doors, one assumedly propped open by the guards. We rushed inside, found ourselves in the dark confines of the rear kitchen, everything stainless steel and flickering in Dan's flashlight.

Off to the right stood the large doors of a walk-in refrigerated cooler where the restaurant stored much of its fresh meat and produce, no doubt. A heavy metal chain was coiled around the doors and secured by two padlocks.

"Well, they got the food locked up. That'll slow us down if we want to get in there," Dan said. "Wine for now."

We pushed on through the cone of light, through an adjacent hall, to a door that Dan identified as leading toward the wine cellar. We passed through there, descended a small staircase, then Dan roared back and booted open a door, shattering the small lock and opening into the climate-controlled cellar. James found a light switch, flicked it on.

We all swore over the remarkable collection—thousands and thousands of bottles lining every wall, every niche, some with years' worth of dust on them, others newer with piles of invoice slips nearby. Barrels lined several walls, and wooden crates containing more wine were stacked to the ceiling, the scent of pine shavings heavy in the air. The cellar was actually multiple rooms, the connecting halls filled to capacity with more racks of bottles. I was certainly no connoisseur of wines, but the names and dates struck me as remarkably expensive.

And just as remarkably, the first thing Dan did was grab a bottle, tear off the label, and dig up a corkscrew from atop one of the barrels.

I shook my head. "What are you doing?"

"I'm thirsty."

"Now?"

"Loosen up, Charles." He popped the cork, took a long swig, then exhaled loudly and handed me the bottle. I took a tentative sip, then a much longer one before the bottle was wrenched out of my mouth by James.

"Save some for me," he said in a stage whisper.

"No rationing now, huh?" Dan asked.

"Nope."

"Charles, go bring up the car. I'll call Alexandre to meet us. Go!"

I rushed out, up the stairs, and bounded through the kitchen, down the steps, and back onto the street.

Down below, near the docks, the fireworks continued, punctuated by the distinct crack of a gunshot.

My breath escaped for a moment, then I picked up the pace, reached the car, and got her going. Reflexively, I switched on the headlights and roared up the hill. I came in loud and well lit, about as stealthy as an elephant wearing sequins in a Las Vegas circus. I cursed at my error as I pulled up, shut off the lights, and turned off the engine.

I rushed up the stairs, into the kitchen, and back down into the wine cellar.

What I found there sent my hand reaching to my waistband for the pistol, but that didn't matter.

I was already too late.

TEN

"JESUS, Charles, don't shoot from that angle. We need the wine bottles!"

I froze, staring at my brother, my pistol still tucked in my waistband.

They say there is no greater loss than the loss of a child. Parents are never prepared for it and often descend into the deepest of depressions brought on by guilt and grief. Our job as parents is to teach them, protect them, and love them, and when we fail to do that, some say we have failed at our true purpose in this world.

I have mixed feelings about saying I have a true purpose, and I'm unsure if it's to be a parent. I'm a lot of things, and not so good at most of them. I do concur that losing a child is the greatest emotional pain a human being can suffer; thus when I entered that cellar and took in the scene before me, like something ripped from one of my more recent nightmares, I thought, *James, I have failed you. I have failed to stand up to my brother. I have allowed him to interfere with my skills as a parent. I allowed him to place you in this position. And it will be, in the end, my fault. No one else's.*

I held my breath.

Rousseau's personal bodyguard, the black man with the front end of a Peterbilt truck and a radiator grill of gold teeth, swiveled his head toward me, even as he pointed a large pistol at the back of James's head.

Dan stood opposite them, his pistol trained on another man, a blond, ruggedly handsome actor type also familiar to me. He'd been close to Rousseau during that dispute outside the hotel. He, too, held a Beretta on Dan's head as he stood beside his buddy, facing slightly away me.

As Dan finished his sentence about the wine bottles, which itself was just a diversion, he gave me the look, an intent gaze and slightest nod toward the bodyguard, indicating he wanted me to make my move and shoot the bastard. I was only five feet away. Even an English professor could make that shot. But the guy had that gun jammed into James's head. There was no margin for error, and I was hardly prepared. My eyes burned.

How far would you go to save your child's life? Would you ask that question during the moment? No. You would simply run into that burning building, lift that twenty-five-hundred pound car with pure adrenaline, or strangle that kidnapper with your bare hands. I wasn't sure if the fear of being late or fear of taking another person's life made me hesitate. Or maybe I was just spending time intellectualizing the moment, trying to find each player's true motivation, rationale, and factor in the odds of who had the intestinal fortitude to kill a man and who did not. Bookies in Vegas were breathing heavily into my ears.

However, to this day, I'm still unsure why I floated there,

trapped in a bubble of indecision, my hand hanging in midair, like an unfinished sentence that would end with the word "dead."

And all of it happened in that million-year second that leaves you so exhausted, so spent, that even two days in bed is not enough time to recover.

Dan's cry to me caused the blond guy to turn his head and fleetingly drop his guard—and that was enough for my brother. Just enough.

The muzzle of Dan's gun flashed like an antique camera bulb in that dimly lit room, and the boom came so loudly that I could no longer hear a thing as I tripped backward, falling and reaching frantically for my gun while the blond guy's head jerked back.

At the same time, James wrenched out of the bodyguard's grip and hit the deck, colliding with the nearest wine shelf, knocking off several bottles that smashed open on the floor.

I could barely get my hand around the pistol as the bodyguard spun in the direction of the first shot, bringing himself to bear on Dan's waiting pistol.

Within that same heartbeat, Dan fired once more, striking the big guy directly in the chest, the shot muffled because my ears were still ringing from the first one. Another boom followed, and I wasn't sure if Dan had fired a third time or the bodyguard had squeezed off a round before staggering backward, clutching his heart, then collapsing onto several cases of wine, the wood splintering under his girth. "Aw, dude, you killed me, man! You killed me!" He coughed up bright red blood that raced down his chin and neck. Then he began choking.

My gaze panned to the blond guy, now on his back, his forehead opened up like a banana peel. The blood puddles began to swell.

James was shivering and uttering "Oh my God" over and over,

his cheek dappled by a crimson mist that had erupted from the bodyguard's chest.

Dan came forward, the smoke still literally pouring from the barrel of his pistol. He was shaking badly, swallowing, and gaping at the dead men. He rushed to the bodyguard, checked for a pulse.

"What have you done?" I asked, my voice burred by the horror of it all.

"I saved our asses is what I did. You should've taken that shot, like I told you." He cursed through a sigh, then added, "We got lucky. Let's start loading up. We're not walking out of here with nothing. They heard the shots. We have to move."

I grabbed the nearest case of wine, thrust it into James's hands, and urged him to go up the stairs. I followed close behind with two cases of my own, listening as Dan called Marcos and Bento on the radio.

For once my brother and I agreed on something—if we had been forced to kill two men, we sure as hell weren't walking out empty-handed.

Outside, we found Alexandre waiting with a third car, another subcompact. We left the cases with him to load and rushed back into the hotel, where Dan was already charging out with two more boxes, his face a mask of sweat and stress.

We made two more runs and got out about ten cases of wine before Marcos and Bento told us their diversion was all but over and they were coming around.

As I climbed into the Suzuki, the roar of a car engine rose at the top of the hill, and suddenly the rearview mirror at my shoulder shattered. For a moment, I looked at the mirror, wondering what the hell had just happened, and then it dawned on me (dummy) that the men above had fired at us. I'd never had anyone trying to shoot me before, and I just locked up, in shock.

Alexandre, standing just off to my left, whirled and began firing at the oncoming car, even as a gunman hanging from the passenger's side window fired back.

Dan was screaming for us to go, and James was hollering at me while my head was spinning because I had just witnessed a double murder and was now thrust into a gun battle. I shuddered back to the moment, yet every gunshot sent me flinching and gasping as I shakily started the engine (reflecting now on those clichéd film moments where at this point in the story the engine does not start, but the Suzuki kicked right over), and we went barreling down the hill, with the oncoming car just behind us. And I'd thought the radiation would kill me.

Alexandre delivered a few more shots as the car passed, then— although I didn't see him—he jumped in his car and raced up behind the men chasing us.

"Looks like just two," said Dan, rolling down the rear passenger's side window. He thrust himself through it, hung out, and fired twice at the car, a darkly painted subcompact, both shots burrowing into the windshield, but the car kept on, and the passenger returned to his windowsill, sending two rounds through our rear window, the bullets whirring past my head and punching out the front glass. We all ducked, and for a moment, I lost sight of the road, then dragged the wheel to the left, making the next turn, driving all of us toward the right and clutching anything for support. The tires squealed, and I thought the car rose up on two wheels.

Twin booms sounded behind us, and when I checked the mirror, I saw that Alexandre had accelerated up alongside our pursuers and had cut his wheel, forcing them into the brick wall lining the road. As he did that, Dan opened fire once more, taking out one of their tires. Meanwhile, Alexandre cut his wheel back and raced ahead of them, coming up behind us. Then he hit his brakes.

"They stopped, they stopped!" cried James.

I checked the mirror again. The car remained at the wall, and the driver's side door slowly opened. Alexandre accelerated once more, charging up behind us.

"We need to get back," said Dan. "In case this asshole plans to retaliate."

"Oh, I don't think he needs plans," I said. "You killed his bodyguard, maybe his best friend."

"Well, I didn't plan to kill anyone."

"What do you think they would've done to us? I doubt they would've shot us."

"Still got a lot to learn, Charles."

"Well, I have learned that we killed two guys just for some wine we could've picked up at one of the other cellars."

"No, the other cellars have already been looted. We checked 'em. And this was nothing."

"Well, excuse me for being incorrect on that small point—"

Dan smote his fist on the back of the seat. "Charles, just shut up!"

"Dad?" called James. "Let's just . . . not talk, okay?"

"You shut up, too," I told my son. "You keep playing soldier with him, you'll get hurt."

"Sorry, Dad, we don't have a choice now."

"You always have a choice."

AN hour later I was seated in our room, still rubbing my tired eyes and listening to Vanessa trying to comfort me. I didn't hear her words, but her tone was soothing, and that's all I needed at the moment. Dan might have already ignited a powder keg, and the thought left a deep pit in my stomach.

"Dan just needs to back off," Vanessa said, as I began to pay attention to her.

I agreed but added, "If he wasn't aggressive tonight, James would be dead."

"It's Dan's fault that James was out there."

"No, it's mine."

"You know what? We're talking about him like he's still our little boy. He needs to make his own decisions, and all we can do is guide him, despite your brother. I was thinking about that today, about how this whole mess has me wanting to overprotect them, like our instincts are kicking in, but really, they're both adults now."

I didn't respond to that. My thoughts were already rewinding. "Vanessa, when I got down in that cellar, he just looked at me. And you know brothers, you can read each other. And he was asking me to take the shot. I was supposed to kill the guy holding James. I should've done it. I mean it was our son right there."

"What?"

I hadn't told her the whole story, only that we'd stolen wine and nearly gotten caught. I couldn't bear the burden of what I'd done (or failed to do), so I just sat there and confessed, and when I was finished, she nodded and said, "Dan was trained to react in those situations. You were thinking about what would happen if you missed, or if you shot the guy and he still managed to shoot James."

"And now I'm thinking that if something like that happens again, I'm going to kill someone. That's what it's come down to. That's what it's always been coming down to, and I just didn't want to admit it. We're going to kill each other on this island. We're a month out, and it's already starting. We don't have a choice. Jesus . . ."

She let that thought hang for a minute, and I was about to apologize for sounding so depressing when automatic gunfire echoed from outside.

"Stay here!" I cried, then snatched up my pistol from the bed and darted out of the room.

I pounded down the wooden staircase, turning toward a group of about ten men standing on the beach, facing the hotel. The gunfire had come from them, someone shooting in the air to get our attention, I hoped.

"Who's in charge?" came a familiar voice. I squinted and saw Rousseau detaching himself from the others and coming forward, some kind of machine gun clutched in his hands, his shirttails hanging out. "Get down here now!"

Dan, Marcos, Bento, and Alexandre headed out to the beach, armed now with rifles and shotguns. It was like the goddamned O.K. Corral, illuminated by the beach lights someone in the restaurant had turned on, the now eerie Eden Rock logo glowing otherworldly on the sand, a clever light display that we'd done away with to conserve power.

Part of me couldn't believe that Dan would march out there to square off with this guy. I assumed he would consider that strategy a grave tactical error as I did.

I didn't realize that Dan was going to play dumb until I reached them, struggling to regain my breath.

"Someone killed my bodyguard and one of my friends," said Rousseau, speaking clearly through perfectly straight, laser-whitened teeth.

"Sorry to hear that," Dan answered. "Now, are we going to see

if those guns work, or are we going to talk all night? Or maybe
you boys want to go home? It's late. We're all tired."

Rousseau snorted. "We know you guys did it. And you'll
pay—with interest."

"Haven't you heard? Money's no good. Dollar's worth zero.
There is no interest rate. Ever. It's the end of the world."

Rousseau took a step closer to Dan. "It's the end of your
world."

"Hey, Hollywood, you come over here with your guns and
your big attitude because you played cops and robbers in a few
movies. Go home. We didn't kill anybody."

"Your cars are here. Maybe we can go up and have a look at
the broken glass and the holes."

"Mr. Rousseau," I began, "you should go back to your hotel,
and maybe we can help you find who shot your friends in the
morning."

"Who the hell is this?"

"He's my brother," said Dan. "And he's right. We'll go sleep it
off and give you a hand in the morning."

"What's your name again?" Rousseau asked.

"Like it even matters to you?"

The actor's eyes widened, and in the starlight they took on a
frightening sheen. "Oh, it matters. More than you know."

Dan grinned. "Well, then, my name is Dan Spencer. And
I might call your attention to that .50 caliber machine gun we
have up on the roof. Why don't you give a nice wave to my friend
Heverton up there. He used to be a waiter, but now he likes to
play with big guns."

"You don't think we're well armed? You don't think I have
connections all over the Caribbean? All over the world?"

"Why are you still here, then?"

The question seemed to catch the celebrity off guard. It was my belief then that all of Mr. Rousseau's connections had abandoned him because there was no longer any need to feed off his celebrity. He had only a few true friends, and he'd probably come to realize that in the past few weeks. He also might have thought as we did—that it would probably be no better someplace else, more than likely worse.

Rousseau finally began to nod, as though he'd reached some conclusion about Dan's question and intended to ignore it. "Watch your back, Danny. And all of you. Watch your backs! You've all made a fatal mistake!" With that, Rousseau spun around and marched off, his minions trailing in his wake.

"He's going to come in the middle of the night," I said in my brother's ear.

"I don't care. Everyone, to your posts!"

I remained on the beach a few moments longer, watching Rousseau's party head back toward the road. They got in their cars and squealed off. The man's ego would not allow him to suffer long.

ELEVEN

THE next morning during my English class, the waiters and waitresses in attendance, eight in all, entered bleary-eyed and dragging their feet. Bento told me they'd been up all night discussing what had happened at the Carl Gustaf, and Chef Dayreis, who came by a few minutes late, said that Dan had made a terrible mistake and now the entire group was at risk. Dayreis was, in fact, furious over Dan's plan, waving his hands and raising his voice to say the others were thinking about going to Dan and demanding that he cease and desist from any further raids.

I listened to them complain for a few more moments, growing more agitated because I, too, had barely slept and my patience was now threadbare. As they went on and on, I found myself defending my brother, initially because I deemed the restaurant crew as too quick to turn on him and ungrateful for all he had done. I know now they were only speaking out of fear, and you couldn't blame them. But I stood there and took a long breath and said, "What happened at the Carl Gustaf was an accident.

No one planned for anyone else to get hurt, let alone killed. We were slipping in there to get some wine and get out. That's it. You can't blame Dan for that. Water is our number one priority right now. And you can't stop believing that what he's doing is the right thing for us. He's a soldier and trained his whole life for these kinds of things. He's the guy we need. And we have to trust him. I'm sorry, but that's the way it is."

"But, Mr. Charles, we know you don't like him," said Bento. "Why are you saying these things?"

I tried to repress my grin. They could detect BS as effectively as I could. "He's my brother. I've been fighting with him all my life. You don't have to like him to trust him. He's the best guy for this job. Is there anyone else here who knows as much as he does about defending this place?"

"What about the old man, Vacher?" asked Dayreis. "He was a soldier, too."

"Yeah, but he's taking care of my father, and that's the best place for him."

"Then please talk to Dan," said Bento. "We don't want them to come and start shooting."

"It may be too late for that," cried Dayreis, drawing murmurs of agreement from the others.

"Let me ask all of you something. When the supplies start running out and we're down to just fishing and looking for whatever water we can find in the cisterns, the gutters, the puddles, the leaves on trees . . . will you still be worried about this? No, you won't. All you'll be thinking about is the next sip of water. And that's the great irony of being on an island, right? There was an old poet named Coleridge who wrote, 'Water, water, every where, nor any drop to drink.' "

They stared at me, some trying to translate in their heads.

Dayreis shrugged and finally said, "When the time comes, I will kill a stranger for his water. I think we all will."

LATER that day, I told Dan he had lost the group's confidence. I told him I'd tried to win them back but that *he* needed to do something positive to regain their trust. He asked me what, and I couldn't answer.

VANESSA and I spent a few hours that evening watching the news reports from South America. More than half the group sat along with us in the restaurant. The Brazilians were planning to launch a new weather/communications satellite and park it over the equator. The device would measure wind speeds and directions based on sea-surface wave action, current detection software, and five independent radiation-sampling sensors. I was surprised by the speed and efficiency of the government; then again, these were extraordinary times and early-warning radiation detection could save millions on that continent. The reporter said the satellite would be ready for launch in about six weeks. He went on to add that the channel would be adding an English-language broadcast to accommodate the thousands of new viewers now watching and listening to them.

Alexandre shook a fist in the air and told everyone how proud he was of his countrymen. In the face of utter disaster, the Brazilians had come through. "See, we do a lot more than just play soccer!" he cried.

The news was, indeed, a source of encouragement for us all and suggested that somewhere out there, people were fighting as we were to recover some sense of normalcy.

I glanced over at Vanessa, who seemed less hopeful than the others. "Good news, right?"

"Yeah, I guess so."

"Are you having a 'Charles Moment'?"

She almost smiled. "Is that what we're calling them?"

I nodded. "Doom and gloom is my middle name."

"Well, it's not that. It's just . . ." She lowered her voice and tossed a look to our daughter, who now sat at the other end of the room with Alexandre and a few of his colleagues. "You know what Chloe said to me this morning?"

I shook my head.

"She said that when the power dies, so will the music. I asked her what she meant, and she said she couldn't recharge her iPod, so there wouldn't be any more music. Ever. And I told her we'd make our own music."

"I'm sure that went over big."

"It's going to be more real when that power goes off, isn't it? It's not like we're really sacrificing anything yet. We've lost a little weight, but that's all."

"Remember Hurricane Gloria? I caught up on a lot of reading that week."

"Don't change the subject."

"I'm not."

"You know without the TV we won't know what's going on out there."

"And you really want to know?"

"Charles, you're right about the news being good. Maybe we can go to South America . . . or Australia. We'll go somewhere. We can't stay here forever. It's all going to crash pretty soon. I don't want to be here when it does."

"We'll see."

She sighed and tucked her head into my shoulder. God, she felt good.

THAT night I lay awake in bed, tears streaming down my cheeks. I couldn't get Chloe's words out of my head. Our lives were now wired to the power generator, and when its fuel supply ran dry, so would the last dregs of our denial. Dan was already investigating how many portable generators might be on the island and which ones we might secure. Even so, the fuel to run them would become increasingly scarce. Generators would buy us only a little more time.

My thoughts began to fray, shifting erratically from memory to memory, and I kept coming back to my bicycle when I was ten years old. It was black, with a long banana seat, and I referred to it as my black chopper. Dan had a purple bike, same kind of seat, and we took old pieces of plywood and built ramps and did jumps and wiped out on the asphalt so many times that our knees and elbows were almost always covered with Band-Aids. No one wore helmets back in those days, the days of drinking from garden hoses and riding two miles from your house and still feeling safe. We popped wheelies and used clothespins to fix baseball cards to our bike frames so the cards would "tick" through the spokes as we pedaled. I had a couple of pinwheels my mom had bought me at a carnival, and I had taped them onto my handlebars so I could watch them turn like propellers as I rode faster and faster. I remember one Halloween, it was early, only four p.m., and I was racing down the block to check on one of my friends to see what his costume would be, and when I got to his house, his mom came out and told me that he wasn't going trick-or-treating because his older brother who'd been sent to Vietnam had been killed.

I just said, "Okay," and left and raced all the way home and told my mom.

I don't remember how I felt, but I do remember just listening to those pinwheels humming as I road home, accompanied by the wonderful racket of those baseball cards. And as I lay there in that hotel bed, I could hear those sounds as clearly and distinctly as I had on that early Halloween night.

And just like that, I sat up and realized why the hell I was thinking about riding my bike and baseball cards and pinwheels. I shuddered with chills.

Before heading down to the island, I'd been reading some local news posted on one of the many websites, and there'd been a story about a wind-powered turbine installed at a private residence in the hills of Lurin and that there'd been plans to construct more. I didn't remember the details, but if there was a wind-powered generator up there, then maybe, just maybe, the music wouldn't die after all. That's what we needed: a renewable source of energy. A renewable source of hope.

DAN shrugged when I told him I wanted to head up to Lurin with a small party. "Take a couple of the guys and go up there. See if they've got that thing rigged to the house. Bring something to plug in."

"Uh, I got that covered," I said, perhaps a little too sarcastically.

"I've been thinking about winning back the guys. One minute I want to apologize, the next I want to scare the hell out of them, keep them loyal through fear. Works for most dictators."

"I wouldn't do that. But I would get more sleep, because you look horrible."

"I can't sleep, knowing that he's coming. I keep seeing myself going up there and taking him out. I got rings around my eyes from staring through the binoculars."

"Just stop."

We'd been standing on the back terrace, and he faced south, toward the Gustaf on the other side of mountains dotted with palms and cacti. "He's up there, in the hills, watching us right now."

"Probably."

"Take Alexandre with you, too. In case there's trouble."

"Okay. We're going up on bikes."

"Sounds good."

"You better get out of your funk," I told him. "Only us academics can have mood swings. You ain't paid to think. You're paid to fight."

He snorted.

I went back inside and asked Chloe for her iPod, recharger, and power transformer, since the island operated on 220 AC, sixty cycles. She gave me a quizzical look, as though I were insane for wanting to listen to her music. I told her what we were doing, and she begged me to come along. She argued. I caved.

A pair of iguanas sat sunning themselves on a large rock beside the mountain road, and as we rode by, they didn't give us the time of day. Behind them stood a remarkable wall of colorful plants: bougainvillea, purple allamanda, golden trumpet, hibiscus with red and yellow flowers, and oleander. Riding the bike gave me a whole new perspective on the island, and I realized how much I'd already missed by allowing the landscape to blur by as a car driver or passenger.

I had Marcos, Alexandre, and another waiter, Carlos, as well as Chloe with me, and we were all well armed as we pedaled steadily up the hill. It was about eighty-five degrees, a bit humid, and we were already soaked with sweat when we came upon the four bodies dumped like litter on the shoulder.

They were young men in hotel uniforms, each having suffered multiple gunshot wounds. They'd been dumped maybe twelve hours prior, maybe less. The flies were buzzing, but there were hardly any signs of sun damage or real decay.

"We're not stopping," I said. "Keep riding!"

"Oh my God," muttered Chloe.

Alexandre shouted something in Portuguese to the others, and I asked what he'd said.

"We know one of them. He used to work for us, but then he went to the Le Village Hotel."

"Just keep pedaling," I told them.

"Dad, what do you think happened?"

"I don't know. We don't care."

We rode with a heightened sense of urgency, the guys repeatedly checking over their shoulders and slowing as we reached the crest of the next hill.

A white Mini Cooper with the top down was coming up the other side, and I shouted for everyone to pull over. As the car drew near, the driver, a white-haired man seated beside a woman about as old, accelerated hard and raced on by, his eyes widening for a moment before he swiveled his head back and stared straight ahead, as though not looking at us would somehow conceal him.

We just watched him descend, the tires squealing around the next corner, the engine's hum fading.

"That was weird," said Chloe.

"They saw our guns," I pointed out.

"Where do you think they're going?" asked Alexandre.

"Well, they're not looking for a wind-powered turbine, that's for sure."

"Dad?" Chloe called. "I have to go to the bathroom."

I looked at my daughter, flashing back to those thousands of times we'd been shopping and just when we got to the back of the store and were as far as we could possibly be from the restrooms, she'd utter those deadly words.

"You better hang on," I told her, "because we're not stopping till we get up there."

She huffed and climbed back on her bike.

WE finally approached the private villa about an hour later. I sent the men in first, told them to see if anyone was home. If not, they were to break through one of the doors. Ten minutes later they returned to where we were waiting in the woods near the driveway and said they got inside and no one was there. Good. Chloe jogged all the way back with Alexandre and rushed inside to use the bathroom.

I went directly to the back patio, where near one corner stood a large tower rising some thirty feet into the air. Four large rotor blades extended outward, turning lazily in the breeze. Behind the blade was a large nacelle inside which I would later learn were the gearbox and generator. What troubled me, though, was that two access panels on the nacelle had both been lifted up, exposing the turbine's innards. And off to the right stood a portable scissors lift with a large basket to accommodate one or two people.

"Where do I plug in my iPod?" Chloe asked from behind me.

I turned back. "Hang on. Alexandre, check the house for

papers or anything else you can find. It looks like they were working on this thing. Got the lift right here; the panels are open up there. I hope the thing's not broken."

Alexandre nodded and headed back into the villa. Carlos and Marcos took up positions at the bottom of the driveway.

"It's pretty cool looking, Dad."

"Yeah, it is."

"Mr. Charles?" called Alexandre. "I have something here."

I rushed back into the villa, where I met Alexandre in the kitchen. He was holding a small stack of papers. "It looks like, yes, there was something wrong with the turbine. Something with brake system. Some electrical problem. They said they had to order a part."

"So it's not working now."

"I don't think so."

"Do we know anyone who could fix it?"

He pursed his lips, shook his head.

Chloe plopped down hard onto the couch. "There's no God, and we have no luck at all. Can I hate my life any more than this?"

"Well, while we're here, let's go through this place and see what we got."

"Fine," she spat, then rose and headed into one of the bedrooms, from where she screamed.

TWELVE

MARCOS, Alexandre, and Carlos had told me they'd cleared the house, so I hadn't given Chloe's trip to the bedroom a second thought.

I bolted out of the kitchen, down a narrow hall whose walls were jammed with dozens of framed photographs. I knocked off a few pictures as I brushed against the wall and burst into a bedroom, my blood ringing in my ears.

Chloe stood just inside, shaking and aiming her pistol at a young woman standing near a half-open window. She couldn't be much older than Chloe, with blond dreadlocks curling like serpents around her shoulders. She had a large hoop impaling her nose and dozens of bead necklaces hung loosely down her chest. Her long dress was the type you'd see on some women in Greenwich Village, its floral pattern harkening back to the 1960s and much too heavy to be wearing in this hot climate. And of course, she wore Birkenstocks. I'd had many students like her over the years, Rastafarian wannabes, and they were all the same—

brilliant writers who never came to class and flunked because of attendance. They had great sensibility as artists and no common sense when it came to simple things like setting an alarm clock or buying a textbook.

"Bitch, if you shoot me, they will kill you," she told Chloe.

"You're American. Who are you?" I demanded.

"Me? Who are you? And what are you doing in my house?"

I snorted. "This isn't your house."

"The hell it isn't."

"Where were you hiding?" I asked.

"Dad, relax. She's just scared," Chloe said, lowering her pistol.

Alexandre, who was in the doorway behind me, muttered something in Portuguese and kept his gun on the woman. I glanced at him, then faced our visitor and took a step toward her. "Answer my question."

She regarded the window, and I could almost see her thoughts as she calculated how quickly she could tug it all the way open and leap out. "All right," she finally said. "I heard you break in. I was under the bed."

"What's your name?"

"Jodi. I've been here for a couple of days."

"What's your story?"

"I don't have one. The world ended, and I got stuck here."

Chloe snickered. "Same as me."

"Aren't you with anyone?" I asked.

"I was."

"What happened?"

"She went back to the ship. She got scared. She was an idiot."

"What ship? What're you talking about?"

"We got here a couple of days after it all happened."

I realized she was referring to the small cruise ship that had anchored off the coast, near Gustavia. The ship was called the *Silver Whisper*, and Dan had mentioned that if it remained, we might go out to raid it for supplies—but that was before the wine raid on the Carl Gustaf.

"So you were on vacation?" I asked her.

"Yeah, some vacation."

"And you don't want to go back to the ship?"

"The crew's taken over. They've got the guns like you do. Their plan is to stay there, and then, when the supplies run out, they'll come ashore. They think they can take over because they have a few pistols and rifles. But some people didn't want to listen to them. Sheila and I got out because a couple of the crew members didn't want to stay either. We went with them, two bartenders and a housekeeper. I don't know where they are now."

"How did your friend get back to the ship?"

"Some guy with a yacht took her."

"What guy?"

"I don't know. She just got on his boat and took off. He was good-looking."

I nodded. "What're your plans now?"

"I don't know."

"You want to come with us?" asked Chloe.

"That's not your decision to make," I suddenly told her. "Don't even offer that."

"Why can't she come?"

"Because we're rationing everything, and we're not taking on any more people—"

"Unless they got skills, huh, like your doctor friend?"

"Chloe, I think we need to be careful," said Alexandre. "We cannot help everyone."

"I don't want your help," snapped Jodi. "I just want you out. I'm staying here right now."

"You can't stay," said Chloe. "Someone will come for you. There are no police anymore. It's do whatever you want. And they'll do you, know what I'm saying? You should come with us."

"Screw you."

Chloe raised her voice. "I mean it."

"It's not your decision," I told my daughter. "She's not coming."

"Well, if Uncle Danny decides, then he'll do what I say."

Jodi's expression turned incredulous. "I'm not going with you people."

"No, you're not," I said. "There's nothing here, and we're wasting our time."

"Wasting our time?" Chloe asked darkly. "You need to be someplace, Dad? We've got all the time in the world, what's left of it."

"I'm out of here," said Jodi as she started for the window.

"Wait, please," urged Chloe, rushing to Jodi and seizing her arm. "If you don't come with us, you'll die."

"Hey, Dad," called Jodi, "can you come get the drama queen off me?"

"Chloe, let her go."

"You can't do this."

"Why not? You suddenly care? You're suddenly my friend?"

Chloe hesitated. "Yeah, I am."

"You're nuts." Jodi tugged free her arm and began climbing through the open window. Then she stopped. "What the hell am I doing? I told you guys to get out."

"And we're leaving," I said, then gestured with my head for Chloe to exit.

"We're at the Eden Rock Hotel," she said quickly. "If you change your mind."

My daughter could've played Lady Macbeth. She had the evil eyes, the slight exposure of the teeth, and telltale puff of air down pat as she stomped past me.

I faced Jodi. "I'm sorry."

"For what?"

I shrugged and turned back for the hallway.

Alexandre rushed up to my side. "Why does Chloe want that girl to come with us?"

"Because she's spent her whole life saving puppies."

"What does that mean?"

"It means my daughter's got a big heart, maybe too big for this world now."

"But you're the one who gave her that heart."

I paused in the living room and regarded Alexandre with a pained look. "You're right."

BACK at the hotel, we shared the not-so-good news with Dan, who was sitting out on the terrace with Vacher and my father.

"Unless we find a good electrician or engineer, I don't think we can get any power out of that turbine," I said.

Chloe sat on the couch behind us, her face buried in a pillow.

"What's the matter with her?" Dan asked.

I told him about Jodi.

"She still up there?"

"I guess so."

He nodded. "She knows we're down here?"

"Chloe told her before we left."

"Then she'll be back. Unfortunately, we're not taking on any more strays."

"That's what I told her."

"You? Mr. Liberal-Wants-To-Save-Them-All?"

"Yeah, then Chloe said we only take them if they have skills, like Nicole."

"That's right. What skills does this girl have?"

"She's got an attitude. That's all I could tell. So . . . what now?"

He was about to answer when something out on the beach caught his eye. One of the fishing boats, a "flats" boat with a large canopy, was speeding in toward the shoreline, but I couldn't see any men on board.

We both stared curiously as the boat hopped the waves and hummed directly in toward the beach. It neither slowed nor changed course; it simply ran aground, the outboard wailing and churning up sand.

"What the hell?" I gasped.

"Come on," Dan cried, then sprang from his chair.

WE had to call Marcos and Bento to help us with the boat and the bodies. We hauled the four fishermen onto the beach and lined them up. They were former employees of the Sand Bar, Alexandre's friends, who'd become part of our fishing team and were on the water everyday for the past few weeks. Their weapons and catch had been stolen, all four of them had been executed, and their motor had been rigged at full throttle to express mail them to us.

And it all had happened in broad daylight. Dan had seen

another boat out in the bay, but he'd assumed it was our second fishing boat, not someone else's.

Alexandre came running out to us, fell to his knees, and began sobbing over the dead men, not a one of them older than twenty-five.

No one said his name, but everyone knew who was responsible, and when Alexandre composed himself, he rose and walked up to Dan. "We need to stop this."

Dan took a long breath. "I know. We're going to go over there and kill him."

"Should we go tonight?"

I shifted up to them. "You can't do that."

"An eye for an eye, brother."

"We have to talk. We have to stop this now."

"Talk?" asked Alexandre, pointing to the dead men. "Mr. Charles, I don't think there is anything else to say."

He was right, but I didn't want to admit that. Not then. But I should have, because Rousseau had more plans, many more plans for us.

DAN decided that hitting Rousseau that same night would be too obvious and that the man would be expecting him. So we'd wait a few days, try to catch him when he least suspected it. I kept trying to talk him out of it, saying maybe we could capture Rousseau or even join forces with him, but Dan would have none of that. He'd found himself an enemy and had created a war. He was in his element, and no one, probably not even Dad, could stop him.

I volunteered to take one of the night watches, along with James, and we both went up to the machine gun nest on the roof. James manned the .50 caliber, and I had one of the high-powered rifles. In the silvery glow of the stars we sat there, surveying the beach and surrounding mountains. The radiation meter remained silent. We were quiet for a long time, just watching and listening.

Then James suddenly said, "I feel bad for Hannah."

"Hannah? Why?"

"Uncle Dan's been ignoring her. She kind of wanders around like a lost cat. He doesn't give her anything to do. Just tells her to look pretty and shut up. I think she's getting really depressed."

"I haven't seen much of her."

"Because she spends all her time in their room, just sleeping."

"Why are you so worried about her?"

"I don't know. I just feel bad."

I eyed him suspiciously. "Okay."

"Dad, can I ask you something?"

I groaned. "What now?"

"Do you think we'll be all right?"

"What do you mean?"

"I mean how long are we going to live?"

"You're asking me that? Okay, you'll live another four years and twelve days, but then you'll slip in the shower and hit your head."

"I'm serious."

"I don't know. I just don't. I don't know if the fallout will ever get down here or if that idiot out there will start shooting and kill us. I don't know. How can you expect me to answer that?"

"Sorry."

I wrung my hands, realized I was taking out my frustration on him. "James, we'll be okay. Like Mom says, we were placed here for a reason."

He nodded, lowered his binoculars. "It's so quiet up here."

"We've never spent enough time together, have we?"

"That's because we don't want to hate each other, right? Every time we've been on vacation, we've spent more time fighting than having fun."

"And that's our family, huh?"

"Everybody's like that. Can't live with 'em, can't live without 'em."

"And now we can fight all we want. We have no jobs, no money, just this rock to defend. I was looking at my school ID the other night, and it was like a relic from another time. I feel like we've been here for years."

"Me, too."

I put a hand on his shoulder. "I'm proud of you."

"Why you saying that now?"

"I just want you to know it."

"I already know it, Dad."

I wanted to ask if he was proud of me, but I was too frightened of the answer, and even if he said he was, I'd be listening for the lie in his tone.

We sat there for another hour, making banal small talk and maintaining our watch. I began to doze off when James whispered, "Dad! I think they're coming!"

With a gasp and bolt of lightning shuddering through me, I rolled and peered up above our pile of sandbags. "Where? Where?"

"On the road. Two cars. No lights. See 'em?"

"No."

"Look harder."

I squinted through the night, the air filled with a kind of moist static that wavered like heat off a barbecue. And then, finally, two subcompacts in silhouette slowly materialized and rumbled down the road, toward us. I checked my watch: 2:35 a.m. They thought they'd catch us off guard. And they would have been right, were it not for James. Perhaps, too, they'd grown frustrated over Dan's failure to attack.

I got on one of the walkie-talkies with its failing battery and called Marcos, who was at his post below at the foot of the restaurant's staircase. He saw the cars and would alert the others.

"Maybe we shouldn't let them get any closer," James said, swiveling the big gun around and lowering his aim to the road. "Maybe I should take them out right now."

"You wait. There's something wrong here. If they wanted to attack us, they wouldn't be driving right up to the hotel. They'd be coming up on foot."

Automatic weapons fire rattled from somewhere in the southern hills, followed by more shots from the beach.

"Maybe they're doing both!" James cried, and before I could stop him, he cut loose with the machine gun, the rattle shockingly loud, the hot brass streaming at my knees as I screamed for him to stop, but he was on a mission, ordained by my brother as a minister of death.

I swung my head down and looked to the road, where James's rounds chewed into the first car, stitching their way up the hood and into the windshield. The car veered off the road, and a second later burst into flames, even as James shifted his fire to the second car, which had already stopped and was trying to make a U-turn. The driver was too late. The windshield shattered, and smoke began pouring from the hood a moment before James ceased fire. The passenger's side door on the second car swung open, and a man rushed out.

I lifted my rifle and sighted him, but he was as quickly gone into the woods.

James ceased fire, his breath heavy, eyes bulging. "You see that! You see that!" I'd never seen him so pumped up and shaking with adrenaline.

"I saw it." More gunfire reverberated from below. "Stay here. I'm going down."

I shouldered my rifle and climbed down the rope ladder and reached the top of the staircase. By the time I leapt onto the wood, another wave of gunfire ripped into the wall beside me. I hit the deck but lost my balance and went tumbling down the stairs. I stopped abruptly and felt a hand seizing my shirt collar, trying to lift me.

"What the hell, Charles?"

It was old Vacher, pistol in hand, come out to fight one last battle for himself.

I got shakily to my feet, sharp pains ripping through my shoulders and back, but nothing felt broken.

Two more rounds rose from the beach, and Vacher took off, moving at a remarkably swift pace. I fell in behind the old man, still blinking off the dizziness. I wanted to go up to our room to check on Vanessa and Chloe, but they already knew what to do in the event of shooting. We'd all discussed it, so I kept on after Vacher, and by the time we reached the sand, my heart sank over what we found there.

THIRTEEN

DAN, Marcos, Bento, and a few other men from Dan's teams had shot and killed four more people from Rousseau's party, with a fifth seriously wounded. The movie star's loyal troops were all young guys in their twenties, no doubt whipped up into a frenzy by their deranged leader. I called for Nicole, who came down to the beach and said the wounded man was losing too much blood. Dan insisted that she do what she could to keep him conscious, and my brother grilled the guy for everything he could about Rousseau. It was difficult to watch my brother act that cold and heartlessly.

After that, I went up with two more men to check out the cars James had taken out. The first one was still burning, the tires now puddles beneath the rims, smoke billowing in long, black banners. I glanced up at James, still in the machine gun nest, but I couldn't see his face. He waved. I just shook my head.

The stench of gasoline kept me from getting too close to the second car, but I did note a man slumped over the wheel. I didn't think the car would catch fire since it was far enough away from the first, so I told the others we'd come back in the morning to siphon off the remaining gas in the tank. There wasn't much else we could do there but stand in the eerie, hypnotic glow and reflect upon what had just happened. After a moment, we hustled back to the hotel.

On the beach, I shared what I'd seen with Dan, thanked him for turning my son into a murderer, then abruptly started off toward the stairs.

"You'll come down off your high horse someday, Charles. Trust me."

I froze. "High horse? We haven't even run out of stuff and we're already killing each other. High horse? Jesus Christ, Dan. Wake up!"

"This is how it goes. Maybe we get the fighting out of the way early and buy ourselves even more time."

"Or less."

IN our room, Vanessa was huddled in a corner with Chloe sleeping in her arms. She sat there, tense, biting her lip, her eyes swollen, and she jerked when she noticed me. "I can't take it anymore, Charles. I just can't."

"I know. I'll talk to Rousseau myself. I'll put an end to this." I wanted to tell her about James, but I didn't have the heart. He later confessed, and the shock that she had raised a murderer left her speechless for a long while. But she would let it pass, and so would I. We'd had no idea how much darker the days would become. "I'll put an end to this," I repeated.

"You're not doing anything. You go there, he'll kill you."

"We need a truce. That's all we need. Just a truce, even for a little while."

"I'll do it," came a voice from the doorway.

It was my father.

"Dad, go back to sleep."

"No one's sleeping now."

"You're not going anywhere."

"Listen, let me and Luc go over there. What the hell can that bastard do to us? Kill a couple of old men? He doesn't have the balls. Let us go. Let us be useful. I'm tired of waiting around to die."

I looked at Vanessa, who rolled her eyes.

"Dad, forget it."

"If I can rally the troops around here, I sure as hell can get that idiot to stop shooting. I'm sure he's taking flack for the five guys he just lost. They got girlfriends over there, relatives, and they're all screaming at Rousseau to put an end to this. They were just people on vacation, not soldiers. They can't handle this."

"We can't either," snapped Vanessa.

I studied my old man's expression, the one eye vacant, the jaw set.

"What do you think you can say to him?"

"Do you know how many leaders of opposing forces I've negotiated with? Do you understand the complexities of international diplomacy? Do you know how to cleverly and subtly maneuver your opponent in a conversation to get what you want from him? Son, I've been doing that all my life."

FEAR and dread rolled in like a fog off St. Jean Bay and devoured the hotel. Smiles were a rarity. A team of men had been assembled to bury the bodies from both groups, and services would be performed by one of the kitchen employees whose brother was a Catholic priest (that was the closest we could find to clergy). I detached myself from all of that and spent most of the day coaching my father and Vacher and reminding them they were sworn to secrecy.

"Do you realize who you are talking to?" Vacher reminded me. "Do you know what kind of security clearances I've held over the years? There were days when I knew more than the president of France!"

I sighed. He and my father were cut from the same cloth all right. "Okay, Luc, then you know the expression: loose lips sink ships."

"Of course."

The two geezers would head out to the Carl Gustaf just after dinner. James and I would drive them, and we'd wait to link up with them on the north side of the hotel, not far from where we'd staged our wine run.

I maintained an air of calm. Inside, I was on a torture rack, my heartstrings being torn apart. I kept wondering if I was just using my father and old Vacher, throwing them to wolves on a hunch that maybe Rousseau would listen and succumbing to their belief that they were now key diplomats in our group, our little tribe at Eden Rock. I imagined Rousseau putting a bullet in my father's head for opening his big mouth. And I shuddered. Then again, he'd go out in the blaze of glory he'd always wanted, fighting "the enemy." In some bizarre, sick way, I would be giving him a final gift. Damn, I just couldn't get my feelings wrapped around any of it, but I knew if we failed to at least try to negotiate with Rousseau, the attacks would continue, and none of us could handle that kind of paranoia and stress for much longer, even his high-ness Dan Almighty, who was already starting to unravel.

After dinner, James told me that Dan would be "busy." How did he know, I asked. He'd talked to Hannah and had asked her to keep Dan occupied, that the men were planning a little thank-you party for him, and, in fact, a few of them were doing just that, so Hannah would keep him occupied.

Before we headed out, I asked James if he was all right.

"Yeah," he said, surprised.

"How do you feel about what happened last night?"

"I don't know."

I tensed. "You don't know?"

"What do you want me to say? I feel bad? They attacked us. We defended ourselves. I don't feel bad at all—"

"About killing those people," I finished.

"Well, I guess I do. But, Dad, I hate to say this, it wasn't that much different than a video game. Better force feedback. My senses were fully engaged. But the imagery was pretty much the same."

"There are consequences for your actions, you know that. That's why your grandfather and Vacher are going out there tonight."

"Not because of me."

"No, because of everything. And you'd better start realizing that you can't be numb to all of this. You can't justify murder like this."

"I'm not justifying it. I'm just saying we defended ourselves."

"Okay."

"Dad, if it's us or them, I choose us. That's all I'm saying."

"So do I. They try to kill you, I kill them."

"Really?"

I grew more tense. "Yeah."

"Good, because I'd kill for you. I did last night."

"I just don't want us to be proud of that, to be bragging about it. This is horrible, James."

He shrugged.

I tried to repress my deep sigh of frustration and failed. He'd killed, had little to no remorse, and compared it to a video game. Was this the generation we had raised? Or was this his defense mechanism so he could process it all and still function? I felt certain I hadn't raised a murderer, but the families of the men we had hauled out of those cars would beg to differ.

WE drove up to the Carl Gustaf, and James remarked that we didn't see a single other car or person along the way. They were hiding and/or watching us from the road. Some had probably heard the gunfire and realized that we'd all descended to yet another level of hell. There was no more traveling alone, out in the open, and most would avoid a confrontation at all costs.

We dropped off my father and Vacher about two blocks from the hotel, and they shuffled up toward the main entrance, Vacher guiding my father by the arm, as the setting sun shown through a veil of lavender and saffron.

"This is crazy," said James.

"Can I live with myself?"

"What?" he asked.

I hadn't realized I'd said that aloud. "I'm worried about your grandfather. If he doesn't stick to the plan, they might shoot him."

"Dad, I should tell you something."

"What?"

"I was worried about this. I didn't think it was such a good idea—"

"So you told your uncle? Aw, James, man, now—"

"No, I didn't do that."

"Then what?"

"I told Alexandre. He's out here with Marcos right now, in case we get into it. I have one of the walkie-talkies in my backpack. I just thought you should know."

"Well, thanks for the vote of confidence."

"Dad, you've said it yourself. You're out of your element here."

"And you're the expert?"

"No, but it's good to have more help."

"And you don't think they told Dan?"

"No, because, well, I have something on Alexandre, and he owes me."

"Oh yeah?"

"I'll tell you later. But right now, I can't sit here and wait."

"Neither can I. So I guess we're not sticking to the plan. Let's get in closer."

JAMES and I left the car and slipped down into the hills around the hotel. As we descended, Rousseau's voice began to echo and rise, and I realized that we had picked a perfectly good or perfectly bad time to send in our "overqualified" diplomats. We crouched in the cover of several palms and gazed out across the hillside, where the megacelebrity himself had gathered all one hundred or so of his followers. They sat on the rocks and the grass as though in a stadium, with their leader at the bottom, wearing a pink silk shirt and raising his arms in the flagrant gestures of a televangelist.

"There is nothing in this world that we need anymore. The spoils of mankind are meaningless to us, and soon, very soon, we'll be packing up and leaving this pathetic meat that binds us to a scorched and poisoned rock." Rousseau beat a fist on his chest, then continued. "You and the Earth are not one. You have never been one. Remember, we are thetans, merely visitors, and soon detoxification will be complete. So there is nothing to fear, my friends. The destruction of this world has opened the gates for us to continue our journey out there, among the stars."

"Oh man. He sounds like Captain Kirk on acid," said James.

I snorted. "Even Captain Kirk would agree. And that's not Scientology he's preaching. I've studied it, and he's got a pretty skewed take on it all."

A young man dashed up to Rousseau and whispered in his ear. The movie star's eyes bugged out. "Bring them forward then!" He reached down, took a sip from a glass full of wine, then said, "My friends, we have visitors from Eden Rock, from those murderers who've killed seven of us already! And they have the audacity to come here! Bring them forward!"

"Oh my God, we're screwed," James muttered.

"Calm down. Trust your grandfather."

"Like you do? This guy's a lunatic."

"Grandpa's pretty crazy, too . . ."

I tried to hide my apprehension as my father and Vacher were escorted down to Rousseau by two shaggy-haired men holding rifles. Someone at the top of the hill switched on the floodlights of the nearest villa, and now the group was cast in a harsh, interrogator's glare.

"What do you have to say to us before we lock you up and leave you to die?" the movie star asked.

"Everyone!" my father cried, turning away to face the group. "We're calling for a cease-fire! No more blood! No more violence!"

"But you perpetrated the first act of evil!" Rousseau's finger-pointing—both literal and figurative—drew cries of agreement from his minions.

"That was an accident. I know my son is very sorry for what happened that night."

"Your son. So it's your boy who is leading that band of killers at the Eden Rock, the same bastard who turned us away when we were hungry."

"Look, Mr. Rousseau, we came here to talk cease-fire. No one wants to lose any more people. It's going to get hard enough without us killing each other."

"People, are you listening to what he's saying?" Rousseau extended his arms to the crowd, then once more pointed flagrantly at my father. I'd seen many of Rousseau's other performances, but this one was as over the top as they came, sans any director to reign him in.

"I hope they're listening—because all we have to do now is leave each other alone," my father said. "We're willing to make a promise, right here, right now, that we won't touch you again. Can you make that promise? Come on, Rousseau. We're all stuck on the same island. We're calling for a truce. That's all. Nothing else."

Rousseau thought a moment, then began rubbing his eyes. Suddenly, he pulled a pistol from his waistband and shoved it into my father's head.

"Wait!" cried Vacher.

"He killed my best friend," cried Rousseau. "Him and his sons!"

People screamed from the hillside, and a woman shouted, "No more! No more, William. We want peace!"

"Go ahead and shoot me," shouted my father. "I'm already dying. I want the bullet. But when you pull that trigger, you'll lose them all. You want to be a leader? You want them to follow? Fear only works for so long. You want them fiercely loyal? The only way you build that kind of trust is through smart leadership—and compassion. Trust me, young man, you call a truce, you let us walk out of here, and we'll honor that. We're men of our word. And in this screwed-up world, that's all we have left."

I wasn't sure, but I thought I saw Rousseau slowly, almost painfully, begin to nod. He lowered his gun and turned to face the audience. "They want a truce. What say you?"

A shirtless young man rose from the hillside. "Make love not war, man!"

Several others shouted their assent, and for a moment I felt as though we'd been time-warped back to Haight Ashbury, circa 1969, the "Summer of Love."

"All right, then. We'll give them their truce, with the promise that if they break it, we will come down on them with a spiritual force so powerful that none will survive it!"

"Whatever, dude," called the shirtless man. "Just no more shooting!"

"It's working," said James. "Grandpa's a bad ass."

"Yeah, he is." I groaned. "Of course, there will be no living with him now."

"I wouldn't worry about him," James began. "It's Uncle Danny. When he finds out what we did here—"

"I think he'll just need time to realize that for once he was wrong."

We picked up my father and Vacher a few minutes later, and the two old coots couldn't be more pleased with themselves, joking and laughing and replaying the scene, Vacher doing a terrible impression of Rousseau. We have our truce, they kept repeating, but all we really had was a temporary cease-fire because deep down, all of us knew, every one of us, that when supplies grew scarce, the violence would return, and only the fit would survive.

FOURTEEN

Today the power finally went down. My iPod wasn't fully charged, and I've only got about five hours of play time left. After that, the music dies forever, unless Dad and Uncle Dave figure out where we're going from here. I don't want to cry, and Alexandre has been trying to make me laugh by singing really, really bad versions of pop songs in Portuguese. I pretend to laugh. Sometimes I just want to kill myself, but I'm too scared because I don't know how to do it without feeling any pain. Nicole has all the medicine locked up in one of the hotel safes, so OD-ing on pills is out. I don't even know why I'm writing this. No one's going to read it. I hate this. I hate this so much I don't know what to do anymore. I really don't. I don't even know what I'm talking about now.

I gasped as I set down my daughter's journal and quickly left the room. I knew I would regret my snooping, as I had in the past, and I was literally sick to my stomach. Once more I learned just how distraught Chloe had become. Like me, she did a good job of hiding it. I groped for ways to help her find value in her life, to feel important and most of all, loved.

We'd been on the island for ten weeks, and the power had lasted a bit longer than we had anticipated. We had neither seen nor heard from Rousseau and his people, nor most anyone else for that matter, save for a few people who now and again wandered across our beach and were met with harsh orders to head away by our guards. All complied, though all begged us for help. I watched through the restaurant windows, and my heart broke each time. Dan went out to talk to one couple, honeymooners who were beginning to look emaciated. They'd been turned away by people from their own hotel and every other they'd visited because as the young man had said, "They were too good-looking and everyone hated them for that." They'd said the entire island was divided into a bunch of prison camps. They'd docked their small yacht in Gustavia after they'd run out of food. Dan told them to leave, but they were also low on fuel. He told them he was sorry and walked away, leaving them standing there. The woman broke down and fell to her knees. I wanted to go out there, but Vanessa grabbed my wrist and looked at me.

Dan got over the fact that I had sent our father to negotiate with Rousseau. Sure, it took him a week or so before he finally calmed down. Word of what I had done spread among the group, and I thought I saw them looking at me differently. Or maybe that was just wishful thinking.

DURING the next two weeks, I formed a scavenging party (because scavenging sounded so much better than what it really was, looting). Marcos, Bento, Chloe, Alexandre, Carlos, and I worked on foot, keeping off the main roads and carrying back-packs to fill with whatever might be useful—even just pens, paper, and old books we could (God help us) burn if needed. Chloe kept a pair of earbuds glued to her ears, even though her iPod had long since run out of juice. She said they made her feel more normal. We went back up to the wind turbine for another look, and there was no sign of Jodi, and I once more studied the turbine. I checked out the lift, and it was still operational. Then we went down into Gustavia and rummaged through the shops, ever wary of encounters. The downtown area was in a shambles, with debris blowing across roads speckled with broken glass and parked cars lined up, their gas caps dangling from their sides, their fuel long since siphoned. The people left on the island were survivors with too much time on their hands, so by three months into our fight most of the obvious stuff had been secured, to use one of Dan's words. The mannequins stood nude in shattered shop displays, some headless, some batted apart. In one clothing store we found a well-dressed corpse lying behind the counter, a distinguished looking Frenchman whose wallet had been rifled through and whose chest bore a large bullet hole. He reeked. We didn't stay long.

Chloe moved through the buildings with enviable efficiency, her eyes the keenest of the group. She'd find batteries and boxes of matches and other items overlooked by the first wave of looters because they hadn't dug as deeply as she did. Marcos, Bento, and I would go in first to clear a building, then the second team of Chloe, Alexandre, and Carlos would move in behind us and sweep for materials. We were absolutely systematic in our approach and left no door, drawer, or drapery unexplored.

At night, when we returned to the hotel, Chloe would pour over the maps and pick our next hunting ground. I thought keeping her busy had worked to lift her spirits, and I repeatedly told her how proud I was of her.

One evening, as we sat at a table alone in the restaurant, after Vanessa and most of the others had turned in, she finally opened her heart to me.

"I know you've been reading my journal."

"Only a few times. I'm sorry."

"It's okay. I guess after I found out, I started writing it for you. Sometimes it's easier to just write, you know?"

"You're talking to an English professor. At least I used to be . . ."

"You still are. The language lessons are still pretty fun the guys say."

"Good. You know, I wish your brother would talk to me."

"He doesn't say much to me either. He's spending most of his time with Uncle Dan and Hannah."

"That's what worries me."

"How are you doing?"

I blinked. Hard. "Excuse me?"

"How are *you* doing?"

"Me, I'm okay."

She laughed under her breath. "Why is that surprising?"

"Your question? Well, it's nice to be asked."

"Mom never asks you?"

"Sure she does."

"But I don't."

"It's okay." I rose, came around the table, and gave her a hug. "You know I love you."

"I know. And thanks for letting me come along to get stuff."

"You're the best stuff getter we have."

"I was hoping for bigger things."

"You know, I was thinking the other day that as terrible as all this is, it's also pretty extraordinary."

She frowned. "Wow, that's a weird word to use."

"No, I mean it. I was thinking that for the most part we all would've lived pretty ordinary lives. Eat, crap, die, right? Nothing unusual. Now look at us. This is anything but ordinary. We're fighting to stay alive on an island in the Caribbean after a nuclear war. Even after saying it, even after all this time, it's still hard to comprehend."

"You're a strange guy, Dad."

"I've been up and down and sideways and all over the place with this. Now I'm just trying to be positive. Who knows what's going to happen to us, but I promise you, it won't be boring."

"I believe you, Dad."

"And I have a surprise. Uncle Dan got his hands on a few small generators. We gassed them up. We should have enough power to recharge your iPod."

"Are you kidding me?"

I held her closer. "No, I'm not."

A few days later—I'm not sure how many, they all began to blur into each other—I was standing in front of the mirror, wearing just my boxers, when Vanessa come into the bathroom behind me and her jaw dropped.

"Almost thirty pounds," I said, seeing my ribs for the first time in almost as many years.

"I'm down only fifteen," she said. "But you know, we can't lose much more."

"It's a metamorphosis. That's what it is."

"Oh God, here we go," she groaned. "You're going to get

philosophical about food rationing and how we've lost weight and the symbolism of all this. Charles, there's nothing symbolic about this."

"Sure there is. Sloughing off the fat of our old lives. Transforming ourselves."

"We're just refugees."

"No, like you said, we were saved for a reason. And things are beginning to change for us."

She wrapped her arms around my waist. "I don't want any more change."

JAMES woke me up in the middle of the night and called me to a meeting with Dan and a few of the guards down in the restaurant. Emilia, one of the Portuguese waitresses who'd been well trained by Dan and whose English skills had been honed by me, stood before the group in flickering candlelight, holding her rifle, her binoculars hanging from the cord around her neck. She spoke quickly and breathlessly:

"We saw four of them in the hills, watching us. They moved in closer on the southwest side, then stayed there for about an hour. Then Bento called me to say he saw another three at his post, and Marcos, you saw two more down the beach, right?"

Marcos nodded. "They were armed, too."

"You think it's Rousseau's people? Or a group from another hotel?" I asked.

Dan shrugged. "Only way to find out is to confront Rousseau. He's honored the truce for this long. Maybe they got a little too hedonistic and burned out all their supplies."

"Maybe."

"All right, everyone. Keep a tight watch tonight."

Back near the door, I spotted my father and Vacher. The old Frenchman whispered something in my father's ear, then they left.

I told Dan I'd see him in the morning, went back upstairs to my room, and slipped into bed with Vanessa.

"What was it?"

"Aw, more people watching us. Could be Rousseau. We'll have to find out in the morning."

I thought my heart had stopped. The shock sent me bolting upright in bed. My ears rang, and for a moment, I wasn't sure what had happened until I was fully conscious. My watch read 4:41 a.m. I'd only been asleep for a couple hours after being wrestled awake by James.

A single gunshot had exploded in the night like a bomb in a quiet town on Christmas Eve.

The shot had come from within our villa.

I blinked hard, grabbed my flashlight and my pistol from the nightstand.

"Charles, I'm coming with you," Vanessa whispered.

"Get in the closet," I whispered back. "Now!"

Vanessa slipped out of the bed, but instead of going to the closet, she fell in behind me and said, "Let's go."

There was no argument in her tone.

I rushed out as a voice from the other side of the villa cried out. The voice was French. Vacher. What was he saying?

Then came Hannah's voice, high-pitched, whimpering at first, then breaking into a bone-chilling cry.

My pulse leapt, and I broke into a run.

James shouted, "Oh my God!"

And Chloe echoed with, "Oh no, what happened?"

"I don't know! I don't know!" shouted my father.

A voice was missing from that group, and suddenly a pit formed in the bottom of my stomach, and then a hole, and then all of my courage poured from that hole like dark wine.

There were two of them at the bus stop who would always harass me, Anthony and John Schema. And I would take it because I was scared to get into a fight. I was twelve years old and I knew what happened to kids who fought a lot: they got sent away to juvenile detention centers and were forced to pick up garbage and repaint walls sprayed with graffiti. I thought about what my father would do to me if that ever happened. So I told Anthony and John to leave me alone, but they never stopped. Then one day, unbeknownst to even me, Dan hid in the bushes at our corner. And when the two Schema brothers began to shove me, Dan burst out and punched John squarely in the nose. Then my brother turned to Anthony and kicked him in the balls so hard that the kid couldn't get up. Dan shouted in their faces to leave me alone. He shouted again and again, and I got yet another taste of how crazy and violent he could become. Secretly, I was proud of him for helping me. He was my baby brother, yet he was my protector, thus I could barely fathom the sight of him lying on the floor with a gunshot wound to his chest and my father standing above him, clutching the very gun that had delivered the round.

FIFTEEN

MY father's hallucinations had been growing worse during the past few weeks, though I didn't believe they contributed entirely to him shooting my brother. Dad had been worried about an attack from the folks we'd seen watching us earlier in the evening, so he'd gone to bed with a pistol at his side, even though Dan had forbid him to handle any of our weapons.

"It's my fault," said Vacher. "I gave him the gun. I wanted him to feel like he could protect himself. He'd been complaining about that for days. I tried to give him an empty magazine, but he checked to be sure it was loaded."

"Luc, it's not your fault. I shot him," cried my father, and for the first time in my life I saw my Dad break down. Even when his own father had died, he had not cried, at least not that I saw. "Dear God, I shot him."

Dan had come in to check on our father, and in the darkness my father, with his one good eye, had heard him enter, seen a man with a gun, and reacted.

Hannah, who'd dropped to Dan's side, was crying hysteri-cally over him. Chloe and Vanessa pulled her out of the way as I checked my brother's neck for a pulse. I found a weak one, but his shirt was growing more soaked with blood. James ran off to get Nicole while I put pressure on the wound, the way I'd seen her do for Rousseau's man.

My brother's stare seemed vacant, but then he moved his head just a little and focused on me. His mouth opened as if to say something.

I whirled my head and hollered for Chloe and Vanessa to get Hannah out of the room. She was sobbing so loudly I couldn't hear anything else. I put my ear to my brother's mouth, but he didn't talk.

"Danny, I'm so sorry," said my father. "I didn't mean it, son. God, you have to know that. It was an accident!" Vacher helped my father onto the floor, where he clutched one of Dan's hands. "Hang on, my boy. Please, God, let him be okay. Let him get through this. We need him."

I kept the pressure on Dan's chest and felt the blood soak-ing into my hands. My eyes burned and blurred with tears. How much more cruel, more merciless could the world become? How much more were we fated to endure?

Vacher ran off and returned with another flashlight, and by the time he got the beam on Dan's face, I knew.

After a deep breath, I released the pressure on my brother's chest and once more checked his neck for a pulse. I swallowed and gasped, "He's gone."

My father lowered his head and wept like a little boy; it was the most pathetic display I had ever seen, and it scared the hell out of me.

By the time Nicole arrived I was already on my feet, wiping

my bloody hands on my boxer shorts and backhanding the tears from my cheeks.

Without a word, she examined Dan, then glanced up at me. "How did this happen?"

My voice cracked. "It was an accident."

A cluster of our men had gathered outside the bedroom door, their expressions twisted in horror.

I floated outside my body and watched myself go through the motions of calming everyone down, urging everyone back to their beds, and remaining with James and Alexandre to clean up the mess. We wrapped Dan's body in some bed sheets and hauled him down to one of the restaurant's coolers kept running by a few of our small generators. Again, I hovered over the scene, saw myself in the third person: *There was Charles, and his two men, and Charles thought what a gruesome and terrible thing it was to see the absent eyes of the brother he had known for his entire life . . .*

After that, I sat with James in the restaurant, and a few minutes later, Chloe, Vanessa, and Hannah joined us. We were zombies at that table, watching the sun slowly rise, and if there was anything to say it did not occur to us.

We decided to bury Dan at sea. He was a Marine, and it seemed fitting; old Vacher was willing to take us out about a mile offshore with some of the fuel he had left. During our first month on the island he'd moved his yacht from Gustavia and anchored it in the bay so we could keep watch over it. We transported Dan's body in the Zodiac, and then a small group of us went out to lay him to rest via several anchors we'd procured. He'd been wrapped tightly in the multicolored nylon of a parasail that Chloe had found a few weeks ago.

I was hoping everyone would say a few words, everyone except my father, who'd already said he could not bear to speak at the service, although he still wanted to come along. In fact, during the entire boat ride he remained belowdecks, weeping. I feared he would take his own life now, so I asked Vacher to stay with him 24/7, and the old Frenchman reminded me that he was already doing that.

Hannah stood on the aft deck, the morning wind whipping hair into her eyes. The color had vanished from her face, along with any traces of her usual makeup. She uttered half a sentence, choked up, tried to finish it, then waved a hand and returned to her seat. "Give me a minute."

I'd grown to respect her a lot more in the past three months. Somehow she'd put up with my brother and become more than his trophy; she actually provided stability for him, a springboard for ideas. I'd written her off as a ding-dong with a boob job, but when I looked at her sobbing, I thought, she really did love him, and she was smart enough to navigate around his ego to maintain their relationship. I was certain she considered my brother a protector, just as I did, so his passing left both of us feeling scared, vulnerable, and lost.

Chloe, red eyed and somber, stood and said, "Uncle Danny was a good guy. He taught me a lot of things, and even though he was always really tough, he cared a lot about people, which was why, I think, he was so tough. He wanted to bring out the best in us. And he wouldn't want us crying right now. So I'm going to try to do one last thing for him." She nodded, fought back the tears, and had a seat.

James rose and stared down at the body, a mummy strapped with anchors. "Uncle Danny? Thanks. You were always a real character. I guess some people would call you a man's man, which

I guess is the old-school way of saying you were a good leader and a fair guy. It's going to be hard without you." James took a deep breath and started to cry.

Vanessa got up, but I didn't pay much attention to what she said. Call me a horrible (or typical) husband, but I knew I would be next and was beginning to panic. I'd made two attempts to write out a little speech, and both had failed miserably.

Hannah suddenly gave it one more try, but all she managed was, "I love you, Dan."

We all sat a moment in the bob and wave of the bay, the wind growing warmer on our necks.

Then it was my turn, and I would be the last to speak before we committed Dan to the sea. I stumbled at first, but then I launched into stories of our childhood. I told them about the *Playboy* magazine and riding our bikes and Dan defending me at the bus stop, stories none of them had ever heard because my anger and resentment had kept them locked away for far too long.

I told them about the time when Dan and I had been Cub Scouts and we'd both entered the pinewood derby model-car race. Dad had been firm about not helping us build our little cars out of the supplied piece of pine that came with the kit, and so Dan had gone out to the garage and constructed a fabulous little racer with sandpaper and files and wood glue. I'd sat in the living room and sobbed for an hour. Dan returned and told me he'd help me build my car. And so he did, and it was one of those glorious moments when two brothers stopped fighting for a few hours on a Sunday afternoon and created something rudimentary but remarkable.

And the rub came when my car beat Dan's and most other cars in the big derby. I took second place, while he got eleventh, and even though he had, in effect, built my car, he wasn't bothered very much by losing because he knew the car was also his and that he had done a good thing by helping his brother. He congratulated me and asked if he could hold the trophy to see what it felt like.

These are the memories that make me sob like I did that Sunday afternoon when I felt totally helpless. These are the memories that all brothers carry because we are blood, because we will give our lives for each other. I knew the kind of man Dan wanted me to be. I just didn't know if I could be all of that.

James and I rolled Dan off the deck and into turquoise depths, and we watched him plunge, the nylon fluttering about his body like angels' wings. As I watched, I tried to remember the last thing I'd said to him down in the restaurant; it was a phrase as banal and pedestrian as any other: see you in the morning.

I cleared my throat and spoke as his corpse faded into the depths. "See you in the morning, Dan."

DURING the boat ride back, I went below with Vanessa and told her we'd have to find someone to lead the group and that maybe Dayreis would be a good choice.

"Are you kidding?" she asked. "They'll expect you."

"Me? I can't do it."

"Why not?"

"Because . . . I don't know. Because I'm not *them*."

"You mean your father and brother? Uh, yes, you are them. And yes, we need you now. You're the smartest man we've got. We need someone who thinks outside the box. Someone a little unconventional."

"What about Vacher?"

"Give me a break, Charles. Besides, he's really got his hands full with your father."

"I think we should put it out there and let them decide."

"That could work, but I think they're expecting you to step up and carry on your brother's work. If you come out strong, they'll be even more loyal. If you show them you're unsure, then you come across as weak. It's time for you to lead. They trust you to do that. They haven't forgotten about the truce with Rousseau. You did that. Not your brother."

"I don't want this."

"You think any of us did?"

"I can't do it the way Dan did."

"Then be yourself, and do what you think is best. And we'll stand behind you all the way."

"Vanessa, I'm scared."

"Me, too."

We held each other, and once more the tears came hard. I heard my brother whisper all his favorite idioms in my ear: *Are you going to cry like a pansy—or are you going to come down from the mountain, step up to the plate, and get with the program?*

WHEN we returned to the hotel, Marcos, Bento, and Alexandre were standing on the beach, confronted by a group of eight women, one of whom I recognized.

"Jodi!" Chloe hopped out of the Zodiac and started up the beach as the young girl with the dreadlocks broke off from the group and padded across the sand toward my daughter.

"Who's she?" Vanessa asked.

"The girl we ran into up in Lurin."

"Really?"

"Yeah, come on."

We left the boat to James, who would head back to the yacht

to fetch Hannah, Vacher, and my father. I asked Alexandre what was going on.

"They came from the cruise ship, and they're looking for help," he said, sounding exhausted.

"All right, ladies—" I began.

"Before you go any further," interrupted a lean woman barely five feet tall with a crew cut. "I want to know if you're the guy in charge, because we can't get anything out of these guys."

I glanced to Vanessa, who hoisted her brows.

Then I took a deep breath. "Yeah, I'm the guy in charge." The words came out easier than I'd thought. I introduced myself, Vanessa, and Chloe, who was still near the back of the group, talking to Jodi.

"Charles Spencer. Why does that name sound familiar?"

"I don't know. Who are you?"

She proffered her hand. "Cindy Berkerson. And this is my partner, Jane Marshall."

A taller woman with longer hair and bony arms smiled wanly at me.

"Well, Cindy, I'm sure you came here looking for help, but we don't have much ourselves. There are a lot of hotels. Maybe you'll have better luck with them."

Cindy's expression darkened. "We've been to most of them. This is the third day we haven't eaten. Even all the fruit trees have been picked clean. Jodi insisted we come here. She said you offered to help her. Now I'm asking you, please, help us."

"I'm sorry."

"Come on, Cindy, let's go," said her partner, throwing her arms in the air. "They're just like all the rest."

"Where are you guys from?" I suddenly asked, feeling the guilt take hold like my mother's hand.

"We're both from Seattle. We came down with the group here. This was supposed to be the vacation of a lifetime with people we really enjoy."

"Yeah."

"Well, you guys have the guns and food. And all we can do is grovel."

"Dad, what's going on?" asked Chloe, pushing up to me with Jodi at her side.

"They were just leaving."

"Leaving, why? They need help."

I took a long breath. "Chloe, we've talked about this, and I won't have this conversation right now."

"So we're telling them to just go off and die?"

I couldn't face those women anymore, their sunken cheeks and pleading eyes, their wrinkled clothes and sunburned shoulders. Then I remembered what Dan and I had discussed about taking in strays.

With a deep sigh, I faced them once more. "Ladies, tell me something. What did each of you do back in the world?"

"Why does that matter?" asked Cindy. "It's all gone. They're all dead. The president killed them."

I sharpened my tone. "What did you do?"

She frowned. "I was a group fitness instructor."

"And I was an electrical engineer," said Jane.

"Excuse me?"

"I was an electrical engineer."

"You ever work on any wind-powered generators."

She shook her head. "I've done a lot of work with solar, though."

"That's good. And what about the rest of you?"

We had two teachers, one elementary, one college; a VP of

sales for a clothing store; a dentil hygienist; a loan officer for a bank; and then there was Jodi, who was partnered with the hygienist, Sheila, and whose answer was, "I've done a lot of different things, most of which are none of your business."

It seemed to me that only Jane had a skill we needed at the present moment, and that might be enough to justify giving them a little food to tide them over—if Jane agreed to go up and have a look at the wind turbine.

I discussed the idea with them, and she quickly agreed. I told them we could only spare enough food for a day or two, and even then it wouldn't be much. They didn't care.

I told them to wait down on the beach while I went up to the restaurant to discuss the trade with Dayreis. The old chef protested vehemently. "You don't even know if she can help with the turbine. I say you wait to see if she can help, and if she can, then you give them some food."

"Or we give them some food now and we have their loyalty."

"Mr. Charles, ask yourself, would your brother have made this trade?"

"Probably not. He would've dismissed them and the help we could've received. We can't just turn everyone away. And if we can get some power up in that villa, we can get the news again. We need the news."

"But listen to me, Mr. Charles. We can't feed all of them without starving ourselves! Next week, we will only have fish. All of the other food will be gone!"

"I understand. Just go along with me on this one. We'll need that turbine. We need to get back in touch with South America. We need power."

"Take what you want. I'll tell the others about your decision."

"Thank you."

"For what? You are in charge now, right? I have no say in the matter."

"Yes, you do. I'll lead this group, but not the way my brother did."

"Be careful, Charles. Too much compassion is not good now. Your brother was correct on this: we must be fighters. Otherwise, we will die."

"I think we can be fighters—and still not forget who we are."

"Okay. I am glad we had this talk. Fate has stepped into your life, Mr. Charles. I hope you will pay attention to the signs."

"I hope so, too."

SIXTEEN

THOSE poor women tore into the grilled dorado and almonds and quenettes we gave them, and one slightly pudgy woman in her late forties threw up because she'd eaten too fast. Then she began crying, and Chloe gave her a half dozen crackers she'd been hording in her backpack.

"This is how we're going to die," said Jane. "We'll watch each other starve to death, and there's nothing we can do about it. Nothing."

"That's not true," I said. "We can teach you how to fish. We can loan you some gear. There are plenty of small boats left. It's up to you. And so far the fish are safe. We've scanned them. There's a lot of wood here to burn. We can help you get a fire started, so you're not eating sushi every day."

She thought about that and eventually nodded.

I took Jane and a small team of four men back up to the turbine. She went up on the scissors lift and had a close look at the nacelle and the turbine's internal parts, a spaghetti of wires and different colored boxes that resembled the pile of Christmas lights I'd had in a box in my attic, in a house that had since been reduced to a charred concrete slab peaking out between piles of ash.

"The papers we found said there was a problem with the brake system," I called up to her.

"Yeah, there's a short. I can see it."

"Glad you can. Can you fix it?"

"Maybe."

"They said they had to order a part."

"They always say that because it's easier to replace than fix."

We'd packed a small tool kit that Chef Dayreis kept in his kitchen. Jane reached down into that box and produced a socket wrench, then she got to work. I opted to remain on the ground for the rest of the repair. The wind rattled the lift and definitely unnerved me. She seemed unfazed by it.

ABOUT ten minutes later, just as Jane was calling me over, Alexandre came charging up the driveway. "Five men coming. One is Rousseau."

My shoulders slumped. "Damn."

"Jane, it's broken. You can't fix it."

"I understand," she said.

Rousseau and his group strode cockily into the backyard, covered by my men. The celebrity wore a baby blue silk shirt; however, it was torn at the shoulder, and a long, dark slash stained the left breast. He'd grown a beard, with a touch of gray appearing at his chin, and he was a little skinnier than I remembered.

"What are you people doing to my wind turbine?" Rousseau asked.

"It's nobody's now. Can't be fixed," I said.

He swung around to face me. "You again. Where is your brother?"

"He's dead."

Rousseau sighed. "I bet his mouth got him killed."

"Yours might, too."

"Whoa. That gave me a chill. And how is your father?"

"Why do you ask?"

"Because I respect the man. He came as a sheep into a den of wolves."

"Isn't that a line from one of your movies?"

"I don't remember." He shielded his face from the glare and turned up to Jane. "And you up there? What are you doing?"

"Nothing."

"You can't fix it?"

"No, the brake system is gone. Won't work."

"I see." He faced me. "Well, Mr. Spencer, it seems you and I have a common problem. We both need power. Do you know what month this is?"

"Yeah, it's March."

"And by June we'll be into hurricane season. We'll need those weather reports from South America."

"You're right."

"And who knows what a storm could do to the fallout."

I shrugged.

"I'm told you have a radiation detector. You got it up at the hospital."

"Who told you that?"

"Doesn't matter. If those readings go up, you owe it to everybody left on this island to let us know, so we can take some cover."

"Of course. But why even stay? Why don't you take your group and sail off. There's still some boats left in Gustavia."

"We sent a group down to Cartagena and Caracas. Some of them went ashore and were arrested. They'll rot away in jail. No food to spare for prisoners. There's no sanctuary for us there."

"I don't believe that."

"You want to talk to the ones that came back? I can arrange a meeting."

I shook my head. "I'm told your people are doing a lot more fishing now."

"Like you."

"Do you have any food left?"

"Why do you care?"

"I'm just curious."

"Then you tell me."

"We have some. Mostly canned goods. The fresh stuff is long gone."

"Are you still drinking my wine?"

"We haven't touched it yet."

"Well then, you'd be correct in returning it to us." He cocked a brow.

"I'll consider that."

"All right, then." He whistled, and his men turned around to leave.

"Hey, Rousseau?"

He glanced sidelong at me.

"Good luck to you."

My sentiments were met by a deep frown before he ambled away.

Alexandre, who'd been standing at my shoulder, said, "He's

not the same anymore. He looks old and tired. I thought he would be arrogant until the day he died."

"We just caught him on a good day. I heard he was manic depressive. And he's been off his meds for three months. We can tell him what he wants to hear, but we do not trust him."

"You're right, Mr. Charles."

I glanced back up at Jane, whose arms were elbow deep in wires, and gestured with my hands for a report.

She raised a thumb.

"Great. Thank you."

I waved Alexandre into the shade of the back porch. "I've been wanting to talk to you about something. Two things, actually."

He lowered his gaze to the concrete. "I'm sorry, Mr. Charles. I did not mean to disrespect you."

"So you know what's coming."

"I think so, sir."

"Well, it was hardly a surprise. I just want to be brutally honest with you. My daughter is young and vulnerable and the last thing she needs right now is a pregnancy. Do you understand?"

"Of course, sir."

"Good."

"Now what's this I hear about you taking off at night?"

"What do you mean?"

"James followed you. He saw you meet two men at a boat. Are you passing them food?"

He closed his eyes. "Yes, but only some of my rations. I have not stolen anything."

"Who are they?"

"Just friends I used to work with. They have nothing and need my help."

I put a hand on his shoulder. "I know what it feels like, but there's only so much we can do."

"I understand. I won't meet them anymore."

"You mean you won't get caught again."

"No, sir."

"All right, that's it for now."

He was a good kid with a heavy heart. Chloe could have done a whole lot worse, and perhaps he gave her hope. I couldn't interfere with that.

Jane descended on the scissors lift and said, "Okay, only two more wires to connect."

"Down here?"

"No, up there."

"Then let's go."

She shook her head. "How bad do you want power?"

"We already had a deal."

"You can't throw us out there to die."

"I still don't know if it works."

"Doesn't matter. You need to do the right thing."

"Yeah, protect my family."

"And to hell with everyone else? You can teach us to fish, but we need protection. Just let us stay with you. We'll get our own food, like you said. Just let us stay."

Maybe I was tired of being pushed, tired of being taken advantage of, tired of being tired, I wasn't sure. But that violence that lurked in my genes finally reared its ugly head. I drew my pistol from my waistband, shoved it into Jane's head, and screamed, "Back on the lift! You're fixing it right now, or I'm going to blow your brains out!"

Her eyes brimmed with tears, her lower lip beginning to tremble, as she said, "Go ahead. I don't care anymore."

"Mr. Charles!" cried Alexandre.

I pressed the muzzle even harder into Jane's head. "Do it, right now!"

She grimaced and slowly turned and started back toward the lift, with me behind her, the pistol now trained on the back of her head.

We ascended together, and weeping, she finished the job on the turbine and slammed shut the access doors.

"It had better work," I warned her.

"It will," she gasped.

We went to the side of the villa, where beneath a long awning sat several large pieces of machinery that Jane said were the batteries and alternator for the turbine. There were several outlets built into the alternator unit itself, as well as a status panel with an indicator that now glowed red. Jane told Alexandre to get a lamp. He did and when he plugged it in, a tiny light appeared inside the bulb. "Satisfied?" she asked. "The batteries are still drained, but they'll charge up now and that light will turn green."

I lowered my pistol. "You have to understand the position I'm in."

"Oh, I understand it perfectly. All I was asking for was protection."

I rubbed my eyes and thought a moment. What the hell had I just done? "All right. You got it."

BACK at the hotel I explained to Dayreis and the others what our arrangement was with the women, and they were okay with it so long as none of our food and water was given to them. They had to catch their own fish, and if they found any nuts or fruit in the hills, so be it.

The gasoline we had siphoned from all the vehicles was just about gone, and the small generators we'd been using to keep one of the restaurant's coolers running would soon shut down. We'd sent two more teams to the island's gas stations, and all the tanks had been, for the most part, emptied. Our guys returned with about five gallons and had been watched the entire time by a group of five black men with dreadlocks. They'd asked for help, but as our men were instructed, they said nothing and left.

Alexandre, Dayreis, Marcos, Bento, James, and I were sitting in the restaurant and discussing our fuel concerns, with my father and Vacher seated nearby and eavesdropping on the conversation, when Vacher rose and said, "I have an idea."

We all faced him.

"About ten years ago one of my friends bought a villa near Eden House in Marigot Bay. He was a retired officer. Became a mercenary. Anyway, he sold the place a few years back."

"Get to the point, Luc," I said impatiently.

"I will, Charles, I will. Anyway, he was a very thorough man. I remember him asking me about the storms down here, and he said he wanted to be well prepared. I'm not sure what he might have done because we had a falling out not long after, but it might be worth a look."

MARIGOT, we later learned, was on the northeast side of the island, and the road up there was tortuous to say the least, with steep drop-offs on either side. We formed a bike expedition, six of us in all, with James riding up front. We passed a small group of five people, tourists we assumed, walking down the road, and they quickly threw themselves to the embankment in a pathetic attempt to hide from us as we rode on by. I glanced back at them, trying to harden myself against the pain in their expressions.

Vacher, with the help of a local phone book, was able to remember the exact address so we didn't have to drag him up there. As we neared Marigot, and the bay slowly scrolled up into view as though a shade were being drawn open, a gunshot rang out from the forest to the south, and we stopped short, threw down our bikes, and dropped to the ground.

Another shot hit the pavement not a foot from James. I screamed to him as Alexandre and Marcos fired two rounds apiece into the woods.

"Hold your fire!" I told them. "Don't waste the ammo till we know what we got! Get over here!"

I waved them all forward, to where James had found a ditch just off the north side, and they charged over, crouched down, two more rounds hitting the ground behind them.

Although I didn't know much about firearms, I could only assume that our "assailants" were amateurs with bad aim, because they had us out in the open and had failed to score a single hit, unless they were just trying to scare us.

"You down there," cried a man with a deep accent that I guessed was Jamaican. "Leave your packs and your guns in the road, and we'll let you go on your way."

"Alexandre, give me the binoculars," I said, crawling on my belly to the dusty edge of the asphalt. I panned the forest rising at a lazy thirty-degree grade, the palms thrumming in the wind. I couldn't see anyone, damn it.

"We're not giving you anything!" I shouted.

"Dad, keep him talking. I'll go around the side and see if I can flank him."

"No way. Stay here."

"Dad, Uncle Dan taught me what to do. Let me take Marcos."

"You sure?"

"Yeah, I'm sure."

"All right, go." I lifted my voice. "Hey, you'd better come down here right now."

"No, you'd better leave your packs. We know where you are! We can see you!"

I was running out of things to say. "Show yourself, you coward!" I laughed bitterly under my breath. "Oh God, that was lame," I told the others.

Meanwhile, James and Marcos crawled along the edge of the road, then pulled themselves onto the asphalt. Suddenly, they sprinted to the other side, vanishing into the forest.

"We just want your packs."

"Then come down and get them," I cried.

Only the rustle of palms answered. I lay there, pulse throbbing in my ears.

A gunshot rang out, jarring me, and the man screamed.

"James!" I shouted.

"It's all right," my son called. "Looks like just one guy! I shot him and he just gave up!"

"Come on," I ordered the others.

We rushed across the road and climbed into the woods where we found James standing over a black man with dreadlocks who was clutching his thigh. James had already confiscated his weapon.

"Bad move, buddy," I told him. "Bad move."

"Please, I just wanted some water."

"I don't care."

"Don't leave me here to die."

I stepped toward him. "Let me see your leg."

He removed his hand to reveal the gunshot wound on the outer edge. It didn't look very bad.

"You're not going to die," I told him.

"Who are you?" James asked.

"My name is Tremaine."

"Well, Tremaine, you won't get anywhere on this island by taking shots at people," I said.

Marcos pointed his rifle at the guy's head. "You were at the gas station, watching us that day, weren't you?"

Tremaine nodded.

James crouched down beside the man. "Are you from here?"

"No, I'm from the ship. We had a reggae band, but the captain and the crew took over, and they've started throwing people overboard, just trying to get rid of us—so they'll have more food."

"Where's the rest of your band?" asked James.

"We're up at the Eden House with a few more people from the ship, but we're all out of food. The others wanted to stay, but I just left."

"Are they armed, like you?"

"Maybe."

"Tell you what," I began. "If we see anybody up at the Eden House, we'll tell them where you are. And if we don't? Well, tough luck."

"Here," James said, offering the man a small plastic bag with grilled fish and a plastic bottle half full of wine.

"Oh my God, thank you! Thank you so much!" Tremaine said, tears coming into his eyes.

I shook my head over James's generosity. Not long ago I'd been shaking my head over his work with the machine gun and his lack of conscience, and I wondered when the tug and pull of our existence would finally tear us apart.

While Tremaine ate, we cut some pieces from his jacket and used them to fasten a makeshift tourniquet for his leg. Then we got him to his feet, and he tested the leg. "I think I can walk a little."

"That's good," James said.

I sharpened my tone. "Well, Tremaine, we won't be returning your gun, lest you shoot someone else." I faced the others. "Let's go."

As we walked away, James said, "Poor guy."

I didn't answer. I could already feel the ice forming inside, spreading in thick veins.

SEVENTEEN

IF Eden House was occupied, we saw no evidence. Tremaine's friends might have been hiding or away, hunting for food. Out of guilt, I told James that on the way back we'd see if the man was still there, and if so, we'd give him a ride up the hill, even though he'd tried to kill us—I had to add in that last remark, and when I did, I shuddered over how much I sounded like my brother. I think even James noticed that.

We forged on to the villa: twenty-five hundred square feet of opulence carved into the hillside. Its walls shone behind lush tropical gardens, and the hibiscus planted in perimeter rows were in full bloom. As with many of the other vacation homes on the island, there was a keen sense of symmetry between the architecture and the landscape that appealed greatly to Vanessa's feng shui sensibility. I just thought the homes blended well into the mountains.

Unsurprisingly, the place had already been looted. We entered through a shattered door and cleared the rooms, military style,

as Dan had taught us all. Certain we were alone, we relaxed and
began a search. The refrigerator was empty. The cistern had
already been drained, and the drawers had been yanked from the
pricey antique furniture. We found some dog-eared paperback
novels, a few pieces of clothing that looked as though they'd been
on the hangers for two years, some maps and travel brochures.

"Damn, what do people pay for these things?" James said,
marveling over the sprawling living room.

"They pay nothing."

"You know what I mean, Dad."

"Big bucks. Come on, let's see if there's anything else here or
if we wasted our time on an old man's memory."

Alexandre had ventured back outside, and he called for us to
come. We joined him on the east side of the villa. "What do you
got?" I asked.

"Mr. Charles, this over here is a big generator, and in the
ground here is a fuel tank. I don't know how many gallons, but it
looks nearly full." He shone his flashlight into a pipe jutting from
the ground. A heavy metal cap was chained to the pipe and swung
back and forth.

I bent down and took a look; I could smell the fuel. "We need
to dig this out a little bit."

We found a shovel and a small rake in a detached garage and
began excavating around the pipe, exposing more of a cylindrical
tank. James unearthed a section that had a metal label attached
with rivets. The label said the tank had an eighteen-hundred-liter
capacity, nearly five hundred gallons.

"Alexandre, you did it, brother! This is it! A mother lode right
here!" I cried.

We all broke out into laughter, and I shook Alexandre by the
shoulders and said, "Who's the man? You're the man."

"No, Mr. Charles, you are the man."

"We are all men," said Marcos, wearing a silly smile.

When we calmed down, I frowned and thought about how we would transfer that much fuel all the way back to the Eden Rock. We couldn't fill small containers. That would take far too much time and leave us exposed to attacks. We needed to remove the tank in one fell swoop.

"All right, let's cover it back up, get something to throw over the ground," I said.

We cut some fronds and spread them across the fresh earth, making sure no one would spot our digging. Then I told everyone we were heading back.

We rode as giddy as ever, only later on remembering that we did not see Tremaine in the road; however, we would see him again.

We gave Vacher a good excuse to get drunk, and he did, along with my father. Dayreis cooked us a nice supper, and we dined like royalty. I, too, had far too much wine. It was about time something positive happened on the island. That night Vanessa and I made love, and she told me I had never been so warm or so passionate. Afterward, as I lay staring at the ceiling, I saw my pistol pressed into Jane's head, and very slowly, in a near whisper, I told Vanessa what I had done.

THE next morning, one of our fishing crews came in with a significant catch of wahoo and tuna, and despite my throbbing hangover, I still felt generous and I told our lead fisherman Lefort to give some of our catch to the women (referred to by James as the "lesbian tribe") from the cruise ship. The man looked at me with sun-bleached hair dangling across his brown cheek and a roadmap of deep lines spanning his forehead. He was an old salt all right, and I told him it was the right thing to do. He finally nodded.

Alexandre, Marcos, and Bento were already bursting with ideas of how to get that fuel back down to the hotel. Alexandre said there was a tow truck parked behind one of the rental car agencies at the airport. The truck had a long flatbed, and while he was certain its gas tank was dry, he said we could transport five gallons or so from the big tank over to the truck, then drive it up to Marigot.

I agreed. We could use the truck's winch to drag the tank from the ground and onto the flatbed. I didn't like the idea that we'd have to make yet another trip up to the villa and that we'd have to ride back with five gasoline canisters, but we didn't have much choice. Marcos and Bento removed the tires from a Mini Moke and built a small trailer that could be towed by a bike. Bento, the heaviest and strongest of us, was commissioned as pack mule.

We decided we would leave at four a.m. the next morning, while it was still dark. We would arrive forty minutes or so later, siphon the gas out during sunrise, and then be on our way while the rest of the island hopefully slept.

I gave Vanessa a big hug good-bye, and she told me she was going crazy being stuck at the hotel and wanted to come. I told her that she was going to be in charge when I was gone and that I would notify the others. They would answer to her. She told me I was just placating her, but I said I wasn't, that I didn't trust anyone as much as her to make decisions if something happened. She frowned, agreed, and swore she was coming on the next "expedition."

I notified the guards, then met up with the others down in

the parking lot. A chill hung in the air as we pedaled off, all of us dressed in dark clothes.

ABOUT halfway to the villa I grew irritated over the creaking and rattling of Bento's cart, which I felt certain would give us away. I called for a halt and went back to examine the wheels and wooden planks. "Can't you make this thing any quieter?"

He frowned and finally said, "It's okay, Mr. Charles."

"No, it's not."

Marcos and Alexandre came back and began spitting on the axle as James muttered, "Gross."

But the salvia helped a little.

I got back on my bike and we resumed our trek, the road now a streak of black ink wandering away from us. A waning gibbous moon as pale yellow as an elephant's tusk hung at our backs, and somewhere in the distance, cook fires rose, the scent of burning wood drifting toward us. Someone was already awake.

I wasn't sure why, but I began thinking about my brother, about the way he died and how unfair the world was and how my life had now been reduced to riding a bicycle to go steal gasoline. He would not want me to feel sorry for myself. He would be proud of what we'd done so far.

But there are always moments of weakness, and by the time we reached the villa, I had already palmed away a stream of tears that I kept well hid from the others.

We worked quickly, siphoning the gas into the containers and loading them back onto the cart. I supervised the operation, wary of every shifting shadow. By the time we finished, my breath had grown so shallow that I needed to compose myself before speaking. "All right, this is great. Are we ready?" I whispered.

They were.

"If anything happens on the way back, Bento, you get away from the gas, okay? Someone fires a shot—"

"I know, I know. I don't want to explode."

I winked. "Good man."

OUR ride back was tense, my ears pricked up the entire time, my pulse elevated. But nothing happened. We reached the tow truck just as long reefs of clouds on the horizon glowed saffron, and with the reverence of men delivering holy water to a cathedral, we lifted the containers and slowly emptied them into the tow truck's tank. Alexandre had already made sure that we had the keys—he'd found them inside the rental car agency, hanging on a wall peg.

Now we had a decision to make. Should we take the truck to the villa and begin our operation? Or should we wait until the next morning and attempt to remove the tank during those wee hours?

We'd already had a heated discussion, and I had not reached a final decision, but I knew where most of them stood. We were going to create a lot of noise, which would, of course, attract some attention. If we were attacked, we would have a better chance of identifying our attackers and their positions during the day. Our attackers would, however, always have the advantage because we were forced to remain in position near the tank. Driving up at night would, in fact, provide us with better cover and decrease our chances of encountering anyone, so I decided that we would wait one more day, and leave a bit later, about five a.m., so we would arrive and get our operation underway during sunrise.

Once the last canister was empty, Alexandre climbed into the cab, inserted the key, and turned it, drawing a rat-tat-tat from the engine.

"Aw, the battery's dead," I said, then launched into a string of curses.

In fact most of the cars had not been driven for a few months, so it could be possible that their batteries were also dead. None of us had anticipated that.

Consequently, it was just as well that we waited another day. I sent Alexandre and a few men up to the turbine, along with the tow truck's battery and a battery charger we had found inside one of the toolboxes bungee-corded to a side panel. Meanwhile, James and I stood guard at the tow truck. I feared it would be a long, nerve-wracking day, and I was right. As we stared out past the runway toward the bay, James spotted a large yacht on the horizon, motoring eastward.

"You see it?" he asked, drawing a pair of binoculars from his pack.

"Yeah."

"I don't see any flags."

"They're not coming in. They're sailing around. Maybe they'll dock at Gustavia."

"They probably came from St. Martin."

"Maybe. Surprising they still have fuel."

"Dad, maybe we should think about leaving. Or at least come up with a plan."

"I have been thinking about it. It's the plan that's the problem. Where do we go and how do we get there? And will it be better there? We already decided that it wouldn't."

"I mean when it gets bad here."

"If we can keep fishing and collecting rainwater, we can buy ourselves some serious time."

"I guess we'll see."

The boat left a shimmering wake as it disappeared around Point Milou.

Chloe and Jodi arrived ten minutes later, both on bikes, and Chloe's expression troubled me. "What're you doing here? You don't even have a guard with you? Jesus, Chloe . . ."

"Dad, it's Grandpa."

NICOLE and Vacher were with my father in his bedroom. I froze in the doorway. "Has he passed?" I braced myself.

"No, but I think he's slipped into a coma," said Nicole. "He's unresponsive."

"Is there anything else we can do for him?"

"Just keep him as comfortable as possible. I've given him some pain medication. It could be any time now, so you may want to begin saying your good byes."

I nodded.

Vacher glanced at me and pursed his lips. "I am very sorry for you, Charles. I know your father loves you very much."

"Thank you."

With a deep breath, I turned and left the room. It didn't hit me until I was down on the beach. My father was going to die, and I'd never had that talk with him, the one Vacher had urged me to have. It was already too late. My cheeks caved in, and I thought I would vomit.

I went back to the tow truck, and James asked about his grandfather. I told him the truth. He choked up and said, "So sorry, Dad."

"It's okay. He had a good run. That's how he'd put it. And he said he wasn't going to walk around and feel sorry for himself. He didn't."

"Dad, you need to go back up there. Let me take charge of this. You should be with Grandpa. I can do this. You shouldn't be here, not now."

"I'll stay with you till they get back with the battery. We'll get the truck to the hotel, then tomorrow morning, we'll see what happens. Grandpa could already be gone by then."

WE remained there until midafternoon, since the battery would take several hours to recharge. The men returned from Lurin with good news, and the truck fired up immediately with the recharged battery in place. We all climbed onto the flatbed, and Alexandre drove us back to the hotel. I hadn't realized how much I missed riding in a gas-powered vehicle and became acutely aware of the world's addiction to them.

I spent the rest of the day sitting in a chair, watching my father, occasionally holding his hand and talking to him, telling him all the things I wanted to say but never could, not with him facing me, with him reacting to my complaints, defending himself, and once again squashing my independence. I actually liked him in his coma. He was quite agreeable. Trouble was, every time I spoke, I could hear him in my head. I knew him far too well. He could just lie there and say nothing because he'd already said everything.

BY five a.m. the next morning, Dad was still hanging on, and James begged me to let him lead the crew up to fetch the tank. They had gathered everything they needed to strap it up and haul it away.

I asked Vanessa what I should do.

"I don't want to make this decision for you," she said. "You and only you need to be comfortable with this."

"If it were your father, what would you do?"

"I'd do what I did. I'd stay with him. But that was a different world, Charles."

"He's in a coma, for God's sake."

"At this point it's not about him anymore. It's about you and what you can live with."

"What if we send James up there and something happens? And I'm not there."

"What if something happens and you are there?"

"Then maybe I can help."

"Maybe you can't."

"Aw, I need to go. I can't just sit here."

"And you'll be okay with that, if he passes while you're gone?"

I said, "Yeah," but I still wasn't sure. I knew I didn't want my son going up there without my help—a decision that sounded very much like one my own father would make.

Charles senior didn't trust me. I didn't trust James. And maybe that was the whole problem, wasn't it?

I went down to the tow truck, where James, Alexandre, Marcos, Bento, Carlos, and Dayreis were waiting. "Get that tank back here, all right? I'll be waiting."

James's eyes grew wide. "Really?"

"Just . . . be . . . careful."

"Absolutely. All right, guys, let's do it!"

Alexandre started the truck, and they thundered off into the darkness as I grew chilled over what I had just done.

I returned to my father's room to find Vacher with his head down on my father's chest. He was whispering something in French, and when he looked up, he said, "He just passed, Charles. He is with God now."

EIGHTEEN

I had the shakes all morning, and I couldn't sit still. My father had just died and my son was . . . *out there*.

I paced the beach, then went up to the hotel roof to check on our guy manning the .50 caliber. I went down to the restaurant where Chloe was letting Jane and Jodi listen to her iPod, then I found Vanessa standing on the terrace, gazing out across the bay. I didn't know what to do with myself, but she seemed completely in control.

"How can you be so calm?"

"I'm a wreck."

"You fooled me. I want to go up there so badly I can taste it."

"Don't. They'll come back."

I nodded and shut my eyes. "We buried my brother, and now we bury my father."

"Charles, did he have a will? Do you know what he wanted?"

I laughed bitterly. "I'm not even sure."

"Well, I guess he would've told Vacher. Go ask him. I'm sure he knows something."

"I will."

She nodded, seemed to think a moment, then said, "How much more time can we buy, Charles, before we run out of everything?"

"Whoa. Let's put that on pause, just for today. But really, I don't know. Next time it rains, we need to get more organized about collecting the water."

"You want me to work on that?"

"Yeah, and see if you can get Cindy and the rest of her women involved."

"I will."

"Charles, I'm so sorry."

"Well, the old man got the last laugh on us, like he said."

She nodded, then her expression changed. "Listen. You hear that?" Her brows lifted.

I nearly fell down the stairs as I raced to the hotel entrance, where the tow truck came rumbling forward, the fuel tank firmly strapped on the flatbed, with James standing tall and clutching his rifle, along with the others. Alexandre, who was at the wheel, threw the truck in neutral and brought the vehicle to a squealing stop.

"Dad, I thought you'd be smiling," cried James. "Look, we got it!"

"I know. Great job. I'm proud of you guys. All of you. And we can't thank you enough for this. James, come on over here."

I pulled him aside and told him about his grandfather. He fought back the tears and hung on. "Sorry, Dad. So sorry."

"He lived a good life."

"I'll help with whatever you need."

"I know."

VACHER told me that my father wanted to be cremated but that the dignified burial at sea we had given Dan would be perfect for him. None of us had any intentions of creating a funeral pyre on the beach because of the attention it would draw and the odor. I didn't say much at the service, just that my father was strong willed and a great leader of men and that he would be deeply missed. Strangely enough, during the ride back, I whispered aloud, "We forgive each other." And I thought I heard him answer, *Yes*.

I spent the next week helping the men with more fuel transfers from the big tank, which we kept strapped to the tow truck. The fuel was vulnerable in that tank, so we began emptying it as quickly as possible, even using wine bottles when necessary. Consequently, we had a huge supply of Molotov cocktails waiting to be assembled if we needed them.

On Friday morning Cindy and Jane came to me with some interesting news. They'd spied on a group up in Lorient who were holed up inside the Catholic church. I'd read in one of the brochures that the place had been built by women using local stone and that conch shells served as holy water basins. I remembered Vanessa telling me she wanted to see it a few days before we'd left New York. Maybe now she would get her chance. Cindy estimated there were about twenty people there, but more important, they had about a dozen or more hens and a rooster, meaning they had fresh eggs—a renewable food supply. I thought it might be worth going up there to see if we could trade some fish for eggs. Cindy was skeptical, since she'd seen a few men with rifles outside the building.

I told her we'd send up our own recon team and make a final decision in the next few days. Meanwhile, we needed to come up with a systematic plan for raiding the island's cisterns, especially after the rain showers, which occurred mostly at night or in the early morning hours. The coming hurricane season—as pointed out by Rousseau—would be a blessing and a curse. A storm would bring with it much needed rainfall during the hot and usually dry summer months. In fact, I was afraid that if we didn't get a good storm, we might not survive past July. Alexandre had reported that the desalinization plant near Public Beach was out of power and useless because our turbine would be impossible to connect and hardly provide enough power to operate all the machinery.

With our fuel issues temporarily addressed, we were all about water collection. Vanessa, Chloe, Jane, Cindy, and Jodi began making backpacks that contained jugs for "water raiders" to use on their hunts. We also had garden hoses for siphons and became adept at transferring the precious fluid from cistern to jug and jug to bottle. Dayreis suggested that we construct some more significant water collection units on the hotel's roof, since the place had relied much more on city water. I loved the idea and put him in charge of that. We could remove gutter and tube systems from surrounding villas and reconstruct them in and around the hotel.

During one of our water raids, Marcos and Bento spotted solar panels on the garage roofs of two villas just north of Gustavia. They broke in and found stations for charging some of the new electric cars that were being imported onto the island before the attack. There was no sign of the cars, but the batteries supplied by Energies Saint-Barth were fully charged. I would get Jane involved and have those units taken apart and brought back to the hotel.

WE got started immediately on both our water project and on acquiring those solar power units. I was placing more and more trust in James and had him lead the team to dismantle the power units. He said he wanted to take Hannah along. He argued that she'd been deeply depressed over Uncle Dan's death and needed to keep busy and feel important. I had already suspected that his concern for her went beyond sympathy, and I felt squeamish over the idea that my son had a crush on my dead brother's girlfriend. They were much closer in age, certainly a more traditional couple, but I couldn't help feeling the heat of my brother's gaze as I told him it was his responsibility to keep her safe. He thanked me, and I opened my mouth, wanting to address the issue head-on, but I let him leave.

I told Vanessa about them, and she gave me a funny look. "Of course," she said.

"And you're okay with this?"

"Let them be happy, any way they can."

"Does that go for us, too?"

She winked. "Believe it."

LATER in the afternoon, as I was helping Dayreis sketch out rough plans for our water collection system, James and his group returned, announcing themselves with loud cries for help. Dayreis and I rushed down to meet them.

They'd taken the tow truck up to Gustavia, had dismantled and loaded all the solar panels and parts, but on the way back, they'd been attacked. The truck was riddled with bullet holes, and as I rushed around the passenger's side, I saw a shirtless James helping Hannah out of the cab. His shirt, now blood soaked, was wrapped around her left arm.

"Dad, we didn't even see them," James cried. "They fired from the woods. I have no idea who they were."

"Jesus, are you okay?"

"Don't worry about us. We need Nicole. It's Carlos. He's in the back. I think he's stopped breathing."

I craned my head, saw Vanessa standing at the top of the stairs, and shouted for her to get the doctor.

Then I hustled past them and climbed up onto the flatbed, where Alexandre and Marcos were giving CPR to Carlos, who had been shot several times in the abdomen.

He was such a quiet and unassuming young man, utterly shy to the point that speaking aloud during our English lessons left him exhausted for an hour afterward. He'd told me as much in private.

Alexandre and Marcos were crying as they frantically worked on him, blood pooling across the flatbed like paint, the poor boy just lying there.

Nicole arrived breathlessly, and I helped her up onto the truck. She ordered Marcos and Alexandre away, then grimaced and quickly examined Carlos, but I could tell from her expression that he was already gone. She took a deep breath and sat back, just staring at him.

Marcos and Alexandre embraced each other, and Bento stood near the front of the truck, wiping away his tears.

I glanced back up at the staircase, where Vanessa and Chloe

gazed down at the scene. I imagined how grim we all must've looked. I wanted to feel something other than the fear of showing weakness. If I was going to lead these men, I had to do as my brother did during wartime. He had once told me that you cannot dwell on the dead. You save your grieving for another time, another place, when you're alone.

I lifted my voice. "Carlos was a good man, a great help to us, and his life meant something. It did. So let's make sure we get these panels together and use this power. That's what he would have wanted."

"Yes, Mr. Charles. You are right," cried Marcos.

A few hours later, Alexandre and I went up to the Carl Gustaf Hotel and called for Rousseau. He came down to meet us, looking even more disheveled than the last time we'd seen him.

"Some of my guys were attacked up near here," I said.

"We heard."

"I thought we had a truce."

"Where's my wine?"

"I'm still thinking about that. Right now, I want to know, did you break the truce?"

Rousseau moved uncomfortably close. "You know, sometimes when we shoot we need to get like this for the cameras. Do you know how unnatural that is? Trying to have a conversation with someone with their face in yours?"

"I asked you a question. Enough with the BS."

"Tough guy now, huh?"

I turned to Alexandre. "Let's go."

"Wait," Rousseau called out.

My glare refocused on him.

"It wasn't us," he continued. "I don't know who hit your guys, but twice we've seen some speedboats out in the bay. Don't know where they come from. Don't know if it was those guys. If they hit you, they're going to hit us."

"Then you'd better watch yourselves." I walked back up to Alexandre.

"Hey, Spencer?" Rousseau called.

I groaned and raised my brows.

"You got solar power over there now?" he asked.

"If a storm's coming, I'll let you know. Don't have to worry about that."

"Oh, a storm is coming."

"More movie dialogue?"

"No, only facts."

I smiled crookedly. "See ya."

THE men decided to bury Carlos on the hillside, and I helped them to dig the grave and said a few words because they said I talked nicely, though I doubted they understood everything I said. I even quoted Shakespeare just to hear the words, the beautiful words: "When sorrows come, they come not single spies, but in battalions . . ."

Afterward, the men got to work on the panels, mounting them on the rooftops of the northeast side of the hotel for maximum exposure. They worked with a fervor under Jane's supervision; they worked for Carlos, for all of us, and didn't quit until the stars began to flicker on in the deep blue sky. I'd told Chloe we would use her iPod as the first "test device," and it charged up without a hitch. She was thrilled because I told her our trips up to the turbine would be limited and primarily for getting news reports from South America. Now we would check the TV daily via the solar power cells.

Nicole treated Hannah for her gunshot wound and said she would fully recover but have a very nice scar to show for it. James remained at her side, but before going to bed, he came to me and said, "I shouldn't have brought her."

"You know, I thought it was odd that Uncle Danny wanted your mother and Chloe to learn how to shoot, but he never bothered to teach her."

"I guess he wanted her to be more . . . feminine."

"Well, I think you should teach her how to shoot, get her into the program, and you bring her along on the next run, because we're all in this together."

He almost laughed.

"What?"

"Dad, that sounds so weird coming from you."

"I know."

"All right, I'll do that. And thanks."

"For what?"

"For not making me feel bad."

"You came back with the panels."

He nodded, pursed his lips, and padded off toward his bedroom. I smiled to myself.

SOME time during the night I awoke to the sound of distant gunfire, and I stood out on the terrace, just listening to the popping, like corn in hot oil. I called up to our man on the .50 caliber, and he said he couldn't see anything but that the sounds were definitely coming from the northeast.

The popping lasted another minute or so, then nothing save

for the tide and the breeze. I tensed, kept listening, my imagination running wild with images of shadows coming alive and blood erupting and muzzles flashing in the darkness like the eyes of some demon sinking fangs into flesh.

Everyone was awake now, and Marcos and Alexandre ran down across the beach while the rest of us remained where we were, waiting and still listening and wondering when the next gunshot would come, until our eyes grew so heavy that we could do no more than return to our beds, leaving the guards tense and frozen for the rest of the night.

IN the morning, as I reverently sipped six ounces of tea, I surprised Vanessa by telling her we were going up to the church in Lorient to see if we could strike a deal with those people Cindy had told me about. We'd also see if there were any signs of the shooting we'd heard last night. I brought along the usual team of Marcos, Bento, and Alexandre, and I left Dayreis and James back home to hold the fort. Alexandre pulled me aside and asked if it was wise to bring Vanessa; I assured him she was more than capable of holding her own, though deep down I ached with concern. I'd learned to trust James; I needed to trust her and believe that she would make the right choices if something happened to us.

We took the bikes and pedaled our way up into the mountains, and as we neared the church, its elegant stone walls began to rise before us, the mottled browns and grays suggesting the utterly ancient, as though they'd been transported brick by brick from old Europe. Above the drone of my tires and pedals, I heard someone crying. We slowed, got off our bikes, and walked tentatively forward, guns drawn.

"Get behind me," I told Vanessa.

Marcos and Alexandre moved out in front of us, and there, at the foot of the stairs leading into the place, lay the edge of the unimaginable.

"Bento? Take Vanessa and go back there and wait for us," I said.

"No, I'm coming," she insisted.

"You want to see this?"

"I'm here. I don't care."

On the stairs lay four bodies, with more visible through the church's open doors, themselves propped open by another pair of corpses, all of them shot in the chest or head, their limbs twisted at improbable angles. Flies were already buzzing, and in the middle of this scene sat a girl of eight or nine, holding the hand of a bearded man in his thirties who'd taken a round just above his left eye.

Vanessa ran to her, even after I called after her, and she dropped to her knees. "Sweetheart, it's okay, we're here for you."

She looked up, saw our guns, and screamed at the top of her lungs.

I panicked, shouldered my rifle, and grabbed the girl, covering her mouth and whispering in her ear, "Don't do that again. The bad guys will come. Don't do that, again? Okay?"

Her eyes welled with more tears, and she nodded fiercely before I slowly let her go and Vanessa pulled her into her arms, beginning to shush her. "It's okay. It's okay. It's okay . . ."

I rose and shifted with Bento and Alexandre toward the doors, and the scene inside was no better. Both men muttered in Portuguese, and it sounded as though they were praying. How could such horror befall that beautiful place of worship built by the hands of the island's women? I began to count the bodies, and when I got into the teens, I had to shut my eyes, realizing there were over twenty lying on the floor or draped over the pews or shoved up against the wall on stained stone floors, as though they'd been ordered to those spots and summarily executed where they stood. They were mostly locals who lived and worked on the island, with a handful of tourists mixed in, judging from their clothes. There were no children other than the girl we'd found outside, and a sickly sweet stench began to make me gag. I covered my face and headed back toward the wedge of light filtering in through the open doors.

Outside, I gasped for air and looked at Vanessa, still clutching the girl. "Who could've done this?"

"I don't know, but she's coming with us. We don't abandon children, Charles."

I nodded as Alexandre and Bento came up behind me, their boots crunching on dozens of shell casings lying in the street.

"Let's get some of these," I told them. "Maybe Vacher can tell us what kind of ammo they used."

Alexandre's gaze lowered to the street, and he began to rub his watery eyes.

Marcos lifted his chin at me. "Mr. Charles, if these people did this just to steal some hens and a rooster, what will they do to us?"

NINETEEN

THE little girl's name was Trina, and she was almost nine and her address was 27 Grant Street, Austin, Texas. She attended New Highland Park Elementary, where she was in the Young Author's Club and on news crew, and had come down to St. Barts for Christmas vacation. We brought her back to the hotel and fed her and tried to keep her calm, but she was a blond-haired sparrow who flinched as you neared her. In a tremulous voice she said that the bad guys had come during the night and that her mother had hidden her in the church. She'd heard all of the shooting and had waited until morning to come out and look for her parents.

I tried to get more out of her, but she hadn't seen anything. She did say the men spoke in another language, but that was all she knew. My heart ached over the trauma she had been through, and in a moment alone, Vanessa broke down and dampened the shoulder of my T-shirt.

We handed over the shell casings to Vacher, who examined them with a small magnifying glass he used for reading. The old man was absolutely thrilled to be called upon for help, and as I expected, he supplied us with far more information than we needed, though it was interesting nonetheless.

As he studied the casings, he explained that the .45 caliber is a "center-fired" round, meaning that there is a firing cap in the center of the casing and the firing pin has to hit the cap to detonate the round, as opposed to a "rim-fired" round (.22 caliber) where the hammer can hit anywhere on the back of the casing to detonate it. He found at least three different firing pin indentations in the casings, signifying that at least three different .45 caliber pistols had been used. He also said he found a laser-etched alphanumeric symbol, "ADD53," in two places within the casings' extractor grooves. He was speaking Chinese to me, but with some excitement he asked to be taken out to his yacht, where he retrieved a manual from his "firearms library." The manual identified ammo manufacturers' "lot" markings. AAD53 belonged to *Companhia Brasileria de Cartuchos* (CBC). Brazilian weapons manufacturers such as IMBEL *(Industria de Material Belico do Brasil)* and CBC were, according to Vacher and his book, leading suppliers of the M911 .45 caliber automatic pistol.

"I'm sorry, Alexandre, but the pistols probably come from Brazil," Vacher concluded.

"That doesn't mean Brazilians were involved," he said sharply.

"No, it doesn't," I assured him.

Vacher went on to say that since the killing was all "close in" he assumed there'd be no evidence of heavier weapons such as the Brazilian FAL or possibly AK-47s. I told him those were the only type of casings we'd found, then I asked if he thought Rousseau might be responsible. He said it was simple to test that theory by going up to the Carl Gustaf and listening for hens or a rooster. He had a good point.

Curiously, Alexandre was especially hard hit by the church massacre and asked that he be left alone for a few days and be relieved of his duties. I went to Chloe and suggested that she talk to him, and she agreed. She was as worried about him as I was, of course, and she suspected that he knew some of the people who had died, though he hadn't said anything yet.

When I told Cindy and Jane about what we'd seen, Jane gave me a hard look and said, "I'm glad we worked out a deal for protection."

I sighed. "I don't know who these guys are, but if they hit us, they'll be very surprised."

"I wonder why they haven't already," Jane asked.

BY late June a tropical storm blew through, but we were well prepared—not only to gather the precious rainwater but also to batten down the hatches of the hotel and surrounding villas. The storm system hovered over the Leeward Islands for three days, and we couldn't help but rejoice. Our water supply tripled, and there was much more out there in the cisterns of the private villas, waiting to be had. Our water raiders were ready.

The attacks on the island had continued, with very little information gathered regarding the perpetrators. People holed up at a few of the other hotels had been robbed, some beaten, some killed, and all we knew was that a group of dark-skinned men in cigar boats (they were getting fuel from somewhere) would come during the night. Every time we learned of another attack, we wore the news like an infected wound and dragged our feet throughout those days. Rousseau's tribe was not hit. I assumed it was only a matter of time before we were both attacked.

Alexandre had grown even more distant, but he promised that

he would not shirk his responsibilities. In fact, he took on extra guard duties, and James told me that he rarely saw the man sleep. Chloe confirmed that he was depressed. He'd said he couldn't get the sadness out of his heart. She said we just needed to be patient with him.

One morning in the restaurant I approached him and said, "I've told you a hundred times you can talk to us, Alexandre. Talking helps."

"I know, Mr. Charles."

"I don't want you to be distracted, you know? My brother would say we need to stay sharp and focused."

"That's right."

"I wish you'd let us help. You shouldn't be embarrassed. This doesn't make you less of a man."

"I know. You've done everything already. Thank you, Mr. Charles."

My scrutinizing gaze yielded no more than a young man as troubled as he was stubborn. He forced a weak smile and walked away.

ONCE or twice a week sailboats loomed on the glassy horizon, though none ever came toward St. Jean Bay. I sometimes wondered if I was seeing them only because I needed to believe that life existed beyond the island. Perhaps they were only mirages. Of course the news reports confirmed that life had gone on, and the continued low-level radiation readings assured me that life would, at least for the time being, continue on the island.

Marcos had told me that there'd been a small cow, goat, and sheep population on the island, and he thought they were all already gone. Even the sound of a barking dog grew more scarce, and a few of the cats we'd encountered looked diseased and had nasty dispositions. As sanitation deteriorated, the rat and mouse population would increase, and I wondered if those who couldn't fish would resort to them.

Just prior to the tropical storm, we'd found a few more bodies up on the beach: three females in their late twenties. They'd slashed their wrists but already appeared gaunt, their skin clinging like worn suede, their eyes deeply set.

I remember barely reacting, just telling Bento to "clean up the mess before someone sees this." I thought, *This is what it must have been like for Dan.* He'd driven down the "Highway of Death" between Kuwait and Basra during the first Gulf War, and he'd come face-to-face with the demolished vehicles and incinerated bodies and that sweet horrible stench and had steeled himself against it all. He even made glib remarks at parties, and I used to glower at him but understood now that the terrible deeds committed by some people are too much to process.

As a matter of fact, James and Chloe had recently been clinging to the idea that the nuclear attack was simply an accident, one mistake that had unleashed hell and that no one had intentionally decided to "end the world." No one would ever do that.

I estimated that I had lost nearly forty pounds since late December, and on the morning of August 6, after spending eight long months on the island, I frowned at the werewolf in the mirror and wished him a happy birthday. I'd assumed Vanessa had forgotten, as well as James and Chloe, but when I went downstairs, they had a little breakfast party for me, and we had some fruit and fish and I was getting slapped on the back by Dayreis when we heard the plane approach.

It was a Twin Otter like one we'd taken to the island, and he was coming in a little too low, I thought, his wings tipping a bit erratically. Marcos, Bento, James, Alexandre, and I ran onto the beach and westward toward the airstrip.

One of his engines gave out, and the second began to sputter as he vanished over the hillside. He had no doubt run out of fuel and would land on fumes. By the time we reached the airstrip, he had already touched down but had overshot a little and struck one of the rental car buildings, shaving off a section of his left wing.

As the remaining engine died and the scent of hot metal blew toward us, we lifted our weapons and moved tentatively toward the cockpit, where the pilot was just sitting, his head back on the seat. No one else was aboard. James tried the door, but it was locked.

For a moment, we just stood there, looking at the plane, wondering where it had come from, when it dawned on me that "where it had come from" could be bad. Very bad. I shouted for Bento to go get Nicole and the radiation detector, and I was glad I did.

We backed off from the plane and waited. Slowly, the pilot rose from his seat, went back into the cabin, opened the side door. He put a foot down and literally fell out of the plane and hit the tarmac.

James was about to rush to him when I warned him off.

The pilot was lean, Hispanic looking, and his lips were pale and chapped. He rolled over on the tarmac and stared straight up at the sky, his chest rising and falling. He reached up toward the sun for a moment, then draped that arm over his eyes.

"Who are you?" I asked. "Where did you come from?"

Alexandre repeated in Portuguese, and the man turned his head and spoke in Spanish, his voice reed thin, with the word "Cuba" resounding in one of his sentences.

I knew that Alexandre and the pilot could basically understand each other, and Alexandre confirmed that the man had flown in from Cuba.

"Ask him why," I said.

It took a long moment for the man to answer, and after he did, Alexandre eyed me and said, "Everyone started getting sick there. He stole the plane and left."

Marcos turned to me and said, "Can we get sick? Has he brought a plague with him?"

"I don't know."

"Then we know what we have to do."

"We do?"

"Yes, Mr. Charles. He's not welcome with us. He's going to die anyway. If you want to go back, Bento and I will take care of this."

"You know what? Today's my birthday. And we're not executing anyone."

Marcos nodded. "Okay, we will wait until tomorrow."

I rolled my eyes.

The pilot shifted onto his side and began to heave, but nothing would come out.

"Oh God," James said. "What if the fallout's coming down here?"

"We don't know what's happening. The wind could have shifted just a little bit."

James grimaced. "Aw, look at him."

Bento returned with Nicole and the meter, and she strode right toward the pilot.

"Wait, let me get a reading first."

She ignored me and began examining the man.

Indeed, the meter showed a significant increase in radiation as

I waved it over the pilot and his plane. "Nicole, forget it now. It's all contaminated."

"He's completely dehydrated," she said. "We need to get him some water."

"We cannot waste water on him," said Marcos. "He's going to die anyway."

"We can spare a little," said James.

"Nope. No water," I said.

James frowned at me. "The guy's choking."

I sharpened my tone. "Let's go, everybody."

Marcos and Bento nodded. Alexandre shrugged. Nicole scowled at me and said, "If you don't get him some water, I will."

"Then it's your ration."

"Fine." She stomped off.

My son looked at me as though I were the Antichrist.

"Will you give your water to him?" I asked. "Will you?"

He shook his head.

"I thought so."

"It's not our fault." I took a deep breath and swore over the pilot's horrible timing. He had to show up on my birthday, didn't he . . .

"Nicole, when you get back, you're not allowed around anyone till we scrub you down."

"Now you're a radiation expert?"

"You want to get the rest of us sick? You do what I say."

"Yeah, okay," she snapped.

I had no idea how to decontaminate a person. I guessed a little soap and seawater would have to do.

BACK at the hotel, I still argued with Nicole over going back down there, but she insisted. I gave her two men (who were

ordered not to get close to the man or plane) and sat up in the
restaurant, brooding as they left.

Vanessa and the little girl Trina joined me. "James told me
what happened," my wife began.

"We'll need to watch the news, see if they have any more of
those fallout reports."

"Cuba's not far."

"I'm going up to Rousseau's in a little while."

"For what?"

"I'm going to tell him about the plane."

"Really."

"And we haven't heard from him in a while. I'm going to
return a couple cases of his wine—as another peace offering. I'm
thinking we might need to team up if those guys in the fast boats
try to hit us."

"You sure about this?"

"He's the only one we've been able to talk to. All the other
groups just keep hiding."

"Because it's not safe out there."

WE took Bento's cart up to the Carl Gustaf, and I'd brought along
Marcos and Dayreis, who'd been nagging me to get back out again.
I left the chef down to guard the cart while Marcos and I went up
to the front entrance. I told the long-haired guard standing there
to go get Rousseau, that we had some wine for him.

A moment later the celebrity himself fluttered past the door
like a wraith in black silk and squinted in the midmorning light.
He waved us inside, back to the shadows. I looked to Dayreis and
said, "Stay here."

We crossed into the main entrance foyer and back toward the

pool, where under a long awning he motioned for us to take seats among the twenty or so folks strewn lifelessly on loungers and hammocks.

"What's for lunch?" I asked. "I've brought the wine."

Rousseau snorted and began to stroke his long beard. "I'm glad someone is in good spirits."

"Today's my birthday."

"Well, isn't that special."

"I brought you back some of the wine we took. I didn't bring it all."

"I'll take it."

"Just like that? You don't have some epic remarks for me?"

"Look at them," he said, gesturing with his hand toward his disciples. "You know, most of the gendarmes came with me. Now they've all lost the will to live."

"Maybe you need to get back on the mountain and fire them up . . ."

"We're going to get attacked. They know it. The paranoia has sucked the life out of them. I've seen it in the movie business. I've seen it here. And I've tried. I'm getting ready to give up."

"But you're William Rousseau."

He chuckled darkly. "Was . . ."

"Wow, I figured I'd bring you some wine and talk about something more than a truce. Talk about an alliance. But it sounds like you need more than that."

"You've done pretty well for yourself down there. Solar panels, water collection, good fishing operation. I'm lucky if I have four good fishermen here. We're pretty good at getting the water, but I'm tired of this. So tired."

"Why tell me? You've got your religion. Talk to those, uh, whatever, up there."

"I'm telling you because I can. Because maybe you understand this like I do. How's your father?"

"He passed away."

"I'm sorry to hear that."

"He came down here to die. He had a good run."

"We're all down here to die."

"Not me. I'm here to live. Now let me cut to the chase. These assholes who've been hitting the other hotels are coming for us. All I want is a guy on a bike. If you get attacked, that guy rides over the hills to warn us. I do the same for you."

"But you have power. And you have that yacht anchored out in the bay. What about the radio?"

"I didn't think you had any access."

"I've got two yachts down in the harbor. Both batteries are dead. You recharge the battery on one, you give me a little fuel, and we do it that way. I keep a man at the boat every night. You do the same."

"I can do that. But I can't spare the fuel."

"I'll need to run the engines to recharge the battery, otherwise I have to keep coming back."

"We'll see if we can get you a battery recharger, and you can do that up at the turbine. We fixed it."

"Fuel would be easier."

"Not for me."

"All right, we'll use the turbine. Why are you doing this?"

"Because we've got bigger enemies than each other."

He thought about that a moment. "And so we need to trust each other now."

"I guess so."

"Then why haven't you told me about the plane?"

"I was coming to that. Guy flew in from Cuba. He's got radiation poisoning."

Rousseau's expression turned grave. "So the winds have shifted?"

"I don't know yet. Plane's out of fuel, guy's probably going to die, so all we got was a bad omen."

"He have anything else on the plane?"

"I don't know. It's contaminated, and we're just leaving it where it is for now. So if you want, get a few guys and head up to the turbine. I'll meet you there with a recharger. And I'll leave the wine outside for you."

"All right." Rousseau stood. "I don't think your brother would be too happy about this arrangement, but it works for me." He proffered his hand.

I took it, but he suddenly squeezed tight. "Don't go back on your word, Spencer."

"I won't." I tugged free my hand and headed outside with Alexandre.

As I passed through the front door, something flashed in the corner of my eye, and the front deck felt slippery. I looked down.

I was standing in a puddle of blood.

TWENTY

OFF to my right lay Rousseau's guard, his throat slashed, the blood having spilled across the wooden planks and down the stairs.

"I'm sorry, Charles," came a familiar voice.

Dayreis stood near his bike, his hands in the air, his rifle slung over the back of a painfully recognizable man with long, dark dreadlocks who maintained a neck hold on the chef as he pressed a pistol into the chef's temple.

"Okay, okay, okay," purred Tremaine. "You the man I've been waiting for."

"Seems like you've been waiting a very long time. We could've killed you, but we didn't. We even fed you and bandaged you up."

"Your mistake, man. Now come over here. You're the one I want."

"Mr. Charles, don't do it," said Alexandre, his rifle pointed at Tremaine.

The reggae band member widened his eyes. "If you don't come to me, I'm going to kill your boy. You know I will."

"What is this, revenge?" I asked, frowning deeply.

"Oh no. No, no, no. It's much more than that. Now come here, *Mr. Charles*."

Dayreis closed his eyes. "Alexandre, he's going to kill me anyway. So shoot him right now."

I reached out with my hand toward Alexandre. "Just relax, okay?"

And in that second I realized I shouldn't have done that because Tremaine took a step back and screamed, "Nobody move! I'll kill him!"

"Okay," I said, lifting my hands in the air. "Easy. You can take me."

"Just shoot him, Alexandre," cried Dayreis.

"Don't you do it," I warned him.

Alexandre swallowed. "But Mr. Charles—"

"Trust me," I said, then faced Tremaine. "All right, you let him go."

The man pushed Dayreis aside, then rushed forward, shoved his pistol into my head, and relieved me of my own. Then he put me in the same chokehold and said, "Let's go."

"Go where?" I asked.

"Back to your hotel."

"We're going to walk?"

"Yes, we are."

"Don't you have a bad leg?"

"It's better now."

"Why can't we ride? You can hold the gun on me."

"Walk!"

I glanced back at the door, where Rousseau had just appeared, along with two of his men. "What the hell is this?" the movie star cried.

"I'll be a little late getting up to the turbine," I said. "Going to take a little walk with our old friend here."

Rousseau pointed at Tremaine. "I know this asshole. He came here begging for help a few times."

"This is not your business," said Tremaine. "Everybody, let's go." He shoved me forward, and we started down the road.

"Rousseau, just lay back. Don't try to help," I called back.

"No problem," he answered with a snort.

I turned my head toward Tremaine. "Where's the rest of your band?"

"I ask the questions."

"What do you want? Food and water? We'll give you some. No need for this. You know we're reasonable, otherwise we would have killed you that first time."

"Shut up."

I stopped. "I don't want to leave my bike. We need it."

"Too bad." He shoved me again. "Let's go."

"What're you going to do when we get back to the hotel?"

"I said move!"

I flicked my gaze back to Alexandre and Dayreis, widening my eyes ever so slightly on the former, whose head lowered a fraction of an inch in understanding.

Only then did I notice that I'd dug my fingernails so tightly into my palms that I was about to draw blood. I took a deep breath and drove my left hand up, into Tremaine's, knocking the pistol back, even as he fired, and then came the echoing ring and my own breathing as I rolled and broke free from the arm he'd had around my neck. I caught sight of his gun hand and seized the wrist with both of my hands as he fired once more into the air.

He came down, opening his mouth, about to bite my arm, when I brought up my elbow into his nose with a blow so hard that he fell back, and I managed to get one hand onto his gun and pry it free.

He reached down into his waistband for my pistol as blood poured from his nose and drew a red goatee on his stubbly lips and chin.

I've gone over the next five seconds about a thousand times, replaying it from different angles the way detectives examine security camera footage from multiple vantage points. I've even placed myself in the role of Tremaine, starving and desperate, hoping to secure for myself some form of existence in a harsh and terribly unfair new world.

Of course, Tremaine could not have known about the red-hot magma bulging in my gut, and he was utterly unaware of how we Spencers could channel a lifetime's worth of anger into a single explosion without conscience, without forethought, because maybe there was something in our genes, something that harkened back 2.4 million years ago to *Homo habilis*, to Dr. Leakey's "handy man," and underneath we had never evolved.

Once I had the gun in my hands, there was never any doubt of what I would do. I remember thinking, *How dare he challenge my authority? I'm in charge!*

After that I gasped, felt the drool gathering in my mouth, and gritted my teeth as I whirled, pointed the pistol at his head, and saw that fey look come into his eyes as he continued to reach for my pistol.

He knew he was dead as much as I did. Raging aloud, I emptied the magazine, shell casings clinking, his head shuddering with the passage of each bullet. A hand came down on my arm. Dayreis. He said something.

I looked up as Rousseau and his guards came running down the hill, their mouths working, their voices not reaching my ears; there was only the booming and my racing pulse and the struggle to take in more air.

After dropping the pistol, I sat in the middle of the road, staring blankly at Tremaine as the blood wormed its way through dreadlocks splayed across the pavement like black serpents once controlled by a single entity.

It took me a while to realize that in my eyes Tremaine had become the embodiment of everything I hated about my life and the world. I must have thought that killing him would kill the pain. Sure, Alexandre and Dayreis assured me that I struck out in self-defense and that I had saved their lives as well, but that wasn't enough.

"Why did you waste all that ammo?" asked Rousseau, shaking his head at the body. "You're an idiot, Spencer."

I glanced up at him. "Better go get your wine before someone steals it."

"How long till you're up at the turbine?"

I rubbed my eyes. "I don't know. Couple hours."

"All right."

"Can you get somebody to—"

"Hell, no. You clean up your own mess."

"I'm going to leave him here."

Slowly, quite deliberately, I stood and approached Rousseau. My hand found his throat, while he jabbed his rifle into my gut and the muzzles of his guards' rifles neared my head. *"You get rid of him! Do you hear me? You get rid of him right now!"* I squeezed his neck then shoved him back. *"Do you hear me?"*

"Freaking nut job," said Rousseau, his voice burred. "You're losing it."

"Two hours," I snapped.

I marched back up the hill, toward my bike.

ALEXANDRE and Dayreis dared not speak during the ride back to the hotel. About halfway there the shakes took hold, and by the time we rode up to the main entrance my cheeks were caving in. I got off my bike and vomited.

The men tried to comfort me, but I waived them. "Get the battery recharger. And get James."

Alexandre nodded and hurried off. Dayreis helped me back into the restaurant and gave me some water. Vanessa came down, and the chef explained what had happened.

"Oh my God, Charles, I'm sorry."

"Guess I was just fooling myself."

"What do you mean?"

"That I could do this a different way, better than my brother. Smarter. But that doesn't mean anything anymore, does it?"

"Yes, it does."

"No. You'll see what it comes to. You'll see." I closed my eyes and shuddered hard as the first round bored a hole in Tremaine's head, and he lolled back in the slow motion of my memory.

Vanessa placed her hands on my shoulders and whispered in my ear, "You did what you had to do."

No, I didn't have to kill him, and as I sat there, I recalled a conversation I'd had with Dan. I'd asked him about the war and about being a sniper and how he felt about the men he'd killed. He'd killed many. He'd said that every Marine Corps sniper handled it differently. He'd seen guys laugh and brag about their kills. He'd seen others cry as they described them. He'd seen two snipers suffer so badly from combat fatigue that they'd been relieved of duty. I'd asked him how he'd dealt with it all. And he'd just said, "I don't know. I try not to think about it."

And maybe for him, that worked. But I was a man who'd spent most of his adult life contemplating everything—from the flavor of the granola bar I would eat in the morning to the minutiae of an eleven-o'clock news channel's political bias as betrayed by the anchors' tone and the diction used during the broadcast.

Shooting Tremaine in self-defense would have been one thing, but I hadn't just killed him. I'd executed him. I wasn't strong. I wasn't the "alpha male." I was a weak bastard because I'd let the situation turn me into a raging madman. Thank God James had not been present. He would have worn the scars of my violence and would, I felt certain, never look at me the same way again— because I didn't.

WE met Rousseau up at the turbine and began charging his battery. The entire time he just stared at me as though waiting for my next detonation. In a voice barely perceptible, I told him I was sorry for choking him.

"Sorry? You're losing it. You're more bipolar than I am."

I shook my head. "I'm just . . . I don't know."

"Oh yeah? That's a good description."

"Maybe the lucky ones got killed in the blast, huh?"

"Maybe so."

"Are we just running around in a maze here?"

He glanced up at the sky and didn't answer.

"Hey, William," one of his men called out from the villa's living room. The bearded guy appeared past the sliding glass doors. "Got the fallout report on TV. Come on!"

We all rushed inside and watched the Brazilian weatherman

gesture flagrantly to his map. The jet stream had definitely shifted, with more winds blowing down from the north and into Cuba. It was exactly as we'd predicted. The northern winds could become our new worst enemy.

"I don't think that fallout will ever get this far south," said Rousseau.

"Think again," I said.

"Real optimistic guy."

I just shook my head and went back outside, where James was checking on the battery.

"How much longer?"

He shrugged. "About an hour, I guess."

"We could leave them here."

"I wouldn't."

"He's going to have to recharge on his own anyway."

James shrugged.

"Mom tell you what happened?"

He nodded. "Don't feel bad, Dad."

"I never wanted it to come to this. You know that. I said it. God damn it."

"I don't get you. Why is fighting for your family so bad?"

I closed my eyes. "It's not. But we'll all kill each other if something doesn't happen."

"Like what?"

"I don't know. A miracle."

"We make our own miracles. You and me, Dad. That's what we do. That's what we've already done here."

I thought about that and finally nodded. "You're a good kid. Probably had good parents."

He winked. "Yeah, but they smoked pot back in the seventies . . ."

And that nearly raised my smile, even on the day I killed my first human being, August 6. Happy birthday to me.

THE ship appeared during the first week of September, just a glint on the misty morning horizon, the light coruscating off the water and steel, the shimmers enough to send me racing from the beach and back up to the hotel to fetch my binoculars.

I'd been taking early morning walks along the beach because my sleeping pattern had gone to hell, with two hour stretches at the most until the nightmares shook me awake. I diagnosed myself with post-traumatic stress disorder and tried to drink a little wine before bedtime, but that rarely helped. So I was up by five a.m. each day, sometimes earlier, pacing the beach and trying to shake the demon with dreadlocks that warmed my footprints.

And that's why I'd been first to see the ship.

It took two more days before we discerned that she was a military vessel, one Vacher thought might be a destroyer, and judging by the painfully slow approach, we could only assume she was not under power and just drifting. I gave Rousseau's tribe a call on the radio and let them know about her. The celebrity came over with a couple of his men and had a look for himself. Afterward, he left, saying, "You called me for that?"

When the ship drew within a mile from the bay, I decided that James and I would take a couple of the kayaks and paddle out for a closer look (not wanting to waste the precious few gallons of fuel we had left from our once five-hundred-gallon mother lode).

As we dragged our kayaks down to the water, Vanessa, as I expected, tried one last time to talk us out of going.

"We don't know where that ship came from."

"We'll be all right."

"How do you know that?"

"Because it's just drifting. And unless we get attacked by a giant squid, we'll be back in a little while."

She rolled her eyes and looked to Chloe, who said, "We'll be ready when you get back."

I took along the radiation meter, and we donned some neoprene dry suits we'd found months ago aboard one of the yachts we'd raided, figuring a little extra protection couldn't hurt. We also had oxygen tanks and breathing masks, and it was, to say the least, a bitch to paddle wearing all that gear.

The bay was like turquoise gelatin, and our kayaks glided across the surface with razorlike precision. James paddled just off to my right, and my gaze flicked between the meter wrapped in a plastic bag and him. Behind us, out on the beach, anyone who wasn't on guard duty had gathered to watch: Cindy, Jane, and the rest of their crew; Chloe and Vanessa; and a handful of Dayreis's staff. Our fishing team was already out there, and they waved as we passed.

I picked up the probe, pointed it in the direction of the hulking gray ship, and the radiation meter grew active. We rounded the islets and came within a thousand yards, the rust-streaked hull number—749—coming into view. My mouth grew dry as I estimated her length at over three hundred feet. There were no signs of life around the pilot house, bridge wings, or upper decks. We were utterly diminutive, like pilot fish beside a great white shark, and my neck began to hurt as I gazed higher for a better view just as another burst from the meter jarred me back to the moment.

"Get on your mask!" I cried to James. "This thing is hot! Don't get any closer!"

We paddled slowly around the ship toward the stern,

maintaining our distance and hissing into our masks, the meter still crackling. We later learned from an outdated copy of *Jane's Fighting Ships* that Chloe had found in a shop called *La Case aux Livres* that the ship was, in fact, a Cannon class destroyer, commissioned in 1944 and had been a reserve training ship at Key West. We had all of her specs, not that they mattered. She would soon run aground, and I was unsure we could ever move her.

I waved James away, and we paddled back toward the shoreline, my eyes burning, my thoughts focused on that obvious and terribly ironic question: if God had spared us, then why had the wind, the current, the tide, and time conspired to deliver seventeen hundred tons of radioactive debris to St. Jean Bay?

TWENTY-ONE

CHLOE and Vanessa met us back on the beach and tossed out the soap and scrub brushes. We remained in the water beside our kayaks, engaging in our highly sophisticated decontamination process. We checked each other with the meter and scrubbed down once more to be on the safe side. Only then did we leave the water and change clothes.

"You see?" I told Vanessa. "Did you think we were going to get microwaved or something?"

She smirked. "That thing out there. We can't get rid of it, can we?"

I faced the ship, then glanced at her. "It's pretty damn big isn't it."

"Big? It's huge."

"Maybe the old man can help."

WE returned to the hotel, and I sat with Vacher, who was poring over some maps.

"Luc, that ship is full of radiation." I wasn't sure of the technical way to express that, but I knew he understood.

"See here, the naval air facility in Key West?" he asked, maneuvering his index finger over the location and barely reacting to my news. "It's five miles east-northeast of Key West on Boca Chica Key. That's where I think our destroyer came from. Boca Chica was a strategic place to stockpile nuclear warheads, and that made the island a priority target. If the attack was from a submarine-launched missile, perhaps from the Gulf of Mexico side, which would be the least likely direction of attack, there would be no warning and no chance for a defensive countermove. The island and the ships were completely vulnerable when the whistle blew. Maybe the men got out." His tone darkened. "Or maybe they're still on board."

"Luc, that's, uh, really interesting—and I really don't care where she came from. I need to know how to get rid of it. Can we use your yacht and tow it out of here?"

He chuckled under his breath. "You don't know very much about boats, do you?"

I spoke through my teeth. "Educate me."

"Charles, my yacht would never have enough horsepower—and we'd burn up the rest of the fuel just trying. They use big tugboats to move those ships. And even if we had one of those, we'd have to find a volunteer to climb aboard and set up the tow cable."

"I'd do it."

"You'd be a dead man."

"Maybe."

"Forget it."

"So you're saying there's no way to move her."

He hoisted his brows. "None."

"Then we have to leave."

"Now be patient. The ship's contaminated, but if the weather holds, then maybe we'll be all right. You've got the meter to see how that goes. But let me ask you something, did you see anything leaking, or smell any diesel fuel?"

"No, but we didn't get too close."

"Well, if she runs aground, she could very well rupture one of the bulkhead plate seams and start leaking fuel. If that happens, the entire shoreline will become contaminated."

"So it could be even worse. We just don't know yet."

"For now, keep the fishing crews out of the bay."

"They're working out of those last two sailboats. That's going to slow them down."

"You really have no choice." Vacher put his hand above his brow and squinted through the windows at the destroyer flashing in the sunlight. "What are you trying to tell us?"

I frowned at him. "Who are you talking to?"

"God." Suddenly, he laughed, as if over some private joke, then finally said, "Your father would have enjoyed this."

I nodded. "He'd say it was the Navy's revenge against the Marine Corps."

"Yes, he would."

"What do you think he would do? What do you think my brother would do?"

"Those questions are meaningless. What will *you* do? That's the only question that matters. Maybe we'll need to move. Maybe we'll go to the Carl Gustaf. Maybe you'll have to strengthen our alliance with Rousseau."

My blood turned cold. "I just don't know."

* * *

THAT evening, the destroyer ran aground about seven hundred feet from the beach. She came in on a high tide and became entrenched as the outgoing tide dug out the sand beneath her keel. By low tide she began to list about fifteen degrees to port, presenting a clear view of the main deck. She partially eclipsed the three islets and was, by all accounts, a gargantuan, rusting reminder of the death we had wrought on ourselves. That ship, sitting so improbably in our once pristine bay, our oasis, our Shangri-la, raised the gooseflesh on my back.

The after-dinner conversation was, of course, focused on the destroyer, and Cindy must have asked me a dozen times to take another radiation reading and why don't we move to the other side of the island. I told her she and her group were welcome to leave any time they wanted. My sarcastic smile drew a string of curses from her thin lips. James and I decided that in the morning we'd make another inspection of the destroyer to search for leaking fuel and any other potential problems.

Our head fisherman Lefort was manning the radio out at Vacher's yacht, which we'd anchored upwind from the ship, and he flashed the signal light to tell us we were getting a message from Rousseau.

James paddled out on his kayak, and I waited for him on the beach. Ten minutes later he returned, the bow of his kayak scraping up onto the shoreline before I helped him out.

"What?"

"Another attack. This one at the Sunset. Another bad one."

"No one heard the shooting?"

James shook his head. "Most of it probably happened inside."

The Sunset was a small, ten-room hotel near the harbor in Gustavia, and Rousseau had told me a small group of his people had left to join up with another fifteen or so holed up there.

"What happened?"

"They killed about fifteen people and stole all their supplies. They didn't kill everyone, though. Beat up the rest. Same guys in the speedboats. They said the rest of Tremaine's reggae band was there, and they must've fought back, because none of them made it. See, Dad, he would've died anyway."

"We don't know that." I sighed in disgust. "Who are these bastards?"

"They're the guys who are well armed and have fuel. I don't think we should go looking for them—"

"Because they'll eventually find us."

We stood there a moment, just thinking, then James finally said, "There's something wrong here, Dad."

"I know. I've been feeling that since the first attack."

He nodded. "We have the best supplies on the island. They should've hit us first."

"Well, we're also the best defended."

"I don't think that matters to these guys. You know, before we left, a couple buddies from school told me that the drug trade down here was pretty significant. They were joking that I should import some product back to New York. So I'm thinking that the guys we're worried about now were probably pirates or drug dealers here, and now they've got free reign. The stealing and killing is even easier. That group at the church never stood a chance. No one does, except us. Maybe."

"All right, let's think about this. They haven't hit us, and they've hit a couple places near Rousseau. They should've hit him already. Doesn't make any sense."

"Well, if they're drugged up half the time, then they won't make sense."

"Nah, that's not it," I said. "They're not stupid enough to do drugs."

"Yeah, you're probably right. I'm just wondering what they're waiting for."

"Me, too. And that scares the hell out of me."

"Don't tell anyone else that."

I picked up the back end of the kayak and helped him carry it up toward the hotel. We weren't halfway there when Vanessa came running down, shouting my name.

"What now?" I asked with a groan.

"I can't find Chloe."

"What?"

"I can't find her. No one's seen her."

"She probably went up to one of the other villas with Alexandre."

"Well, he's gone, too."

"Well there it is. Calm down. We'll give her the benefit of the doubt, but if she's not back within the hour, then we'll go out."

"She knows not to leave the hotel," said James. "But she's been bitching about privacy."

"So have you," snapped Vanessa.

"All right, let's get upstairs," I said.

I watched Vanessa pace the terrace under a mantle of stars so brilliant they looked manufactured by a Hollywood special effects department. My wife was talking to herself, but I couldn't hear her. I sat in one of the chairs near the television. We'd long since burned out all the candles, but I had a small flashlight with one of only two rechargeable batteries we'd found, and it lay in my lap as I sipped a small glass of wine, convincing myself that Chloe had just gone off with her boyfriend and would be back soon. I refocused my attention on the ship. If the weather turned on us—and it could at any time because hurricane season was hardly over—the entire island could become contaminated. We needed a plan to leave, and that was the most frightening fact of all. Our existence on the island, our sacrifices, paled in comparison to those who might have survived back home. We'd begun forging a new life in a place where the sights, sounds, and smells cast a spell of amnesia on us all.

Leaving meant remembering and risking everything.

And we could never do that without a plan, and I just didn't have one. I didn't know where to go or even how to get there. I kept turning to my left to ask my brother what he thought.

Vanessa slapped a magazine into my pistol, jolting me from my thoughts. "That's it, Charles, I'm going out to look for her. And when I find her, she's going to hear it."

I checked my watch. "It's been a half hour."

"I don't care. Let's go."

"She's still a teenager and just fooling around," I said through a deep sigh.

AFTER calling for James and Marcos to join us, we painstakingly searched each of the hotel's thirty-four houses, suites, rooms, and cottages on the hotel grounds. Consequently, I began to lose it, snapping at Vanessa and my son and cursing and vowing that Chloe would be exiled to her room for a month.

As we stood outside the restaurant in the humid night air, the bugs chirping, James abruptly said, "I think I know where they are."

I went up to him, shoved my face into his the way my brother would when we were kids, and asked, "Really? And this you tell us now?"

He recoiled and backed away. "I just remembered. There's a little fishing village. They call it Corossol. It's on the southwest side of the island. When we were checking out the desalinization plant in Public, Alexandre took us over there, and I remember Chloe saying how beautiful it was and Alexandre saying they would come back someday. He probably took her there."

"Alone? At night?" asked Vanessa.

"I don't believe him." I gasped. "Would he be that stupid? Jesus . . ."

James shrugged.

I swore under my breath. "Let's get the bikes and get going."

"I'm coming," Vanessa said

I knew better than to argue. "James, you'll need to stay here."

"All right, Dad. Take along Bento, too. I'll send him down."

"Good. And James, if we're not back in—"

"Dad, don't get all dramatic. Go get Chloe and bring her home so we can figure out what the hell to do with that ship."

I took a deep breath. "All right."

"Mr. Charles," Marcos began in an ominous tone. "It is not good to ride at night."

"You don't think I know that?"

AS we pedaled along the mountain road toward Gustavia and that fishing village James had mentioned, I could literally taste the paranoia in my mouth. Every bend, patch of woods, and swaying frond held the promise of gunfire, of a bullet piercing my wife's heart and her dying in my arms as an apparition with dreadlocks cackled above me.

I would throttle Chloe when we found her.

The road wound down the other side of the hill to reveal a few flickering lights, tiny as they were, near the Carl Gustaf. We pushed on, heading northwest, past Public, until we came to the tiny village, and a few small villas within the heavily wooded hills.

We rode down the street toward the sound of an outboard motor humming below. We reached the docks, where creaking wooden fishing boats had thumped against the rails with the day's catch, and spotted what Vacher would later tell me was a skiff with attached outboard. Two people were in the boat, but I couldn't tell who they were in the dark.

I directed the others to ditch their bikes along the side of the road, and we hunkered down and moved up to a stand of palm trees and just watched.

Their voices were muted, and I swore that we weren't close enough. I hadn't taken along the binoculars either.

Suddenly, Vanessa rose. "It's her."

"Get back here."

"It's her. I'm telling you." She raised her voice. "Chloe? Chloe, it's your mother up here."

I came up behind Vanessa, wrapped my hand around her mouth, then dragged her back to the palm tree as she screamed into my hand.

"You'll get us killed," I whispered in her ear.

"Mom, is that you up there?"

I froze. Then I relaxed my grip and released Vanessa, who

shouted, "Yes, it's me and your father! We're coming down!" She tore away from me and charged toward her bike.

"Marcos? Bento? Hold back here and be ready," I told them, drawing my pistol.

We got on our bikes and road down onto the dock, where Chloe was being helped out of the skiff by another man who finally turned, and to my relief it was Alexandre.

"What're you guys doing here?" Chloe asked.

"Sorry we interrupted your date," I began. "But Jesus Christ, Chloe, what the hell are you thinking here? You want to get raped? You want to get shot? You come out here asking for it? Did you know there was another attack tonight?" Then I turned to Alexandre. "And what the hell were you thinking?"

"It's not his fault," Chloe said.

"It is mine," said Alexandre. "I am to blame for all of this. Me."

I slipped my pistol into my waistband and balled my hands into fists. "I'm just . . . I don't know what to say."

"I'm very sorry, Mr. Charles. Very sorry."

"Dad, I talked him into this. He didn't want to come."

"And what's this boat? Where did this come from? And where'd you get the fuel?"

"Mr. Charles, remember those friends I was helping? Well, this is their boat. It's almost out of fuel anyway."

I took a deep breath. "You should never have done this. Never."

"I understand, Mr. Charles. We won't do it again."

"Now how did you get here?"

"Our bikes are up on the hill."

I nodded, realizing that we should've checked the bike count first before we had even searched for them. "All right, if the boat's nearly out of fuel, then just leave it. Let's go back. Right now."

"Yes, Mr. Charles."

* * *

THANKFULLY, we returned to the hotel without being gunned down to die in pools of our own blood. I brooded during the entire ride, and once up in our villa, I sent Chloe to her room and she cursed at me for treating her like a child.

Then I took Alexandre out onto the beach and pointed at the destroyer sitting right there and screamed, "I don't need this right now. Do you hear me? We've got bigger problems. Much bigger problems here!"

He shuddered. "Yes, Mr. Charles. I know."

Marcos and Bento joined us on the beach, and we all stood there in silence, eyeing the ship, listening to her creak in the wind.

"Well, it seems our days here at Eden Rock are numbered. We have to get ready to leave. Of course, we have no fuel. We don't have a boat big enough, and some of us are too concerned with romance to be worried about life and death."

My sarcasm and hyperbole were wearing thin, even on me. And finally, I turned to all of them, their eyes shining in the star-light, and said in a voice as sincere and genuine as I could muster, "Guys, I need your help."

TWENTY-TWO

THE next morning James and I paddled back out to the destroyer and confirmed the worst: she was leaking diesel on the starboard side. The rank scent was already wafting on the breeze, and an iridescent, slick sheen flashed a rainbow of colors across the waves. Images of the old 1989 *Exxon Valdez* disaster played out in my mind's eye. We paddled back and jogged up to the restaurant, where Vacher had returned to studying his map collection.

"Well, she's leaking," I told the old man.

He didn't look up. "It gets more interesting. Dayreis was watching the news. He tells me there's a hurricane out in the Atlantic. No confirmation that it'll come our way, but we should know more in a few days. We don't seem to have much luck, so I would prepare for the worst."

James swore and said, "There's no way we can stay here. We have to leave."

Vacher cocked a bushy gray brow. "You're right, my boy. But go where? And get there how?"

"Dad, can I talk to you?"

I turned to the doorway, where Chloe stood like a worn and battered Ophelia, her hair disheveled, her eyes bloodshot.

"I'm a little busy trying to save our asses right now—if you don't mind."

"It's important."

With a slight huff I left the table and went over to her, lowering my voice. "What? And wait a second. Aren't you supposed to be in your room?"

She rolled her eyes. "I just wanted to tell you again that it wasn't Alexandre's fault."

"Okay, whatever. I believe you."

"No, really. Alexandre had nothing to do with it. That's the truth. I'm not lying."

"We've been down this road. And you want me to believe you talked him into going up there?"

She hesitated then shook her head. I knew that guilt-stricken expression.

"Chloe, what do want to say?"

"Um, nothing. I mean, well, I saw him take one of the bikes. I didn't know where he was going, so I just followed him."

It took me a moment to process that. Then I asked, "And none of our guards saw you?"

"No."

I tensed. "That's not good."

"Whatever. So he went to that dock in Corossol, and I saw him go out in the boat."

"So the boat was already there?"

"Yeah."

"That's weird."

"Dad, can I finish?"

I nodded vigorously.

"He went up the coast a little to another dock. He got out, went up to a little shack. I didn't see anyone else. He came back about ten minutes later, and that's when I went down there and surprised him."

"What did he say?"

"He said he was meeting his friends again."

"But you didn't see anyone."

"No, but maybe he met them before I got there?"

I made a face.

"So anyway, he didn't want you to know about it, and would I please not tell you. Then he asked me if I wanted to go for a ride, and you guys got there when we were just coming back."

"Did you ask him anything else about his friends?"

"Yeah, I said why doesn't he bring them to meet us."

"And he said?"

"He said he didn't want to divide our supplies any more and that they were really paranoid about meeting anyone else. He said you've said over and over, no strays unless they have something to offer."

"Okay. Thanks, Chloe."

"Like I said, it's not his fault. He didn't ask me to go up there."

"But you shouldn't have followed him. Go back upstairs."

"What are you going to do to him?"

"Nothing. Just go."

I returned to the table, where Vacher was tracing his finger over another map, moving from St. Barts all the way to Australia.

"You have high hopes, don't you," I told him. "We don't have fuel. We don't have a sailboat. We have nothing."

"Australia would be our final destination. I think we can make it down to Tierra del Fuego, right here." He pointed near the southernmost tip of South America, at a group of islands separated from the mainland by the Strait of Magellan. "They call it the land of fire or *el fin del mundo*, the end of the world. How appropriate. We could call it home—at least for a little while."

"Why would we go there?"

"Because the sons of two of my friends are running some of the oil and gas fields. And I think we can get some help from them."

"Come on, Luc. You can't confirm that they're still there. They could've moved on or be dead."

"They love their homes. They wouldn't leave, and their fathers owe me their lives."

"*If* they're there . . ."

He snickered. "I think it's worth the gamble. Do you have any friends in South America?"

After a deep sigh I answered, "All right, so we go to Tierra del Fuego. How the hell do we get there? No sailboat. No fuel."

"And swimming is out of the question."

"You can joke now? Really?"

He smirked then stared hard in thought.

"What're you thinking now? That we should use the contaminated fuel out there?"

Just then Alexandre, Marcos, and Bento came into the dining room, and I widened my eyes on my daughter's young suitor. "We need to talk."

"Yes, Mr. Charles. I know we need to leave the island, and I know how we can do that."

"Oh really."

Alexandre turned to the old Frenchman, who'd begun sketching a picture of a sailboat. "Mr. Vacher, I heard what you said.

You want to make sails for your boat, but we need something better. On St. Martin there is a boat called a Tahiti ketch."

"I know what they are," Vacher snapped.

"This one is about sixty feet long and can hold twelve or more people. It has a diesel engine so we can travel long distances."

"How do you know about it?" asked Vacher.

"Your friends tell you?" I added.

"Mr. Charles, I will be honest. They are more than my friends. Two of them are my cousins, Jima and Santeen. They found the boat. They have some fuel. They plan to fill it up and take it out of St. Martin. We can get to it first."

"So you plan on ripping off your cousin?"

"He wants me to go with them. He will not let me take Chloe, and I love her. I will do anything for her. I've already taken some of my cousin's fuel so we can go get the boat. That's what I was doing last night."

"You've been lying to me all this time about your cousins. Now you want me to trust you? Why didn't you come to me in the first place?"

"Because I wasn't sure I could get the fuel."

"I don't know, Alexandre. I don't know what to believe."

"Mr. Charles, up in Corossol, I have that fuel. It's enough to go to St. Martin on Mr. Luc's yacht and bring back the ketch. Then after that, there is another place we can get more."

I walked up to the young man and seized him by the neck. "You know of another place we can get fuel? What the hell is this? You've been holding out on us?"

"Please, Mr. Charles," he gasped.

"Mr. Charles, let him finish," said Marcos. "Let him finish."

I relaxed my grip on his neck, then finally lowered my hand.

"Maybe I should shoot you right here. What else aren't you telling us? *What else?*"

He actually started to cry, right there, the kid I had trusted with everything—including my daughter—just broke down, then backhanded away the tears and said, "I just want to help us. That's all I want to do. I didn't think I could turn against my cousin. But I have to now. That's why I didn't say anything. I didn't know if I could do it."

"Oh, man, this is a pretty good sob story you have."

"You don't understand, Mr. Charles. But you have to believe me when I say the ketch is there and we need to go get it. I can help."

"Why do we need to get it so badly? Why can't we just use Luc's yacht or the ones that Rousseau has?" I asked.

Alexandre sighed, his expression tightening in frustration.

Vacher decided to answer for him. "Charles, I've been sailing all my life, and we can't use my boat. You've seen the hull—it's v-shaped and won't do well in heavy seas or hurricanes. I bought it for sailing in fair weather. It looks pretty and moves fast, but it was never designed for a long trip on the open ocean. Same goes for Rousseau's boats. Now that ketch Alexandre talks about. That is a work horse, with one of the most seaworthy hulls around. She does very well in high seas and moves under minimum sail. She's a world traveler, exactly the kind of boat we need. If we're going to leave the island, then we have to get her. We can't pass up this opportunity."

"So the boat is really that important," I said.

He winked. "I wish you were a sailor."

"Dad, I say we give it a shot," said James. "I mean, what do we have to lose?"

"Maybe he wants us to go off with him so the hotel is vulnerable, then his friends move in to take over. Maybe that's what you want, eh, Alexandre? Maybe there is no ketch. It's just a story to get us away."

"No, Mr. Charles."

"Then I'll tell you what, you and I and James and Luc here will go get the boat. Everyone else stays to protect the hotel. How's that sound?"

He swallowed. "It sounds perfect."

I glanced to the doorway where Chloe had returned and had been watching and listening to it all. She nodded emphatically at me. I eyed James, who shrugged, then I raised my chin at Vacher, who said, "Let's get that fuel."

VACHER'S boat ran on fumes up to Corossol. We were betting everything on Alexandre's plan, and the thought made me nauseous. The Volvo D9s stalled just as we drifted into the harbor and reached the dock. Alexandre had about fifteen large plastic containers of varying size stashed in a shack. James and I helped him transfer the diesel fuel back down to the yacht, and the refueling operation began.

"We'll have to go slow," said Vacher. "And this will be a one-way trip. She consumes about seventy-five liters an hour at twenty-seven knots. That's about twenty gallons an hour at that speed to you Americans."

"Will we have enough to get there?"

"Probably."

"What about getting the ketch back?" I asked.

"We'll sail her back," said Alexandre. "Plenty of wind today."

"Yeah, because there's a storm out there."

He looked at me, his expression full of concern. "I know."

I nodded. He had an answer for everything. But I continued to press because I'd spotted something that made it all click, and I wanted to see if he'd eventually confess. "So, let me understand this. Anybody who had a sailboat here on St. Barts took off to who knows where. Why didn't the owners of this ketch take off?"

"Mr. Charles, I don't know. Maybe they chose to stay on the island."

"So the boat's just been sitting there, waiting to be stolen? You see how that doesn't make a lot of sense?"

"I told you my cousins found the boat. One of their friends is there protecting it until they are ready to leave. They know about the storm coming, too. They told me they are going tomorrow to get it. We'll beat them by one day."

"Why are they waiting until tomorrow?"

"I don't know."

"You do know." I grabbed him by the shirt collar, dragged him off the yacht and back toward the little boat he'd taken Chloe on the night before. I let him go and drew my pistol and ordered him to climb down into the boat.

"See it there, right there by the motor. What is that? Pick that up for me. Hold it up. Show it to James and Luc. Show it to them."

I faced Vacher and my son, ready to witness the shift in their expressions as our most trusted friend extended his arm and held a rooster's elongated tail feather between his fingers.

TWENTY-THREE

"WHAT is that?" James asked, frowning at Alexandre.

"It's a feather," I answered before Alexandre could. "From a rooster's tail."

"So what?" James thought a second, and his expression abruptly shifted. "Oh, wait a minute."

"Yeah, that's right."

James held up his hand. "But how do you know that came from a rooster at the church?"

My cheeks flushed. *"Because he's going to tell us right now!"*

My pistol was trained on Alexandre's head, and tremors were already working through my hand. For a few moments, Alexandre was Tremaine and we were back up at the Carl Gustaf and I was a being of pure hatred. Then I saw the bullies of my past, their faces shortening my breath and sending bolts of anger up and down my spine. My index finger tightened on the trigger.

"Calm down, Charles. Let the boy speak."

I blinked. Looked at Vacher. Realized that all those faces were just Alexandre and that we needed to hear him out. I took a deep breath but held my pistol on him. "Yeah, okay, we'll let him talk. Because his cousins? What were their names? Jima and Santeen? They're the one's who've been hitting all the tribes. We should've seen this coming."

"Are you kidding me?" asked James. "Alex, man, is it true?"

Alexandre dropped to his knees right there in the boat and brought his hands together, his gaze turning glassy and narrowing before he answered, "Please, I'm begging all of you to listen to me."

I snorted. "What can you tell us now? What can you say that will possibly make this any better?"

"Charles," Vacher warned.

My voice cracked. "All right, after nearly a year on this island, we find out we have a spy."

"Dad, I don't think he's a spy," said James. "I think he just got caught in the middle of something."

"Yeah, a massacre. Did you tell them about the chickens at the church?"

Alexandre shook his head. "Mr. Charles, I knew my cousins were out there. They were drug dealers here for years before you came. They wanted me to help, but I never did. I got a job at the hotel, but they forced me to make contact with guests so they could sell the drugs. If I did that for them, they left me alone."

"Your cousins wouldn't be the De Souza brothers, would they?" asked Vacher.

Alexandre recoiled a little. "You know them?"

"Not personally." The old Frenchman's eyes lit as he turned to me. "My God, Charles, they're the guys your father and I were hunting!"

"Well, you might get your wish," I said. "And we've been working with their little errand boy the entire time."

"Mr. Charles, I've never wanted to be like them. And I never thought they would do anything like this. They never killed anyone before."

"Well now they believe they can do whatever they want," said Vacher. "They were already notorious in the Caribbean for piracy and drug running, focusing more on the latter in recent years. They're wanted criminals."

Alexandre nodded. "For years they've wanted me to join them, but I won't. I've told them that my father raised me to live an honest life, and that my lord and savior Jesus Christ won't allow me to be like them."

"I believe you," said James. "See, Dad? I was right. They've been pressuring him, that's all."

"Let him finish."

"Mr. Charles, the only reason they have not come to the hotel is because of me. And I begged them not to hit us or Rousseau's place, but tonight they will steal Rousseau's supplies and kill everyone there. I can't stop them anymore."

"So we'll have to tip off Rousseau," I told James.

"No, you can't do that," said Alexandre. "While they attack the Carl Gustaf, we'll go over to St. Martin and get the ketch. This way we always know where they are. You see, Mr. Charles. Their plan works for us."

"And I'm supposed to sacrifice all those people at that hotel, just like that? I'm supposed to stand here when I know they're going to get attacked, and do nothing?"

"Dad, you saw what they did to the people in that church. They'll do the same thing to us. It's not our fault. We need to get that boat and get the hell out of here. You can't feel sorry for Rousseau. He'd screw us over in a heartbeat. We need to do what's right for us."

"Is that what I've taught you? Is that all you've learned? Me first and to hell with everyone else?"

He came up to me and hardened his expression. "You and I have already killed for our family. I'm not going to apologize for that. And you're not going to apologize for letting Rousseau take the fall for us. Dad, we can't overthink this. Please. Let it go down the way he's saying. They attack Rousseau while we steal the boat."

"Gentlemen, we can finish this conversation back at the hotel," said Vacher. "We don't know where the De Souzas are right now."

"I know where they are. And it's okay," said Alexandre. "They sleep a lot during the day now."

"How many are there?" I asked.

"My two cousins and four more."

I lowered my voice and looked daggers at Alexandre. "If I find out that anything you've told us is a lie, I'm going to shoot you in the head. End of story. I don't care how much you love my daughter or how much you've already done for us. If you've lied, you die."

"Mr. Charles, I understand."

"You'd kill him in a second, after he's done so much for us, but you're worried about Rousseau?" James asked. "Dad, this is the guy who's going to help us."

I snickered and turned back to Alexandre. "If your cousins and their men sleep during the day, why don't we go right now and get the ketch?"

"Because the man they've left on the boat sleeps mostly at night. There was a second man with him, but he ran off onto the island. I don't know what happened to him."

"So we got one guy on the boat, and five more who will be at

Rousseau's tonight," I said. "So all right. Let's get back home and plan this thing."

"Thank you, Mr. Charles. I would never do anything to hurt you or your family. Never."

"We'll see."

Vacher fired up the engines; they sputtered a moment before the new fuel reached them. We shoved off with a little cloud of smoke, and Alexandre wiped away some fresh tears and went below. James gave me a pained look, then went after him.

I shifted up to Vacher, who was at the wheel, and asked, "Maybe we should just move to the other side of the island and take our chances. The kid's story is so convoluted I don't know what to believe. What if it's Eden Rock tonight and Rousseau's tomorrow?"

Vacher glanced down at my waistband, where I'd tucked my pistol. "Might as well shoot yourself right now."

"Yeah, because what this kid wants us to do is insane. Even if we steal the ketch, you don't think his cousins are going to come after us?"

"They're all coming, Charles. You can't stop them. That ship will keep leaking. That storm will hit us. And unless we either take out or escape from Alexandre's cousins, they'll kill us, too. So . . . we get that ketch. We load it up, and we leave. The most interesting question now is who lives and who dies?"

"What do you mean?"

"I mean there is only room for ten, maybe twelve on board that boat. Who decides who comes along? You? I know your brother would have found this interesting. How do you play God? How do you decide which lives are worth more to you and the group? Is there some equation, some formula?"

"Jesus, I just wanted to teach kids to read and write. I didn't want any of this. I'm just a freaking teacher, man. There's no way I can play God."

"You'd better start thinking about it."

"Maybe you and I will stay behind. What do you think of that?"

"I'll stay, but you have to go."

"Oh really?"

"It's your reason to live."

"So you've figured that out for me?"

"Of course, it's not, what do you Americans always say, it's not rocket science. Your reason to live is your family, of course. You do all of this for them."

"I guess you're right. What's your reason to live?"

He put a hand on my shoulder. "You."

WE anchored the yacht almost exactly where she'd been earlier in the morning, upwind of the destroyer, and used the Zodiac to get back to the shoreline, which was already stained by leaking diesel fuel. Vanessa was on the beach, running the meter over the water and shaking her head.

"You hear that?" she asked as the thing ticked away, her hand moving the probe closer to the foul-smelling water.

"Don't worry about it. We won't be here for much longer," I said.

"What's going on?"

"I'm so thirsty. Let's go up and get some water, and I'll tell you."

"Are we going on Luc's boat?"

"No."

"Then where are we going? Over to Gustavia?"

"No."

She hit me. "Then what?"

"I'll tell you."

WE returned to our villa, and I shared the plan. She understood but was worried, of course, and I said we didn't have much choice. If fate had kept us alive, then fate was now telling us to leave.

"That's going to be hard," she said. "I don't know if I can feel safe anywhere else."

"Eden Rock is more of an ideal than a place, and it doesn't matter where we go. We bring that ideal with us. A strong foundation. Our family. And on that we build the rest of our lives."

She began to cry, and I held her tight to my chest. We sat there for a few more minutes until she finally sighed and looked at me.

"I have to make two decisions right now. Do I tip off Rousseau? And if we get that boat from St. Martin, who gets to come along? I think we can fit ten or twelve, and that's pushing it. Maybe thirteen? Fourteen max? The more people we take along, the less distance we can make because of supplies."

She pulled away and wiped her cheeks. "Well, us, that's four. Little Trina, of course. And Hannah, Luc, Alexandre, Marcos, Bento, Dayreis, and Nicole, of course. And what about Cindy and Jane? The rest of Dayreis's staff and the other girls from Cindy's group have to stay behind."

"Half our tribe stays. Lefort and his fishing crews who worked their asses off for us, and everyone else, huh? The guards like Tleverton and Emilia?"

"I know, it's not fair."

"No, it's not."

"Is there any other way to take them, too? Maybe we could tow Vacher's yacht?"

"I don't know. I don't think so."

"How about a little flotilla of ships?"

"And where does all this fuel come from?"

She took a long breath. "We can't let the others find out what we're doing."

"I know. And it's eating me up. We worked so hard together, and now we're supposed to turn our backs on them. Leave them here to get contaminated and slowly die."

"Charles, there's nothing we can do. We have to save ourselves now."

"But we don't have to be happy about it. I'm a murderer, our son has become a killer. Our daughter's in love with a guy being used by drug runners. If you would've told me this last year, I would've laughed my ass off."

"You can't analyze everything. Sometimes you have to keep your head low and keep moving."

"That sounds like something my brother would say."

"Actually, you said it a few years ago, when I was trying to get the business off the ground and I was getting all those rejections."

"Well, I guess it's time for Charlie to practice what he preaches."

I didn't want Vacher to come with us, but he insisted upon piloting his yacht for one last time, and after what he'd said about me being his reason, I granted his wish. I reasoned that he could get us to St. Martin using the least amount of fuel, since he knew the boat better than we did. I took along Alexandre and Marcos and left James, Bento, and Dayreis to hold down the fort.

We thundered away from St. Barts, heading out of the bay, and for the first time in nearly a year, I saw the island from a more distant vantage point, and something inside gave way, like a crumbling balustrade, and I seemed to fall into a deep sense of despair. Vanessa was right. Eden Rock had become our sanctuary, and as I squinted at the hotel rising at the end of our long and foamy wake, pangs of wistfulness struck hard, along with a simmering anger that the universe could be this merciless. I wanted to shake a fist at the stars, but I only stood there beside Vacher, with the wind rushing through my hair and beard. I thought about the man we were about to kill.

TWENTY-FOUR

AS I stood at the bottom of the portside steps, near the stern, all the dreams left behind returned to haunt me. I'd taught Dayreis's staff to speak better English, but I would never stand in front of a college class again. I'd dreamed of gaining my father's respect and recognition, and in the end I might have had his love, but I wondered if that was enough. I'd wanted my brother to look at me with envy in his eyes over my life, over what I'd done, over what it was to be me.

Dreams of better relationships were just the start. Though a good fifteen years away from retirement, I'd already begun to discuss my grand plans. You get older and you associate with an older crowd, your crowd now, and the conversation shifts from children to grandchildren, from buying a new house to paying off the one you have or downsizing to a small condo with lots of amenities because you can't mow the lawn anymore since being diagnosed with that degenerative disc. And you tell your friends that you're going to settle down after retirement and finally write that novel, finally buy that bass fishing boat, finally take a ride to the Grand Canyon or to Mount Rushmore or that giant crater somewhere in Arizona caused by a meteor impact. You get more fascinated by rocks, I guess.

And then there are the simple things, like getting up in the morning and deciding what *you're* going to do for the day, not what a dozen other people need you to do. That's how I thought it would be, anyway. I'm sure if I talked to more retirees, they'd beg to differ.

The moment I had stepped out of that airplane, set foot on St. Barts, all those dreams, clichéd or weatherworn or painfully simple, vanished, and I hadn't even known. I missed them so badly I could taste them on the ocean wind, which got me thinking again about food, a subject that came up so much during the day that sometimes we had to ban it from our discussions. James and Chloe waxed poetic, even evangelic about fast-food burgers and Mexican and Thai and even just a nice draft beer. We could do only so much with the fish we caught, and Dayreis had exhausted his spice collection months ago. I thought I'd probably never have a steak again, that all the cows were dead or dying. But that was all right. Vanessa had been trying to wean me off red meat and other "bad" foods for years. At least the steroids or high fructose corn syrup or yellow dye no. 6 wouldn't kill me.

There was also the dream of finally enjoying my midlife crisis, the one I'd delayed for ten years because I'd been so busy with school and raising kids and with trying to please everyone. I'd told Vanessa that I was going to buy a torch red Corvette and find a mistress, and she had given me that you're-so-pathetic look and told me to finish folding the towels. No, I'd never really had any aspirations to buy a fast car, but I had wanted to drop some weight, get back into some outdoor sports, and return to my own writing. One out of three *is* bad.

So what now? Was it time to develop new dreams in a world where none of us felt like we even deserved to dream? I was too frightened to even imagine the future. The island was something known and seemingly permanent. Once we left, the entire weight of our existence would rest squarely on my shoulders. I almost wished that when we got to St. Martin, we'd find the boat gone or sunk or on fire or something so I wouldn't have to face the truth. I was already on the deck of the ketch during a violent storm, and I watched as Chloe, James, and Vanessa were swept overboard. I was left standing there, alone, in the storm, having lost my world, my family, everything, because of the choices I had made.

During the past six months I'd begun to believe that maybe, just maybe, we'd never have to leave the island. When I'd gone away to college I couldn't wait to get out of that house. I was young and naïve and had little fear of the unknown. I needed to recapture that spirit. I needed to pay more attention to James, who still had a healthy dose of bravado. I was too damned set in my ways. One of my colleagues who taught business classes had once told me that I needed to get out of my comfort zone to achieve more success. *Well, honey, look at me now . . . This good enough for you?*

Alexandre joined me at the stern and lifted his voice above the engines. "I'm so sorry, Mr. Charles."

I nodded.

"I will kill him when we get there—if that's what it takes to prove my loyalty."

"I think you need to prove your innocence more than your loyalty. But you're the best one to get in close to that guy, and you'll need to take him out."

He looked at me a moment longer, gave a weak smile, then headed up toward Vacher.

My faith in him was gone, and he knew it, and even if he did kill that guy, I still wasn't sure that I'd trust him. In fact, the thought had crossed my mind of leaving him behind, but I knew Chloe and James would raise a wall in his defense. Marcos and Bento were much simpler men, quiet, pensive, religious, utterly loyal. Alexandre was as complicated as he was intelligent, and I wondered if he was still plotting down below, still turning the events over and over in his head, calculating which half truths would best keep him alive as he played both sides against the middle.

Marcos, who'd been sitting down near Vacher, shouldered his rifle and came over. He tossed a glance back at the hatch leading below and said, "He is a good man, Mr. Charles. We have known him for a long time. I knew his father. He is telling the truth."

"Thanks, Marcos."

His expression turned sober. "We're going to be okay."

"I should be telling you that."

"I know you are worried. I am, too. But we are fighters." He shook a fist. "We don't give up."

I banged my fist on his. "No, we don't."

OUR trek northwest finally took us to the Dutch side of St. Martin, near the southern coastline, now a stretch of hills gleaming black like carbon fiber and pinpricked by just a few pale orange lights, cook fires no doubt. Alexandre stood beside Vacher, feeding him directions as the wind howled around us. We began to turn north, past the Flamingo Bay Resort and Flamingo Beach, toward a drawbridge whose arms paid permanent homage to the sky. The police station, immigration, and port facilities at the bridge were presumably deserted.

We slid into the channel, lined on both sides by gray and crumbling riprap being pounded by the windswept water. We passed under those great arms of steel to finally enter the lagoon that Vacher assured us was a once bustling seaside community crammed with yachts. The Princess Yacht Club, Vacher then pointed out, looked remarkable without a single boat docked at the nearby piers, its black-windowed buildings huddled together along the shoreline. Vacher rolled the wheel, taking us due north and deeper into the lagoon, with the long strip of the airport off to our left. We glided on by, then Alexandre told Vacher to turn hard left, and we ran once more along the piers and now parallel with the runway until Alexandre pointed at a pier jutting out about thirty feet farther than any of the others. At first glance, I did not see any boats, only some tall towers I thought were for cell phones, but as we drew closer, the ketch's bow shown from the other side of a building rising at the water's edge. Those towers were actually the boat's masts. We'd reached the Turtle Pier Restaurant, its yellow and green sign advertising breakfast, lunch, dinner, and live lobster. The windows were shattered, broken glass flickering, and the main door appeared to have been kicked in, broken in two. There were no signs of anyone, living or dead, at the restaurant, and clearly no sign of any live lobsters.

Vacher killed the engines, and we glided in the last one hundred yards as a figure appeared on the bow of the ketch, holding a rifle. I couldn't see his face, but Alexandre was already calling out in rapid fire Portuguese, his tone somewhere between arrogant and annoyed.

We bumped up to the dock, the old wood groaning in protest, and as Vacher issued me orders to tie her up, Alexandre leapt off onto the pier and strode toward the ketch as it bobbed on the waves. He'd told us not to say anything, so we would let him handle the "negotiations."

My hands were trembling as we tied up Vacher's yacht. Once finished, I glanced over at the old man, who stood there, still gripping the wheel, his head lowered. He was saying good-bye to his baby, and I dared not disturb him.

Marcos came over to me and said, "Alexandre will take care of everything for us."

"I hope so." I craned my head toward the other boat.

Alexandre called out to the man once more, and the guy came around as Alexandre ascended a small gangway and met him at the top. They were hard to see in the darkness and with the wind stinging my eyes, but I saw something flash in Alexandre's hand, and they embraced like old friends.

I held my breath, as one man fell away from the other and dropped quietly to the deck.

"What happened?" I asked Marcos.

"Mr. Charles, I don't know."

"Okay!" cried Alexandre. "Let's go!"

I allowed myself to breathe, and my shoulders slumped.

Marcos jumped off the yacht and charged down the pier, and I went back to Vacher and said, "Luc, it's time."

He glanced up at me and sighed. "Okay."

I helped him off the yacht and we started down the pier, planks creaking under our shoes as something splashed hard nearby. I craned my head as the body of the guard began floating away, carried on the rough waves like a hurricane victim to be found kilometers away from his house.

We ascended the gangway and dropped onto the ketch's deck.

Marcos and I were hardly sailors. Vacher and Alexandre were in their element, and Alexandre said he'd learned to sail when he was a teenager and had worked on several boats. Vacher ordered us to take in all the lines and push away from the pier by hand. He next hit the ignition switch, and I held my breath, then gasped as the diesel rumbled to life, ran for maybe thirty seconds, and abruptly quit.

"Oh, you're kidding me," I said.

I spun to confront Vacher and caught him shaking his head and nurturing a grin of embarrassment.

"Don't worry, Charles. I'll take care of it."

He sent Alexandre below to open the air-intake valve to the engine. I later learned diesels, on rare occasion, can run away and a fuel or air cutoff valve is a requisite safety feature. Vacher scrutinized our rigging as we cleared the spreaders and upper shrouds of adjacent masts and nosed the ketch out into a two-knot current from an outgoing tide. The terminology was all Vacher's, but I was a quick study. I stayed focused on everything happening on board, wary of getting knocked unconscious by a swinging boom and reluctant to spot that corpse floating in the channel.

Vacher informed me that the ketch had an eighty-gallon fuel tank and that it did, in fact, still have about ten gallons—quite extraordinary after all this time. Not so, argued Alexandre. Before his cousins had taken over the ketch, the original owners, two men from Canada, had been on board and guarded what was left with their lives. They'd even added some fuel preservatives to ensure that the diesel didn't go bad over time. Alexandre's cousin figured he would use what was left in the tanks for maneuvering until he could refill them completely.

We sailed back out of the lagoon and into the open water,

toward St. Barts, and I whispered a prayer not to become sea-sick. Alexandre came up to me, pursed his lips, then finally said, "We're on our way."

"Thank you." I extended my hand.

He did likewise, his blood-stained palm shaking. He'd knifed to death one of his cousin's henchmen for me, for my family, and I couldn't help but be grateful. I took his hand and squeezed hard. "No more lies," I said.

"No."

"Good."

"Thank you, Mr. Charles. Thank you." He turned his head into the wind. "That storm is coming."

I nodded. "You said there's more fuel."

"Yes, we're going there right now, to the south side of St. Barts, to an inlet near Mourne Rouge. We can fill up, get back to the hotel, and leave before my cousins realize what happened to the boat. Their plan is to leave Rousseau's and go back to St. Martin and bring back the ketch. They'll find Mr. Luc's yacht, and they'll know we were there."

"Then we should've ditched the yacht somewhere else."

"That wouldn't have mattered. They'll know I did this. They'll be coming for me."

"What if they already know? What if they're using us to bring back the ketch for them?"

Alexandre sighed. "I don't know if they are that clever. Jima has a very bad temper and acts mostly with his emotions. San-teen is more thoughtful. Maybe he would think of something like that. But I don't think so."

I walked up to Vacher, who was at the wheel, his shock of gray hair ablaze in the wind. "How do you like her?"

"Oh, she's a gem. Barely twenty years old, I think. One of the finest boats I've ever piloted."

"So you're our captain now. It's my tribe but your boat, huh?"

"You're a smart boy, Charles. If he gets us the fuel, I'll get us to Tierra del Fuego."

"Alexandre will take you there now."

"That was the plan."

I sighed. "All I'm thinking about now is Rousseau and what might be going on over there."

"What's happening there is keeping us alive. That's all you need to remember."

He was right, but I couldn't accept it so easily. I couldn't switch off my conscience and turn it back on during more convenient times.

When I was six years old I stood in line with my father to buy a fresh-cut Christmas tree, and Dad was complaining about the long wait, and other customers were getting irate, the way people do during the holidays. Suddenly, Dad wrenched me away by the wrist, and we stormed back to our truck and took off, with the Christmas tree tied down in the truck's bed. I stared back through the sliding window and watched the limbs flap in the breeze.

"Dad?" I asked in a hollow voice. "We didn't pay for the Christmas tree, did we?"

"No, we didn't!" he cried. "And those bastards don't deserve our money! They make it goddamned impossible to enjoy the experience of buying a tree because they make you wait on the goddamned line for so long that you forget what Christmas is all about! They turn it into a miserable experience for you because they don't know how to handle their business and keep the line moving and get people in and out! For Christ's sake, all we wanted to do was buy a goddamned tree, and they have to put me through hell to do it!"

I sat there in silence. My dad had stolen our Christmas tree, and when we got home, he pretended that the entire event had never happened. I was sworn to secrecy and didn't even tell my brother. And Dad had his beer and joked around and smiled and acted like everything was hunky-dory. And I just kept looking at him, and looking at that tree, all shimmering with ornaments and tinsel and the baby Jesus in his manger below, and wondering how my father could ignore what he'd done and not show any regret. He must've believed he deserved a free tree and that God had given him one for the inconvenience.

In the days to come, I imagined that the tree itself would turn black and come alive. It would mount the stairs, head into my parents' bedroom, and strangle my father. I kept my distance from that towering monster, and when Christmas was over, I couldn't wait for my father to haul it outside.

"Good job," he said to me, putting a finger to his lip.

I'd made him proud for keeping his lie. And once we were in hell together, staring at a million burning Christmas trees lighting up the crimson sky, he'd tell me what a good boy I was and that sometimes you had to be "forceful" to get things done.

"Charles!" cried Vacher from the wheel. "Come over here! I need your help! The wind's just turned on us!"

TWENTY-FIVE

THE De Souza brothers had plundered their fuel from a grounded tanker eight miles off shore, but Alexandre said that other marauders from the islands had already stolen the rest of the fifty-five gallon drums. Alexandre guided us around to the south side of St. Barts, near a barren islet called Isle Coco that rose from the murky water like the bump on an ancient sea creature's back.

We continued north into the secluded and barren inlet, where a floating pier jutted out forty or fifty feet from the beach and was capped by a perpendicular twenty-foot section forming a letter "T." The shore-to-sea section was made up of empty fifty-five gallon drums with shipboard cargo pallets secured on top for a walking/working surface. While the longer section was obviously makeshift, the shorter twenty-foot end section was commercial work, probably towed out to complete the pier. A piling at each end had been pounded into the seabed through an oversized hole, keeping the entire pier stationary while enabling vertical movement with the rise and fall of the tide. The depth was ten feet at mean low tide, Vacher said. More than enough clearance for our sixty-foot ketch.

Sitting at the pier's end were rows of fifty-five gallon drums full of diesel, thirteen drums by my count. With a lot of shouting and rushing around, I hauled in the mainsail and became hopelessly entangled in yards of damp, wind-whipped Dacron. I clawed my way out of a translucent, white world just in time to see Alexandre leap from the bow to the pier and wrap his line around the piling, affording Vacher the necessary purchase to swing our stern into the pier, where Marcos now stood ready at the other piling. Not only did I need to learn how to furl and unfurl sails, but I also needed to become more observant: I hadn't even heard Vacher fire up the engine to help keep us close to the pier.

"Keep an eye on those lines," Vacher told me. "You'll have to put more slack in them as the tide goes out."

Once moored, the real work began. We realized we could take on board only about six of the drums, stowing three up front between the jib and the mainmast, and another three aft, just forward of the mizzen mast. Vacher said it would've been better if we could get all that weight below to improve the ketch's ability to recover from extreme rolls, but he'd gladly trade a small variance in the boat's stability in order to have the fuel if the winds failed us later on. (Actually, what Vacher said to Alexandre was, "Make sure those drums are stowed on centerline. If I wasn't scared of getting becalmed out in the middle of nowhere, I wouldn't screw with her metacenter." I'm unsure if Alexandre really understood that. I frowned over the nautical jargon.)

I remained on the ketch to tend lines, while Marcos and Alexandre went down onto the undulating pier, tipped the first drum onto its side, and rolled it up the gangway we had dropped between the ketch and the pallets. One after another the barrels came, and it took us a good twenty-five minutes to get all six on board. Then we rolled up a seventh barrel and used one of two portable hand pumps we found in a trunk tied to the dock to top off the ketch's fuel tank. With the drums secured, we pulled out, leaving six full ones behind but taking both the hand pumps. Without them, the six drums would be useless to Alexandre's cousins, unless they could rig up a makeshift siphoning system.

As we sailed back, heading east (carefully avoiding the Carl Gustaf to our west), Marcos worked the hand pump and Alexandre and I began tying down the fuel. Once again, I thought about Rousseau. We'd kept the radio on during our trip to St. Martin, but no call of an attack had come from his tribe. Perhaps their man on the boat had been the first one to die . . . or, perhaps, the attack had shifted to the Eden Rock.

I literally shook with the desire to get back to the hotel as quickly as possible. We sailed all the way around the island and finally pulled into St. Jean Bay, anchoring the ketch upwind of the grounded destroyer as the first hint of dawn shone like a deep blue ribbon behind us. We issued the light signal to the shoreline, and within a few minutes, James was cutting through the waves in Alexandre's small boat to bring us back to the beach.

When he arrived at the ketch, James waved me down into the boat and cried, "Dad, we have a big problem."

"No, we don't. We have the boat and the fuel. Let's get the supplies loaded up. I want to be out of here in the next couple of hours."

"Dad, Alexandre was right. They hit Rousseau. Killed a whole bunch before they stole everything he had. He got away with four of his people, but two of them are shot up pretty bad. Nicole's trying to help them."

"They're here?"

"Yeah, guess they didn't know where to go."

I looked up at Vacher, who cried, "It's going to get nasty, Charles. You need to be ready. I'll stay here."

"Marcos, you stay with him."

"Yes, Mr. Charles."

"Alexandre? Let's go!"

He climbed into the boat with me, and James rolled the throttle and raced us back to the shoreline. Once we pulled up alongside the hotel's small dock, we hustled out. I sent Alexandre back up to the hotel to help Dayreis begin loading the first few crates of supplies that he'd begun packing before we'd left. James and I drew our pistols and headed over to one of the smaller villas, where James said Rousseau and his people had been taken.

Inside the villa's living room stood Rousseau, along with two young men and two women, all of them in their twenties, all dark haired except the tallest man, a blond. Nicole was treating one of the women using the light from Chloe's iPod. The second woman was also shot and groaning softly. My father would've described them all as severely shell-shocked. I went over to Rousseau, whose face was twisted into a knot, and he was muttering something to himself. He looked up at me, his face grainy in the shadows, his eyes barely able to focus. Finally, the recognition took hold. "They got us, Charlie boy."

"I know. I'm sorry. How did you get here?"

"We rode bikes." He gestured to the women. "Even they rode, bleeding all the way here."

"Jesus. Was it the same guys?"

"Yeah. They took off in their speedboats again. Took it all, Charles. Took it all. I thought we'd be ready for them, but they've got Uzis or something, all full auto stuff. Seems like they don't care how much ammo they blow through."

"Now shut up and listen to me. I'm going to give you a little fuel for one of your boats. I'm going to give you a hand pump. There's an inlet near Mourne Rouge. They've got six more fuel drums there. If you can get over there soon, you might have time to get the rest, fill up your boat, and get the hell out of here. No matter what, though, you need to leave."

"I know about the hurricane."

"Then you know when it hits all that wind-driven rain blowing off the hull of that destroyer is going to be like acid rain on steroids. And when the storm quits blowing, every house eave and palm frond is going to be dripping poison. But here's the kicker—just when you think it's safe to come back outside, the breeze will stir all that contaminated dried up, powdery residue into the atmosphere, the air you need to breath. Do you understand what I'm saying? There's no escaping it."

He thought about that and cursed. Then he cursed again, whirled away, and whirled back. "Sounds like you've got this all figured out already."

"That's right."

"Well, if you got an escape plan, count me in."

I took a deep breath, and my expression must've given me away.

"What?" he asked. "You can't take along a few more? What do you got? Another boat?"

"As a matter of fact we do. But no, I can't take you. I can't even take all my people. Now come on. We still have the Zodiac from Vacher's yacht. You can use that."

"No. This is all pretty goddamned cold. You got that down, huh? Your brother taught you that, huh?"

"This place did."

"Well, maybe that's not the way it'll go down. Maybe you didn't factor me into your plans. Big mistake."

Before I could raise my hand, he reached behind his back, and suddenly he had a pistol pointed straight at my head. "Let's go outside and talk about this some more . . ."

"Dad?" called James.

I eyed my son. "Easy. He won't shoot me."

James grimaced. "I'm sorry for letting them in, Dad. They were begging us, and I didn't know what to do. We took all their guns, but he obviously hid that one. I should've searched them better."

"It's all right. You did the right thing letting them in."

"No, I didn't. Now look . . ."

"James, I'm happy about what you did. You still got a heart. I was worried."

"All right, Charles, shut up now," said Rousseau. "I'm taking your gun." He reached down toward my hand.

"You can have it."

Now he had a gun to my head and one to my back. I stepped out of the living room, through the open front door, and into the wind. From our vantage point on the sidewalk we had an unobstructed view of the bay, the ketch's silhouette clearly outlined against the horizon. I'd never seen the bay so rough, and the destroyer creaked under the onslaught.

"So there's your new boat," said Rousseau. "Where'd you get her?"

"I don't have time to talk. They're coming for us. And I don't plan on being here. Either shoot me or let me go."

"You're not afraid to die, are you?"

"Dying would be easy." I slowly turned around and faced him. "I have to tell some of my people they're not coming with us. We've been together for a while now, helped each other, pretty much saved each other's lives. And now we just don't have the room."

"Well, I'll save you that trouble. I'll be taking the boat now."

I narrowed my gaze on him. "No. You won't."

"That's a little cocky, don't you think?"

James had come around behind Rousseau and aimed his gun at Rousseau's head.

"Question is, are you ready to die?" I asked Rousseau. "Ready to travel up there with your aliens?"

Rousseau stole a look over his shoulder. "Kid, you'd better put that away, otherwise Daddy's going bye-bye."

"He won't shoot me, James. But don't shoot him, because I don't trust your aim."

"Thanks a lot, Dad."

"You guys aren't taking me very seriously here. I'm William Rousseau." Then he shouted, "You've forgotten who I am! I've made more money for the movie studios than any actor who's ever lived! I've screwed every beautiful girl in Hollywood that you can think of! I own homes in—"

The shot exploded from somewhere above us, and suddenly my shoulder felt damp as I turned back.

Rousseau was already on the ground, part of his head gone, blood and pink viscera and brain matter splattered across the concrete in a blood trail that fanned out in chaotic brushstrokes. I began panting as I realized how close that bullet had come, and I looked up, toward the hotel's main balcony, where Alexandre came from the darkness and lowered his high-powered rifle.

I glanced at James, who was still frozen, completely stunned over the remarkable shot. But neither of us should have been surprised. My brother had taught Alexandre to shoot, and he'd told me on more than one occasion that the kid was a natural and the best shot we had.

And now I owed him my life. I wasn't sure if I should wave or shout "thank you" or what. I stood there a moment more until James called my name. I hunkered down beside Rousseau and took the pistols. "You stupid bastard. You could've saved yourself. You stupid, stupid bastard." I was so choked up I thought I would gag.

"What should we do with him?" James asked.

"Nothing. We don't have the time. Come on." When I turned back, I found everyone from the villa standing outside the door, their mouths hanging open.

My voice cracked as I spoke. "Nicole, get your bag. You're done here."

She nodded and rushed back to fetch her things.

"What? She's not going to help?" cried one of Rousseau's men, the tall blond. "You can't just stop. They'll die. You can't do this!"

"I'm sorry."

"That's not good enough!"

I took a deep breath and shouted, "Rousseau's dead! And we're leaving! Find yourself a way off this island, otherwise you'll be joining him!"

"Take us with you."

"We can't."

Nicole returned with her bag and hurried past us. James and I followed as the men shouted obscenities and the blond grabbed James's arm.

"Hey!" I cried, raising my pistol. "Let him go."

James lifted his own gun. "Dude, I'll kill you."

"Take us, please!"

I fired a shot an inch away from the guy's head. "Let him go!" He complied, and I added, "If you follow us, I'm going to kill you. James? C'mon."

We jogged back off to the hotel.

EVERYONE had gathered inside the restaurant, where Alexandre and Dayreis were now holding them at gunpoint. No one had gotten much sleep, and to say tempers were flaring would be cliché and an understatement. I heard more four-letter words within the first thirty seconds than I'd heard in the past month on the island.

Cindy and her group had seen the ketch, heard about the attack on Rousseau's tribe, and recently seen Dayreis and Alexandre loading the small fishing boat with water jugs and packages of fish. You didn't need a graduate degree to figure out we were leaving, and the women demanded to know what was happening.

I pulled Cindy and Jane into the back kitchen and spoke slowly, deliberately. "Okay, I'm going to be honest with you. So we're leaving in a few hours. There's only room on board for you two. The other six in your group can't come." I looked at Cindy. "You have to make your plans now. Figure out how you're going to handle that. I suggest you just keep quiet till the last minute, all right?"

"What're you talking about?"

"I'm talking about that storm coming. I'm talking about living through this. Do you want to live? It's a simple question."

"Oh my god," said Jane. "You've already made a list, haven't you? You've decided who lives and who dies."

I didn't know how to respond, so I just went on. "You need

to say something to them. Get them distracted or something, I don't know. But they can't interfere with the loading. When the time comes, I'll get you two. And that's it."

"Why us?"

I closed my eyes. "I don't know. Maybe you just got lucky."

"Because I helped you with the turbine, huh?" asked Jane. "So I get to live, but the others don't. And Cindy gets to live because . . ."

"I'm not going," said Cindy. "I'm not telling them anything. Either we all go, or none of us."

Jane turned to her. "He's willing to save us." Her lip began to quiver. "We have to go."

"Then you tell them. You tell them they get to stay and die, because I sure as hell won't."

"Cindy, they got the boat, and this *is* it. You can't stay here and die. I won't let you."

Cindy widened her eyes on me. "Did you consider any of this? Did you think about what this would do to us? You can't put people in positions like this."

I guess I'd had enough, because I grabbed her by the throat, pushed my face into hers, and said, "The world's gone. You come or you stay. I don't care either way. I got two slots. One for you. One for her."

I let her go, and she began to break down. "Christ, it's just not fair! It's not!"

"If I overload the boat, the odds of any of us making it decrease. That's the way it is."

"Where are we going?"

"South America."

"We can't go there."

I threw up my hands, turned, and marched out of the kitchen

and back into the restaurant, where the two men from Rousseau's party were standing at the doorway, their hands raised, and one of them, the shaggy-haired blond, was screaming at the top of his lungs, "Your leader Charles is a murderer, and you want to follow him? Do you think God will bless a murderer? He's not leading you to salvation! He's leading you to hell!"

"You guys are all aliens," I shouted. "You don't know anything about God. And I told you what I'd do if you followed us." I turned and saw Bento, rifle in hand, and ordered him to get them outside.

They refused to leave.

"All right, then," I said. "Bento, shoot them."

"Yes, Mr. Charles." He raised his rifle. "Which one do I shoot first?"

A half dozen gasps filled the room. I had no doubt that Bento would carry out the order.

And, apparently, so did the blond. He and his buddy suddenly raised their hands and fled through the doors.

Dayreis rushed over to me and lowered his voice. "My entire staff thinks they are coming."

"You lied to them?"

"I had to. But I sent all of them to the Carl Gustaf and the other hotels up there to find what they could. I told them the orders were yours. We need to leave before they get back. Please, Charles."

"Thank you. And you're right. We need to go, otherwise we'll have a riot on our hands."

"I hate this."

"I hate it even more."

"We will never live down this night. You know that."

I took a deep breath. "I know."

TWENTY-SIX

I estimated the wind gusts at about thirty miles per hour as James and I loaded another pair of crates onto the small fishing boat. My gaze was torn between the work at hand and the destroyer, which had listed a few more degrees and was taking a battering from the waves. A foamy band of diesel fuel lined the shore, and that stench mixed with the smell of forthcoming rain in the air.

The dark clouds had already broken off into long tendrils as the storm's outer bands began to reach us. The news reports said that Hurricane Karl's eye would strike the leeward islands in another thirty-six hours and that the storm was one of the largest ever recorded in the area. Karl was taking a northeast track, so if we sailed directly south and made our turn west around Guadalupe, we could skirt those more destructive winds and avoid disaster. I wondered if the nuclear strike had anything to do with the hurricane's intensity. Probably not. It was just our bad luck.

Once the fishing boat was full, James and Alexandre took off for another run out to the ketch. I put Bento in the Zodiac, which we'd refueled, and he transported the lighter stuff: smaller jugs of water, bags of clothing, and Nicole's medical supplies, along with the good doctor herself and the little girl Trina. I assumed that even if Alexandre's cousins left Gustavia and traveled directly to St. Martin to pick up the ketch, then we still had a couple of hours. James had told me he'd learned that the De Souzas had attacked Rousseau's place approximately two hours ago. I felt certain that we could load up and leave before they came looking for us. However, if the brothers had gone back to their fuel supply first, then we'd have a problem. I wished we'd had the time to engage in some elaborate ruse, like taking the fuel but leaving the empty drums so the brothers might not realize they'd been ripped off.

Before I could return to the restaurant, Chloe grabbed me by the arm, her face full of tears. "Jodi told me what you're doing."

"Chloe, you're supposed to be upstairs."

"I don't believe you! You don't have the right to do this! You have no right!"

"Jesus Christ, Chloe, get back up there with your mother till I call for you or I swear to God—"

"You'll what? Leave me behind, just like them?"

"We don't have the room."

"Then why didn't we do a lottery? Why do you get to play God?"

"Get back upstairs!"

"Why can't they all come? Leave somebody else behind. Like Marcos and Bento. Leave them. Leave Dayreis. Jodi said she's going to die here because of you."

I seized my daughter by the shoulders. "Look at me. I'm doing the best I can. I'm doing what's best for us. The people going on that boat are the ones we need."

"Oh, and that's not selfish? That's not playing God? How do you know we'll need them? You can see the future? What the hell is this, Dad?"

"Right now, I don't care if you hate me for this, but I can't stand here anymore. We need to get loaded!"

"What did you think? Just because my boyfriend's on the list that I'd be happy? You thought you could shut me up like that?"

"Get upstairs!"

"Yeah, whatever!" She cursed at me and ran off.

I wasn't sure if I wanted to kill someone or just break down and cry. I kept telling myself that no one should ever have to make decisions like this, but if no one did, then we'd all die. My father and brother would tell me that I was making a less-bad choice in an imperfect situation, and that there was no shame in it. Great leaders had made similar choices for thousands of years.

A gunshot resounded from inside the restaurant.

"What the—"

I shuddered and took the steps two at a time and burst through the terrace door to find Dayreis holding a pistol over Cindy, who was lying on her back and clutching her chest while Jane screamed for the doctor.

"She's already on her way out to the boat," I said. "What the hell happened?"

Blood began soaking through Cindy's sweatshirt. The rest of her group stood behind, with Chloe's friend Jodi in the far back, her dreadlocks reminding me of Tremaine and making me more tense. She stood crying beside my daughter.

"They wanted the food. She hit me with that, Charles," said Dayreis, pointing at the piece of pipe under a nearby table. He trembled and tripped over his words. "She came twice. I warned her. I didn't want to shoot. They wanted the rest of the food. That's what they said. I told them to leave. I wouldn't give them the food. I couldn't." The chef's eyes widened, his mouth opening further in agony.

Jane cursed at me and said, "They were right about you! Rousseau's people were right! You *are* a murderer! You are! He's the one we should kill! Let's kill him and take the boat. Look at what they've done to Cindy!"

The other six women screamed in agreement, and a few came toward me, though they were all unarmed. Dayreis and I shifted beside each other, waving our pistols.

"Dad? Don't let this happen," Chloe hollered. "Just take them all. We'll figure it out somehow."

"Chloe, shut up, God damn it!"

"No."

"She's dead," cried Jane. "Cindy, oh my god! Cindy!" The lithe woman's body had, indeed, gone limp, and Jane's sobbing forced a chilling silence among the rest of us.

My gaze was focused on Jane, on the utter pain in her eyes, and I could easily put myself in her position and imagine what it would feel like to lose Vanessa. I was so caught up in that moment that I didn't notice Chloe and Jodi slipping out the back door. I wonder how differently the future would have played out if I had been paying better attention.

I cleared my throat. "Ladies, nobody wanted this to happen. I never wanted to leave here, but now we don't have a choice. I can't take all of you. I'm taking Jane. Another slot has opened up. Another one of you can come. I'll let you decide. Now, you need to step away and let us finish loading."

Jane rose slowly and stepped up to me, ignoring the pistol.

"You smug bastard. You think you can just stand there and dictate to us what we should do? After he just killed all I had in this godforsaken world?"

I hardened my tone. "Jane, we didn't want this to happen. You and Cindy had your chance. She chose to do this. You can still save yourself."

She folded her arms across her chest and said she wasn't moving. Not one inch.

Up to that point I'd tried to remain somewhat civilized; after all, I was hardly a British schoolboy stuck on a deserted island, and I'd tried—really tried—to sympathize with them. But we were fast running out of time.

So I put my gun to her head as the other women screamed and cried, believing I meant to shoot her.

"Are you ready to die, then?" I asked at the top of my lungs. "Are you ready to die?"

"Do it, you murderer! Do it! You should have killed me back at the turbine, when you had the chance!" She launched into a string of curses, spitting as she spoke.

"Charles?" called Dayreis. "Charles! Look outside!"

I turned back toward the wide windows, where I spotted the Zodiac still piloted by Bento skipping across the waves. He had Jodi and Chloe on board and was headed back toward the ketch.

However, knifing into the bay was a sleek, high-performance boat that Vacher would tell me was a Rogue Jet deployed by St. Martin law enforcement; it even had the word "Police" painted in large blue letters on its hull.

There was little doubt who was piloting that boat, and Alexandre later confirmed that his cousins never used the Rogue Jet during their other raids on the island, which was why no one had ever described seeing a police boat leaving the scene, only smaller speedboats.

The Rogue Jet veered off, and the man at the wheel aimed directly for Bento, Chloe, and Jodi.

I might have gasped or said "Oh my God," or cursed, I don't remember. My instincts as a father kicked in. I slammed my way through the women and bolted past the open door. I staggered down the stairs and reached the dock where James and Alexandre were standing, in shock, and yelled down to them. "Why did you let Chloe go?"

"Dad, they said you told them to go with Bento," cried James.

"They lied! God! Alexandre, are those your cousins?"

He sighed. "Yes, Mr. Charles. And it seems we're too late."

"Charles, that's Chloe out there," shouted Vanessa from the top of the stairs behind me.

"I know. We'll get her back."

She chambered a round in her pistol. "I'm coming, too."

"Stay here!"

"Don't argue with me, Charles." She came charging down the stairs.

"Fine, we'll all go out and get shot together. Everybody get in the boat."

Alexandre began to pant. "Mr. Charles, I don't know if I can go. Jima will kill me."

"All right, stay here then. We'll go talk to him."

He thought about that. "No, I'll come. Maybe I can explain more to him."

"Are you sure?"

He nodded and took James's hand and was helped over the

rail. My eyes ached, and I thought at any moment I would vomit over the side. I watched as the Rogue Jet came up alongside the Zodiac, and a man came to the rail with a rifle pointed at Bento, Chloe, and Jodi.

James fired up the engine, and we cut through the waves, the bow slapping hard against the whitecaps, the salty spray burning our eyes. I squinted and saw that Bento had already lowered his rifle and raised his hands to catch a line thrown to him by the rifleman. As we drew closer, Alexandre said the rifleman was his cousin Santeen. The guy was in his twenties, tall, with overgrown arms like an ape or adolescent, and with a mop of hair that curled into a nest of electrical wires oscillating in the wind. Even in the grayness of dawn, his malevolent grin flashed as he drew in the line and helped secure the Zodiac to the back of his boat.

"Where are the rest of his guys?" I yelled back above the motor. "You said there were your cousins and four more. You killed the guy at the ketch, so there are three more, right?"

"There should be," he answered. "And I don't see Jima."

We drew closer, and I thought about the massacre at the church, saw little Trina crying over her dead parents. Gooseflesh rippled across my shoulders. My daughter was now in the hands of men who had killed indiscriminately. I glanced over at Alexandre, and he, too, was shivering.

"We're getting Chloe," said Vanessa, her tone sharp, her gaze unflinching.

Chloe, Jodi, and Bento had climbed up onto the Rogue Jet and stood with their hands in the air. Bento was conversing with Santeen, but we could not yet hear them.

Meanwhile, Marcos was now on the ketch's aft deck, pointing his rifle at Santeen. Vacher was still nowhere to be seen. Damn, had the old man gone below to cower? Or was he about to do something very, very rash?

Alexandre began shouting at his cousin. Santeen hollered back, and Alexandre turned to me and said, "They know we stole the fuel and the hand pumps."

Even as Alexandre finished, Santeen whirled, put his rifle to Jodi's chest and fired, sending the poor girl back to the rail and tumbling over the side.

I could barely hear above all the screaming from Alexandre, Vanessa, James, and Chloe. I had opened my mouth, but nothing came.

And while the shot continued to echo in our ears, Bento made his move for Santeen's rifle. As he did so, Vanessa fired a shot from behind me, missing Santeen and striking one of the boat's rails.

I screamed at her to stop.

Santeen, who'd flinched from Vanessa's round, fired, his shot catching Bento in the shoulder and exiting out the top in a fountain of blood that sprayed over the boat's side.

Just then we bumped alongside the Rogue Jet, and I stood in our boat and seized the jet's rail with one hand and pushed up with my pistol to try to get a shot at Santeen's head, but he and Bento turned, and Santeen forced Bento back and fired again into the man's chest. He slumped onto the deck as Chloe screamed again.

"I kill her now," said Santeen in a thick accent. "I kill her!" He shoved his rifle toward Chloe.

"No!" I screamed and threw my pistol onto the deck. "No!"

I pulled myself up and climbed over the rail to grab and hug my daughter as Santeen covered us. He glanced down at Vanessa and Alexandre and ordered them to tie up our boat, then come up.

"Dad, I'm sorry," said Chloe.

"Shhh, it's all right. It's all right."

We stood there, shaking, as Vanessa and James finished with the lines, then climbed aboard.

"We'll just give them everything," said Vanessa, tossing her pistol down. "Everything. We can't die like this, Charles."

"Maybe it's better," I said, choking up. "Better than the slow death here."

Chloe pulled out of my arms and moved behind me.

Alexandre said something to his cousin. Santeen replied curtly, then marched up and smacked Alexandre hard across the face. Then, in his thick accent, he said, "Now we go to our boat that you stole." Santeen turned his head away from us to regard Alexandre once more.

Vanessa said something, but all I heard was the gunshot.

Santeen's left arm came up as he spun toward the rail then suddenly collapsed, blood seeping from the side of his head.

I hadn't seen Chloe drop down, partially concealed by us, and remove the pistol from the back of Bento's waistband. She barely remembered any of it and knew only that she wanted to murder the man who had killed her friend and endangered her family.

I glanced back, and there she was, shaking violently, the pistol clutched in her hand. She swore at Santeen, then the gun tumbled from her hand and she started crying as I snatched her up, into my arms.

Yet even at that horrible moment, my gaze did not stray from the .50 caliber machine gun tucked alongside the deck. Thanks to Chloe, we had just scored some serious firepower to ward off Jima and the rest of his men.

"You saved us, honey," I told her. "You saved us all."

"Not all of us," she gasped.

TWENTY-SEVEN

I'VE always relished historical accounts of improbable victories against impossible odds. A small boy with a slingshot defeats a giant. A determined group of Greeks wards off a massive Persian Army for six days. An incensed English professor exposes a corrupt administration's policies regarding faculty raises and leave time (oh, what a champion I was among the handful of my colleagues!). I'd always held those tales close to my heart because I'd been an underdog for the better part of my life, yet as we took control of the Rogue Jet and, crying, tossed poor Bento and that evil bastard Santeen over the side, I concluded that my life would never end with fanfare or glory. The victories would be small, and the prize would be the strength to utter, "I'm still alive."

James was at the wheel, and I told him to take us back to the ketch.

Chloe's eyes were bloodshot and wide to the point of scary as she spoke to no one in particular about how much Santeen deserved to die and that she was glad she killed him and in the next breath she apologized to Alexandre for doing what she had to do. She was working it all out, the emotional gears grinding like an old four-speed, and there was little we could do but listen and wince and wonder how deep the scars would eventually run. I already knew she and I would have some very long talks about the curly-haired man whose blood she had shed, the man who would haunt her dreams.

Behind us, the three bodies floated swiftly back toward the shoreline. The tide had grown much stronger and began to unnerve me. James throttled up and brought us around, chopping through the waves. Vacher appeared on the ketch's deck and waved us over. We moved slowly as James grew accustomed to the controls while towing both the Zodiac and our fishing boat. We got alongside and carefully transferred Vanessa and Chloe onto the ketch, then I followed. I asked the women to go below with Nicole and the little girl Trina, while Vacher, James, Alexandre, and I discussed our next move, hollering above the wind and the waves lapping at the hulls.

"She's dragging anchor," said Vacher. "We're in twenty-two feet right now. I increased the anchor scope from five to seven times, hoping that'd give it a better bite—but no luck. Marcos and I searched the whole boat for a damned anchor buddy." He sighed in frustration. "We have a spare anchor with two fathoms of leader chain but no extra line to get it down and set the flukes in this sandy bottom."

"Is that bad?"

"It means we're drifting toward the destroyer, and I can't stop us unless I fire up the engine. It's part of the storm surge. The water will get a lot deeper. That's going to be a real problem, Charles."

"Why?"

He muttered something in French, then answered, "The surge will free the destroyer and wash her right up into the hotel."

"No way."

"She'll be on the beach soon."

"Then we have to get the rest of them right now," I said.

"We'll go," said James.

Alexandre nodded. "We have to. I think I know what Jima did. He loaded up the rest of the fuel on his other boat, and he'll be here soon. He sent Santeen here first because this boat is faster than the other big one."

"Big one? What's he got?"

"They have one of the ferries. It's a catamaran. Big engines but real heavy. They used it to move all the oil drums from that tanker."

"Why doesn't he just get out of here on that?"

"Because it uses too much fuel," said Vacher. "He wants the ketch for the same reasons we do."

"Okay, I get it. And so he must be on his way with the rest of his crew."

"Dad, we're going," said James.

I shook my head. "Not without me."

"Charles, look!" cried Vacher.

The destroyer creaked and groaned and began to right herself as long tails of wind-whipped rain streamed from her rails. I half expected the phosphorescent ghosts of dead sailors to appear on her decks, racing urgently to take control of her. And then the rain started pounding us as well, and I shouted to Alexandre and James that I was coming back on board.

"I'll try to buy us some more time," said Vacher. "But I'll have to use some fuel!"

I grimaced. "Just do it!"

As I climbed back down onto the Rogue Jet, the old Frenchman fired up the ketch's engine and tried to hold her position.

James and Alexandre untied us, and within a minute we were rushing across the bay, making a wide path around the destroyer, then jetting straight for the hotel, our bubbling wake as quickly swallowed by the whitecaps.

Only then did I remember how I'd left Dayreis, standing there in the middle of a near riot, and I could only wonder what I'd find once we were back inside.

The water had grown so deep that we could take the Rogue Jet all the way up to the hotel's dock, where we tied her up, then ascended the rain-slick stairs.

Lefort met me at the restaurant's main door with a pistol aimed squarely at my head. The sun-weathered fisherman spoke with an eerie calm, his words clipped by his thick accent. "Sorry, Mr. Charles, but there's been a slight adjustment to the passenger's list." He proffered his hand. "I'll have your pistol."

I pulled my sidearm from my waistband and handed it to him, then I stole a glance back to James and Alexandre. "Give him your guns."

"Dad, I'm going upstairs for Hannah. She's been sick."

"You're not going anywhere," said Lefort. "Your weapons. Now."

They handed over their pistols, and Lefort managed to tuck all three into his own waistband. I thought about the time it would take for me to reach down and snatch one. A wasted thought, no doubt.

"Mr. Charles, you shouldn't have gone," said Dayreis, sitting at a table and rubbing his eyes. He lifted his head at Lefort. "I didn't know you gave him a gun."

"He's always been armed."

"You should have told me," snapped Dayreis.

My voice cracked. "I didn't think it would matter. I thought we were keeping it quiet."

"And you thought you'd leave us behind," added Lefort. "You were too much of a coward to tell us. You should have been honest. Now you stay here."

So there it was. Lefort and one of his fishing crews, three men and two women, had taken over, holding Dayreis, Jane, and the rest of her group hostage. Lefort armed and ordered two of his men to begin loading the rest of our supply crates onto the Rogue Jet, and I interrupted him with, "Listen to me. We're all going. All of us. There's no need to leave us behind. That's why I came back."

"You came back for your friend, the chef. And for your boy's girlfriend, who used to be with your brother. Interesting. That's why you came. But us, the backbone of your tribe, you want to leave us here to die. All our blood, sweat, and tears have meant nothing to you."

Part of me wanted to drop to my knees and beg him for forgiveness. I wished I could have told him what a terrible decision it was, but he wouldn't have listened. All I could do was sigh as the rain drummed along the panoramic windows, and the wind formed a throaty howl at the doorway. Out there in the bay, the destroyer appeared fully upright. Soon, she'd begin drifting toward us.

"Let's all get on the boat, get away from here, away from the storm, then you can have your trial and hang me. Just don't punish everyone else. Not for me." I glanced back at James. "Go get Hannah."

James looked at Lefort. "You're not going to shoot me, are you?"

Lefort shifted his aim back to me. "Go get your girlfriend."

"Thank you." James took off running.

"Mr. Charles, the jet boat's tanks are full, so most of them can follow behind us," said Alexandre.

I knew what he was thinking. Dump them all on the jet. They could escape to another island and at least avoid the storm and the destroyer's radiation. But Lefort, our dear fisherman, would understand the importance of being on the ketch. I had to assume that.

I gave an exaggerated nod to Alexandre, then faced Lefort and said, "Come on. We've busted our asses to stay alive for nearly a year. Let's not throw it away now. What's left? Those crates over there? Come on, I'll give you a hand. Ladies, get downstairs to the boats. You're all going!"

Lefort appraised me with his glance, then cried, "Hold on, everyone. You're all going, but *Mr. Charles* is going to stay here and go down with the hotel, so to speak." He'd uttered my name with enough sarcasm to boil my blood.

My hands balled into fists. I took a long breath and said, "All right. If that's what you want. But I'll help you get loaded up. Let's go."

"Mr. Charles?"

I turned back to Alexandre. "Don't argue with him now."

We hustled over to the stack of wine boxes filled with our supplies and began transferring them down the stairs and out to the boats. Dayreis assumed a position on the dock and accepted each crate. The list of supplies was long, and the Rogue Jet's deck was quickly jammed with boxes, bottles, and long rows of plastic crates filled with clothes, tarpaulins, and too many more items to recall. We switched to the fishing boat, and once we had it loaded down with crates and Jane's group had boarded, Lefort unsurprisingly sent his five people out first on the Rogue Jet. In truth, I didn't know any of them very well, save for their first names. They all spoke French or Portuguese, and they'd only come once or twice to my language classes. I'd always communicated with them through Dayreis or Lefort. They were a tight-knit group, a tribe within a tribe if you will. I was surprised they hadn't already killed Dayreis, and consequently, I thought I could exploit Lefort's compassion. He put the chef at the Zodiac's motor, and Alexandre on the fishing boat. They both started their engines and pulled away from the dock as a particularly nasty gust nearly knocked me off my feet.

Behind us, Hannah and James came slowly down the stairs. Her face was drawn, and she gritted her teeth in pain. James had said she'd been queasy the past couple of days, but I knew she wasn't "sick." Vanessa and I both knew, but none of us had openly discussed the inevitable.

"We'll get in out of the rain and wait for the jet boat to come back," said Lefort.

"Are you really going to leave me here?" I asked him as we turned back and walked along the dock.

"Give me a reason to take you."

"If you don't, the old man out there will kill you."

He laughed. "I bet he would. He likes you for some reason. I guess because of your father."

"All right, that's far enough," came a shout ahead.

Standing between the dock and the staircase were Rousseau's men, the blond and his shorter accomplice, the dark-haired punk with the vampire's grin. They'd come running up with some metal pipes they'd found piled behind the hotel's maintenance area. They beat the pipes against their palms as the vampire boy faced Hannah and James, and the blond faced us.

"Come on, you idiots," shouted James. "Haven't you had enough?"

"You're taking us with you!" cried the blond. "You can't leave us! It's inhumane!"

Lefort marched up to the blond, lifted his pistol, but took aim at the dark-haired kid and fired. The round punched into the kid's chest, and he fell to the concrete.

Hannah screamed, and James pulled her back as the kid rolled over and started groaning.

"No," Lefort answered. "*That's* inhumane!" Then he aimed for the blond. "Are you leaving?"

"Shoot me then! I'm going to die here anyway!" The blond fell to his knees and began sobbing. The rain washed over him as he remained there, utterly pathetic, so much so that I had to turn away for a second, but then I couldn't bear to miss what would happen next, so I looked back in horrid fascination.

Lefort turned his gun down on the blond, ready to put a bullet in the kid's head. Hannah screamed again. James told Lefort not to do it.

The fisherman had a gun in his right hand, and he still had another in his waistband, my gun. He'd given James's and Alexandre's weapons to his men. All of his attention was on the blond. I had a decision to make, and I made it. I couldn't allow Lefort to dictate what would happen, not with my family at stake.

So I launched myself toward him, extended my arms, and knocked him forward, onto the concrete, even as I brought my arms down to pin his arms against his sides. The backs of my hands scraped hard against the concrete as we struck then rolled. He moaned as he fought to pry himself free, and I thought about the gun in his waistband.

I wasn't alone in that. The blond snapped out of his sobbing and dove forward to shove his hand down and wrench free the gun from Lefort's belt. Swearing, the blond jerked back and aimed at my head. He fought for breath and released a shivery cry as he debated his next move.

I looked at him, and there was a moment where we connected, just a second, really, where he remembered that I wasn't the true bad guy. And I saw it, right there, in his eyes.

He switched his aim to Lefort and cried, "You killed Aram! Now you're going to die!"

"Is that . . . the humane . . . thing to do?" asked Lefort, still fighting against my grip.

James broke free from Hannah and rushed toward us. He leapt into the air as the blond turned the pistol on him. All I could do was react, releasing Lefort and driving both hands onto his wrist to direct his gun toward the blond. "Shoot him!" I screamed. "Shoot him!"

The gun went off, and when I looked up, the blond was tumbling back, arms flailing as blood spurted from his upper chest. James crashed on top of him as I drove Lefort's arm skyward.

Reflexively, I brought my knee up into the fisherman's groin, and the pain slackened his grip. The wet gun slipped from his fingers and into my hand, but the barrel was so hot it burned me, and I dropped the pistol between us.

Before Lefort could reach for it, I wrapped my arm around his throat and reared back, beginning to choke him. He dug fingers into my arm, but there wasn't a force in the world that could stop me at that moment. I didn't care that he'd just helped save my son. I saw only my family and the need to protect them and the fact that this man still jeopardized all of that, this man who had spent long, long days on the water, bringing home our meals.

James was shouting that he had the gun and that I could let

go of Lefort, but I kept on choking him, listening to him groan and gasp in my ear, listening to my own panting as the saliva ran down my chin. I grit my teeth, closed my eyes, and squeezed with all my might until Lefort stopped breathing and went limp.

I heard James calling, "Dad!" but the word was meaningless, like my pulse, just out there, somewhere. I shook hard and could barely breathe as I fell back, away from Lefort, and stared up into the rain just as a wave swept over the dock and crashed over me. I jerked and rolled over, looked up, and there was James reaching down, taking me by the wrists and hauling me to my feet. He asked if I was all right, and I stared through him.

He screamed again. "Dad! Dad!"

"Okay! Okay," I finally said.

"Alexandre's on his way back with the boat."

I glanced over at Lefort, then dropped to my hands and knees to check him for a pulse. Weak but there. I told James he was just unconscious and we were taking him on the boat. My son shrugged and pulled Hannah into his chest to shield her from the wind.

TWENTY-EIGHT

LEFORT'S people were still transferring supplies from the Rogue Jet to the ketch as Alexandre reached the dock and tossed us the lines. We tied up the fishing boat, then James helped Hannah down onto the deck. We went back for the still unconscious Lefort and carried him over to the rail, and a confused Alexandre helped us get him onto the deck.

"I'll tell you later," was all I said.

"Dad? Look!" shouted James.

The destroyer had finally broken free from her muddy anchor and was rising and falling with a life of her own. She came forward in the boiling sea with an echoing shriek of steel and clanking chains to spread her invisible death across the entire bay and farther inland. I thought of the unsuspecting survivors in the other hotels, scrimping and saving what food and water they could gather, and all for naught.

I practically fell into the boat as Alexandre steered us northeast, out of the ghost ship's path. We'd been downwind for too

long, and I was certain we'd all been contaminated. We'd run the
meter over ourselves back on the ketch, then scrub down as best
we could.

"Get some of that rope," I told James, referring to a coil near
the stern. "Can't take any chances. We'll tie him up just in case."

We used a knife Alexandre handed us from a small box near
the portside rail. We cut off the lengths of nylon, then tied
Lefort's hands and legs. His eyelids were already flickering open,
and his right arm shifted slightly. He finally looked at me as
I finished tying his wrists.

"I knew one day we'd all kill each other," he said.

"But I'm not going to kill you," I told him. "I'm sorry for all
of this."

"I don't care. Throw me over the side."

"It's not your day. Not mine either. We were friends. I didn't
forget that. I just . . . I had to make a decision."

He smirked and nodded.

Behind us, the solar panels we'd positioned on the hotel's roof
were peeling back at their edges and would soon break off, while
the trees nestled among the buildings shook as though electri-
fied. I could barely see the clay red rooftops through the veils of
mist and rain, and then the destroyer cut across my view with its
gargantuan plates of rust-streaked metal.

I gripped the rail as we reared up through a wave, and as we
settled back, an aching hollowness gripped my chest, an old feeling that summoned up an old wound. My brother and I had gone
away to St. Matthew's Summer Camp when I was eleven. It was
the first time I'd ever been away from my parents. We would be
in upstate New York, on the banks of a beautiful lake, for nearly
ten days. But by the third day I was crying, and there wasn't much
the teenage counselors or priests could do but allow me to call my

parents. My dad ordered me to stop being a pansy, so, with my brother's encouragement, I sucked it up and stuck it out, but that feeling—that feeling I knew so well—returned many times since then, and each time I dreaded its visit. *Please take me back home*, the pain said. *I don't know this place, and I want to go home.*

But my true home was gone. Forever. Obliterated by fools, by greed, by hubris, by us . . . every one of us. We blew it all up, and now we survivors were left to think about that.

I couldn't face the entire truth, though, not then. And now there wouldn't be any real good-bye to our temporary Shangri-la, only a rush to get away like ungrateful children. At that moment, I could not have spoken to anyone.

The destroyer continued southward on its collision course with the beach, and I faced forward as we came up on the ketch and took a line from Marcos.

At the same time, two of Lefort's men, now on the ketch's deck, drew their pistols on James and I and one shouted, "Cut him loose!"

"You see, Dad, we shouldn't have taken him!" my son told me, gritting his teeth and aiming a gun at them.

"We'll just do what they say."

"Charles!"

That was Vacher, at the ketch's wheel, pointing to the east.

I swung around, and there she was, a large, foil-assisted catamaran churning toward us at top speed.

Alexandre pointed himself. "It's Jima!"

I grabbed the knife and reluctantly freed Lefort. "There's a fifty-cal on the jet boat," I said to the fisherman. "We need to get on it and take this guy out. Like I said, my trial can come later. You coming?"

He struggled to sit up. "Yeah."

I took his hand and helped him to his feet. I tossed a glance to his men. "Tell them to back off."

He did and they complied. James helped Hannah onto the ketch while Lefort and I waited, then we brought the boat around to hop onto the Rogue Jet while Marcos secured our ride to the ketch.

"Dad, put me on that fifty," said James.

"Can you operate the gun?" I asked Lefort. He shook his head.

I groaned with some resignation, then nodded to my son. "All right, get your ass over here. Come on!"

Hannah began crying and telling James not to go, but Vanessa came up and wrestled her below as James balanced himself precariously between both boats and hopped onto the jet.

"We'll need you, too," I told Lefort's two men. They looked to their leader, who gave them the nod. They climbed aboard, leaving their three colleagues to maintain control of the ketch.

Along with the the .50 caliber machine gun were three high-powered rifles we'd found in one of the storage cabinets, along with boxes of ammo. I told Lefort I wanted him to take the wheel while we loaded the rifles. He gave me a surprised look but headed for the controls.

Vacher called down from the ketch. "Charles, we need to leave!"

"Go! We'll catch up with you!"

"Okay!" He ordered Marcos to take the anchor line to the deck winch and crank it in to short stay.

With a rumble and hiss, we left the ketch and headed east to intercept the catamaran continuing to plow toward us, its wake spreading like wings as she smashed through the swells. "Do we have any binoculars?" I asked Alexandre.

"I saw a pair in the gun box."

I opened the compartment, found the vinyl case, and removed the binoculars. The catamaran was about a half mile away and closing, and I strained to see Jima's men on the deck, but no one was out yet. I did catch the words "Rapid Explorer" painted on her hull before windblown rain fogged up the lenses.

"I'll try calling him on the radio," said Alexandre.

"No, don't do that," I said. "I want you up on the deck to start waving to him. We don't want him going for the ketch yet. Get him in closer, then Lefort, you're going to turn around, and James, you'll be on the back deck here with the fifty. We don't want to show him the surprise till he's too close, then you'll take him out."

"Gotcha, Dad. But he knows the fifty's on board."

"But he doesn't know who's manning it. Not yet anyway." I turned to Alexandre "Can you do this?"

"I don't know, Mr. Charles. When they see me, they'll just shoot."

"Maybe not. They'll be wondering why you're waving. If I was your cousin, I'd want to talk to you first—or at least get my hands around your throat instead of shooting you from long distance."

"I feel better now, Mr. Charles."

I almost laughed. "They might also call on the radio, but we won't answer." I put a hand on his shoulder. "We're counting on you."

He bit his lip and finally nodded. Then he climbed along the rail and seized the aluminum ladder running up the side of the boat's canopy. He hung from the ladder and began his frantic, one-handed waving, like a battered human sail flapping in the storm. I lifted the binoculars and spotted a dark-haired man through the windshield, piloting the craft, but no one else emerged onto the rear deck.

"His guys must be waiting till we get closer."

"Probably," answered James.

Lefort's two men spoke quickly in French with the fisherman, then he turned to me and said, "They told me they want to kill you three and take over."

"Tell them to wait twenty minutes till we kill those guys," I said, gesturing to the catamaran.

"That is almost funny."

"I might as well laugh," I said through a sigh. "Everyone wants to kill me."

He stared for a long moment, then suddenly said, "I would have made the same choices you did, except I would have taken the fisherman instead of the chef. It is easier to learn to cook than to catch fish!" Suddenly, he burst out laughing, enjoying his joke with an uncomfortable fervor.

I forced a grin, then checked the binoculars once more as the catamaran began to break away. I shifted to my left. The ketch was now about a quarter mile northeast of our position, with the catamaran directly west of us and now turning northwest to intercept.

"Damn it, he's not taking the bait," I cried. "You have to cut him off!"

Lefort rolled the wheel and increased to full throttle, but at that speed he could barely control the boat in the growing swells. I darted to the rail and clung tightly while James, who had set up the .50 caliber's bipod, shoved the weapon down to the deck and tried to pin it there. He looked up at me and nodded, and I didn't understand.

But then he suddenly rose, crashed into one of Lefort's men, drove him to the edge of the rail, rising just above their knees, and shoved him over the side.

I could hardly believe what I had just witnessed, but James was apparently two steps ahead of me. The other guy was hunkered down and one-handing his rifle. He brought it to bear on James, let go of the rail, but tumbled backward as we pounded through a pair of waves.

James crashed into the guy and exploited their momentum to roll him up onto the rail, but the guy snatched one of the aluminum rungs until James ripped off the hand and the guy screamed as he dropped away, into our wake.

A chill ripped through me as I watched two tiny heads vanish into the dark sea. Perhaps they could ride the storm surge back to shore. Perhaps not.

Meanwhile, Lefort was so caught up in his piloting that he hadn't looked back and hadn't heard anything over the numbing drone of the engine, yet as James had released the second guy, the fisherman had stolen a look and now gaped at me as I put my gun to his head. "Keep going!" I screamed.

"You're a fool!"

"I don't care! But we're going to stop that guy! Stay on course!"

I'd forgotten all about Alexandre, who'd been hanging from the ladder and was now crawling his way back along the canopy, fighting to get back onto the deck. James came up and gave him a hand, helping him back down as we continued pounding toward the catamaran.

Then, with no warning, Lefort released his hands from the wheel, raised his palms, and said, "Shoot me, then! Shoot me!"

Alexandre shoved himself between Lefort and the wheel and took over as I ordered Lefort to sit down by the rail and hang on.

"Just shoot him, Dad," yelled James. "Just do it!"

"No, just shut up and get on that fifty and get ready!"

"He's going to kill us all," said Lefort. "How many more guns does he have?"

I ignored the fisherman, kept my gun on him, and stole quick looks ahead as we streaked forward, with the catamaran now running straight toward our portside. As we began to pull slightly ahead, I saw the fifty-gallon drums we'd left on the dock. Jima and his men had loaded them onto the catamaran's rear deck.

"Get us around some more," I told Alexandre. "We need to get in closer, get James on those drums."

"I see 'em, too, Dad. Bring us around and try to hold steady!"

"He's turning again," cried Alexandre. "Not slowing down! Looks like he wants to ram the ketch!"

"What's he doing? He knows we all need that boat!"

"I don't think he cares anymore," answered Alexandre.

"Alexandre, turn again!" shouted James. "I can't even sight the barrels!"

"Okay! Okay!"

"And we still need to get in closer. Two thousand, maybe fifteen hundred yards," I said.

But I also knew that if we didn't slow down, it would be nearly impossible for James to get off any good shots. Between the Rogue Jet rising and falling, along with the catamaran's own movement—and the wind and rain—it'd be ninety percent luck if he caught a barrel at our present range of about three thousand yards.

Alexandre cut the wheel once more, putting us on a head-on collision course with his cousin. "I'll try passing along his side, but you have to fire before we hit his wake!"

"Okay!" James cried.

Jima himself finally appeared near the stern. He was shorter than Santeen, potbellied, with a long ponytail draping down his shoulder and a bushy, Castro-like beard. He hoisted a machine gun, and while the catamaran roared on toward the ketch, he opened fire.

TWENTY-NINE

ALEXANDRE and I dove behind the console as rounds tore into the Rogue Jet's welded aluminum hull and drew spiderwebs in the starboardside windshield. Alexandre kept one hand on the wheel and tried to veer right, as James cut loose on the .50 caliber, the gun rattling over the Rogue Jet's whoosh and whine.

Gunfire also cracked from the ketch, and while I couldn't see who was firing, I later learned that Lefort's remaining three people were armed and trying to defend themselves. Marcos had wanted to join in, but they'd taken over the ketch and disarmed him.

More rounds pinged into the side of the Rogue Jet as we hit the first wave of the catamaran's wake. At that moment, Alexandre rose, got his bearings, and suddenly rolled the wheel as I stood. We slammed up and down through the rest of the wake and circled around, behind the ferry, as James shouted once more for us to get closer and for Alexandre to try to hold her steady.

Meanwhile, unbeknownst to me, Lefort had picked up one of

the rifles and was aiming at the catamaran. He could have as easily turned it on me, but he hadn't. He fired a round, missing Jima
by inches as the man ran along the rear deck to the other side to
once more fire upon us.

Lefort looked up at me from the sight of his weapon, gave a
curt nod, then refocused his attention on the other boat.

We came up on the catamaran's starboardside, buffeted hard
by the waves, and once more James cut loose, brass casings spill-
ing on the deck as his bead stitched along the railing and the
sparks flashed. But his aim went wide as the catamaran dipped
into a swell.

Jima, who'd been ducking away from James's fire, darted
once more to the railing and sprayed our rear deck with bullets.
I screamed for James to take cover.

The ricocheting and sparking seemed to go off everywhere
as a pair of waves swamped the deck, the spray blinding me for
a moment while James and Lefort cried out nearly in unison.
I blinked, tried to see my son as I gripped the rail. James was
pinned against the back deck and clutching his calf with blood
seeping between his fingers. Lefort was lying on his back with
two gunshot wounds to his chest, the blood pooling down and
washing away.

I dove across the wet deck, as seawater and now blood drained
out the back. I reached James and seized his wrist. "Let me see
it!"

"Dad, it stings! It stings real bad!"

"We're coming around again," Alexandre cried.

"All right," I told him, relaxing my grip. "Just keep the pressure on it!" Then I grabbed the .50 caliber and set the bipod back
up, onto the rail.

Jima had taken a position along the portside stern, seated with his arm tucked under the rail as he fired at the ketch now behind us. Then he turned his aim on us just as I squeezed the machine gun's heavy trigger, the gun kicking back, the rounds blasting into the waves behind the boat. I cursed and swung the muzzle back toward the catamaran and fired again, this time striking the hull and hopefully giving Jima pause, as he was seated right behind the fuel drums. As I broke fire, he rushed up into the passenger's cabin. There, however, he and his cronies had ripped out the seats, converting the boat into a cargo carrier now loaded to the gills with boxes and crates. He raced past those rows of supplies, presumably heading back for the controls.

Meanwhile, Alexandre brought us in closer and parallel to the boat, with both of us heading directly toward the ketch. I hazarded a glance at Lefort, who was slumped on the deck, his eyes narrowed to slits, his mouth hanging slightly open. We could have killed each other ten times over, but I wanted to believe that a mutual respect had held us back. He was gone now, and I felt wholly responsible.

There was no doubt now that Jima was alone. He'd double-crossed or killed the rest of his men, which explained why Santeen had come alone. As the bearded madman took back control of the catamaran and cut the wheel toward us, driving his wake into our hull, I told myself, *This is it.* Vacher could not outrun the catamaran with its huge, diesel-guzzling engines. Jima probably figured that if he couldn't have the ketch, then no one would get it. He'd been betrayed by his cousin, and so he would exact his revenge.

I tightened my grip on the .50 caliber, listened to my son crying, "Get him, Dad! Get him!" and opened fire once more, aiming directly for those fifty-five-gallon drums and adjusting my fire with every bob of the Rogue Jet.

At least a half dozen rounds chewed into the drums, springing leaks, but there was no magnificent explosion that I imagined would engulf the catamaran for several hours and leave it drifting there, smoking heavily as the storm took it back toward the hotel. No, there was only a knot of rusting old drums leaking like wooden barrels during a Wild West shootout. And there I was, out of reach and without a match.

"Keep shooting, Dad!" James urged me. "Get a spark on that deck."

A spark. That's all we needed. I swung the barrel around once more and fired again, the rounds flashing momentarily until one hit the rail and a whoosh resounded, followed by a magnesium-white flash that drove my gaze away. A second later twin booms shook our boat as the fuel still left in the drums finally ignited and exploded, blasting a gaping hole in the catamaran's portside and stern and sending showers of burning debris into the high winds, a few pieces dropping across our deck and landing on our canopy.

I lost my breath as the black smoke poured now from the boat and whipped back toward the shoreline. She was slowing down all right, the explosion having damaged something with the engines. I couldn't see Jima at the controls and wondered if he was coming down to try to put out the fire. The ferry was beginning to take on water.

Jima's whereabouts remained a mystery for only a few more seconds. Gunfire came from one of the bridge's windows, which then shattered, and Jima thrust himself through the hole and cut loose with a one-handed bead on us. I ordered Alexandre to get us away and returned fire, driving Jima back into the bridge.

A ten-foot swell rolled up and behind the catamaran, sending torrents of water rushing up and into the cargo area. She began to sink more rapidly as Jima appeared again and sent a fresh salvo tearing into our deck.

The .50 caliber was a belt-fed weapon, and I burned out the last of my ammo keeping Jima at bay as we jetted back toward the ketch, now about a quarter mile ahead of us. Vacher had kept her on a steady course, and I was thankful that the gap between Jima and the ketch continued to widen.

"Do you want to go back for him?" I hollered to Alexandre as I pulled myself over toward James.

"No!" he cried. "Why do you ask that?"

"He might drown!"

"I don't care!"

I looked at him. He was resolute. And that was all I needed. He loved my daughter, and every action was motivated by that. He could do no more to regain my trust.

After a deep breath, I rose, sliding haphazardly across the deck, and grabbed Lefort's body. It took every ounce of strength I had left to get him up to the rail. Alexandre broke away from the wheel for a moment to help me push the corpse over the side. Then I went back to James.

"You'll be all right," I assured him as he continued clutching his leg. "We'll take you right back to Nicole."

"It hurts bad, Dad."

"I know. We're almost there."

I turned back toward the catamaran, where Jima had now climbed up onto the bridge's roof and sat there, still firing at us, his aim terrible now in the wind and growing waves. The ferry began to rise at the bow, and for a few moments, the waves blocked my view. When I looked again, the boat was nearly halfway submerged, and Jima just sat there on the roof, his gaze focused away from us now, back on the island. He had no life jacket, no Zodiac, nothing. I wondered why he wasn't searching frantically for some means of escape, unless he now welcomed death. I knew that feeling.

We were met by Lefort's people at the ketch, the two women and one man who had taken over our boat.

"Put away your guns," I shouted to them. "My son's hurt. And I'm taking him below!"

The man shouted something in French, and Vacher answered for me.

They didn't argue but disarmed us as we came on board while Alexandre and Marcos tied the Rogue Jet to the ketch. The sailboat was sitting low already and definitely overloaded. We had us four, Hannah, Alexandre, Marcos, Dayreis, Vacher, Trina, Nicole, Jane and her four women, and now Lefort's three people. As we rushed James below to be treated by Nicole, Vacher pulled me aside and said, "We won't make it with this many. You know that, Charles. We need to cut our number in half."

"We need to get Lefort's people and Jane's group on the Rogue Jet. We'll tow them as far as we can. Then we'll cut them loose."

"Good luck. They've got the guns and the power now."

I took a deep breath, then waved Marcos and Alexandre to the wheel. "We can't let them have this boat."

They nodded to me.

"All right. I'm going to talk to him," I said, gesturing to the man gripping the line off to my left. He had his pistol pointed at all of us and was glowering.

"You don't even remember his name, do you?" asked Alexandre.

I shook my head. "Starts with an 'M'?"

"It's Pierre. He speaks Portuguese and French. Not much English. Maybe I should talk to him."

"Good idea."

"What do you want me to say?"

"Tell him we need to move Jane's group onto the jet, along with a few more. Tell them we'll go with Jane's people. We don't want any more trouble."

"Really?"

"Yeah, and while you're doing that, Marcos and I will take out the women."

"So I'm just keeping him busy."

"You got it."

"You think he's more dangerous than the women?"

"No. But he's the closest to Vacher, and I don't want him taking the old man hostage. He's the best captain we got here, right? Better than you, right?"

Alexandre nodded.

"Okay, let's go."

I swallowed and, maintaining my grip on the rail, worked my way back to the stern. A glance at the catamaran took my breath away. Only the bow was now visible, and Jima was already in the water, just rising and falling with the waves. I tensed and moved on down the rail, where one of the women had tied herself down to the deck and held her pistol with both hands. She aimed it at me as I approached. I raised a palm and told her to relax. Her name finally came to me, and she was the one with the 'M' name, Margot. I'd met her that first day at the Sand Bar. She'd taken only one English class with me and had left in frustration.

As the ketch crashed through the next swell, I smiled at her, came a little closer as she pointed the pistol at me, and said, "It's okay. I need your help."

"No okay," she snapped.

Then her head came forward, and I realized she was getting

seasick and was about to puke. My first instinct was to shift back, but my moment had come. As her mouth opened and her eyes suddenly shut, I dropped onto her, took her wrists in both hands, and the gun went off, even as she vomited across my back. I shifted one hand up and ripped the pistol out of her grip, then rolled away, coming up with it.

I pointed the pistol back at her, but she was the least of my problems. The other woman, Emilia, who'd been one of our guards, was already on me, directing her pistol at my face, as Pierre and Alexandre came rushing over, along with Marcos. Pierre kept his pistol on me and began shouting in French.

When I looked to Alexandre for a translation, he was already coming behind Pierre and slid his arm beneath the Frenchman's chin and wrenched back—while at the same time, Marcos grabbed Emilia's hand, forcing her gun away.

There was no hesitation. I lifted my pistol and shot Emilia in the chest. Then I burst upright, turned, and shot Pierre just as he and Alexandre had turned to the side and were struggling near the rail. My round caught the man just under his arm and might have penetrated his heart.

While Alexandre and Marcos were still blinking, still entirely stunned, I cried, "Get their guns! Then we'll throw them over the side!"

Margot wailed in Portuguese. I spun around, aimed, and stared into her pleading face for a moment, my hand shaking. "Shut up!" I got down close to her. "Shut up!" Then I rose and helped Alexandre toss Pierre overboard. He was still alive when he hit the water. Marcos and Alexandre took care of Emilia's body, while I went back to Vacher. "She's ours."

He looked at me. "God help us, Charles. God help us all."

"I'm going below. We'll get Jane's group onto the jet."

"They won't like that."

"I don't care."

He grabbed me by the arm. "They can stay until the storm passes."

"You sure?"

He nodded. "It won't get any harder than this. Be strong, Charles.

I took a deep breath and nodded. Only then did I look down and realize I was covered in blood, their blood, and the rain would not wash out the stains.

Yet all I could think about as I went belowdecks was that for now, my family was safe. For now, we would make it. Only later would I have time to reflect and ask others what they would've done were they in my situation—all in a vain attempt to make myself feel better about murdering yet again. I had to kill them, otherwise they would have killed me, right?

But where was the logic? Where were the testaments that we were, indeed, higher-order beings capable of making rational decisions no matter the circumstances? Why hadn't I been able to use the power of my brain to solve these problems? Was my entire education just an artifice? Did it even matter anymore, when all the monuments we had built to celebrate our successes as a species had been destroyed? Perhaps it was just as well—because all those monuments, all those institutions, all those moments of "great enlightenment" had been nothing more than powerful elixirs to make us forget that in the end, we were all nothing more than savages.

THIRTY

I shifted along the ketch's windward side to the cockpit area, just forward of the mizzen mast, and slipped down into the salon. We'd folded down and stowed the table to make more room for Jane and her group. They were jammed into every recess, with the blue cushions barely visible beneath all those bodies. Dayreis was with them, too, an anxious ant surrounded by venomous spiders. I stepped over the floor access hatch and felt the diesel engine's vibration in my feet. Vacher would shut her down at any moment, I knew. I squeezed past the women, under the heat of their gazes, and down into the berthing level, where Vanessa, Nicole, Hannah, Chloe, little Trina, and James turned at my approach.

"We heard the shots," said Vanessa.

"Is Alexandre okay?" asked Chloe.

"We're all okay," I told them. "How is he?"

Nicole was wrapping a bandage around James's leg and paused to regard me. "I removed the bullet and sutured the wound. He'll be okay, as long as we watch for infection."

I sighed deeply, the tension evaporating in my shoulders, at least for the time being. "Thank you."

"There are too many people on this boat," she said. "Are you going to address that?"

Vanessa lifted her brows at me.

Chloe blurted out, "He'll just throw them overboard. Doesn't matter. We're all going to die."

"Shut up, Chloe," snapped James. "Dad knows what to do, and he'll do it. Why do you have to bitch and moan all the time? Does it make it any better?"

"My friend's dead! They killed my friend! So I killed them! Him! Dad, you want me to take care of this?"

"Both of you shut up," I said.

"I'm scared," said Trina. "I want to go back to my hiding place." Vanessa pulled the girl into her arms. The poor child looked at me. "Are we going to die?"

"Not today."

"So what're you going to do, Dad?" asked Chloe. "You keep changing your mind. Why did you bring Jane's group when you know we have to dump them?"

I put my finger to my lips. "Keep your voice down. They would've died on the island. We're giving them another chance."

"But not one with us."

I shook my head. "After the storm passes, we'll work it all out."

Chloe snorted. "I'm sure we will."

After a long breath, I moved in closer to my daughter. "I wish things were different. I really do. But they're not."

She just looked at me for a moment, then turned her head and began to cry.

I headed back up on deck, gripped the standing rigging, and

moved cautiously back to Vacher, who stood there, his boots cemented to the deck like an old pirate, the storm whipping around him as he scowled at her breath. I half expected him to raise his fist, and in French shout, "Is that all you got?" Instead, he got right down to business, informing me that Marcos and Alexandre had transferred all the weapons from the Rogue Jet to the ketch and had locked them up. Everything else was battened down, and now we would ride the edge of the hurricane till we could get on the leeward side of Guadalupe, where he planned to lay anchor. I asked him if he wanted to take a break.

"If I die at this wheel, I'll be happy," he said.

I grinned weakly. "It's your purpose."

"You're learning, Charles. I don't care what your brother said about you."

"I'm just a geek."

He cocked a brow.

BECAUSE the others were not seasoned boat riders, Vacher wanted everyone save for myself, Marcos, and Alexandre below-decks, where we did thorough radiation checks. Even though Marcos and I were hardly more experienced, he and Alexandre would give us on-the-job training once again. Vacher looked to the top of the mizzen mast, where he pointed to a device called the Air-X wind generator; it fed four six-volt golf-cart batteries—the boat's entire electrical system—and worked just like the wind turbine back on St. Barts but didn't have to convert to AC. The boat used 24V-DC power directly from those batteries, and once they were fully charged, the Air-X stopped spinning so as not to overcharge them. The two main batteries for the engine would get topped off once a week by running the diesel.

We sailed for twelve hours, heading south-southeast and using the ketch's onboard GPS to navigate. We finally reached the lee-ward side of Guadalupe, spotting no activity along the shoreline or inland. Not a single light. I forced Vacher to go below, eat, and be examined by Nicole. He was trembling violently now, eyes bloodshot. I told Vanessa to feed him like a king.

I remained up on the deck for most of the night, checking the anchor with Alexandre and debating how I would cut loose Jane's group, along with Margot, leaving just us eleven on board, a manageable number. I decided I couldn't leave them without any supplies, so Alexandre and I discussed moving what we esti-mated to be two days' worth of rations over to the Rogue Jet. They had enough fuel to make it back to one of Guadalupe's coves, Petit Marin, and go ashore there. That was the best we could do for them.

Back on the island, on some of the better mornings, I would wake up and ask myself, *All right, what can I do today to help us survive a little longer?* And I'd get to work. But here on the ketch, after stealing a few hours of sleep in my wife's arms, I shook back awake, dreading the dawn. *What can I do today to help us survive a little longer?*

Abandon seven people.

Vacher met me at the wheel. "You all right?"

"I will be."

"You're a good man, Charles."

"On any other day."

He nodded.

Once everyone was awake, I would need to gather them on the deck, as though preparing each to walk the plank. My stomach churned. Marcos, Alexandre, Vacher, and Dayreis would need to be armed and ready.

Ironically, the weather had turned gorgeous, breezy, with much lower humidity and rays of sun cutting brilliantly across the white-painted deck. I asked the women to come outside, and most of the others followed. In fact, everyone swarmed out, if only to glimpse the sun after so much rain, and I stood there near the wheel, rising and falling with the waves. I cleared my throat. Right until that last second I was trying to gauge my tone. If I wasn't stern enough, we'd have a riot. If I was too sympathetic, we'd have a long debate. I needed to inform them what was about to happen. There would be no conversation, no debate.

But before I could speak, Jane came up to me and lowered her voice. "I know what you're going to do. And we're not going. You'll have to shoot us." She stepped back and nodded, then returned to her group, all of them standing there like concentration camp survivors told they were being freed—only to learn they were getting on the busses for a drive "to the country."

Then Dayreis rushed up to me and whispered in my ear, "Let me talk first. I have a plan. Please . . ."

I studied him, his expression intense. "Why didn't you come to me? What is this plan?"

He took a deep breath, closed his eyes, then faced the group and raised his voice. "Everyone, listen to me. We know the boat is too crowded. There just isn't room or enough supplies. Some of us will be getting off here. We'll take the other boat and go around to a cove we've discussed, and we'll take our chances there. This is one of the biggest islands in the Caribbean, and I'm sure we'll find help. I'll be leading that group, and I'm looking for volunteers."

My eyes widened on him, and I mouthed the word "no."

With tearing eyes, he nodded and said, "Let me do this."

Perhaps he thought he could repay Jane and her group for

shooting Cindy—but I thought they might kill him if he decided he was now their leader. Then again, maybe he was throwing himself to the wolves for his sins.

"He's looking for volunteers," cried Jane, laughing bitterly through her words. "I volunteer Charles and his family for a one-way trip to hell. And take the old man with you. Take Margot. Leave us Alexandre, Marcos, and the little girl. We'll take care of her. You're all backstabbing murderers. Just get the hell off this boat."

I glowered at Dayreis. "You're not going." Then I faced the group, and the tone that came out was my father's, my brother's, the tone of a Spencer man: all military, all business, and I had no control over it. "Listen up, people. Jane? You and your group, along with Margot—get in the other boat. Right now. Do it!"

Jane gave me an incredulous look. "No. I told you we're not going. You'll have to shoot us."

My gaze turned to Vacher. He had no answers for me, only a penetrating stare.

Alexandre raised his pistol at Jane's head.

Dayreis pushed past me and marched up to Jane, gripping his pistol but keeping it tight at his side. "Don't be a fool. He'll kill you just to get the others on board. Come with me now."

She cursed at him and added, "I'll never go anywhere with a murderer!"

"You were there. She would've killed me. Now let's go!"

Without warning, she grabbed Dayreis's wrist, then turned, working her other hand onto the gun.

"Don't shoot!" I ordered Marcos and Alexandre as everyone on the deck dropped under the echoes of shrieks and gasps.

They turned toward me as Marcos and Alexandre moved in closer and Dayreis yelled, "Don't shoot! Please!"

"Jane, don't do this!" I screamed. "You're going to die. Come on, Jane. Let go."

Dayreis finally wrenched her off, spun around, and put the pistol to her head. "Get in the boat."

She stood there, trying to catch her breath, her eyes brimming now with tears, her arm scratched badly and bleeding. "Just shoot me. I don't want to live in this world."

"Jane? *Vamos*," came a voice from behind her. It was Margot, who led the others slowly, deliberately, over the rail, and they began lowering themselves down into the Rogue Jet.

"You see?" said Dayreis. "They don't want to die. We've lived this long already, against it all. So let's keep going." He cocked a thumb back at me. "Their lives will be different than ours. That's just fate. Come on. We have a new island and a new life here." He proffered his hand to her.

She looked at it, took a deep breath, then spun and headed to the rail.

Marcos, Alexandre, and I exchanged looks. They were relieved, and so was I, though I'm sure my expression barely reflected that.

Once all the women were on the Rogue Jet, Dayreis climbed over the rail, saying, "Don't stop me, Charles."

I reached out and took his hand. "Thank you. For everything. For trusting my brother and me on that first day. You didn't have to do that."

"I did. You people can't cook. And besides, we're still alive." He winked. "May God bless you and your family."

"And you, too."

He settled down into the boat, and Alexandre instructed him in starting the engine while Marcos untied the lines and the Rogue Jet began to drift back on the current.

Although I shouldn't have, I found myself looking to Jane, as though she'd offer a final look of forgiveness, an "it's okay" in her eyes. I was a fool for expecting that, selfish even, and she would not meet my gaze.

Vanessa shifted up beside me and threw her arm over my shoulders. "It's okay, Charles."

"I wish it were."

"I love you."

I didn't answer. The engine revved to life, and with a hiss the Rogue Jet turned and roared away from us. Jane and the rest of her group stared at me night after night, the wind rushing through their hair, the sea rising up in a pair of great tidal waves to crash down and splinter their tiny craft as they flailed and tread water for a few moments and begged for me to rescue them, but I was too busy on the deck, shooting Tremaine and killing Lefort's people and telling my daughter that people needed to die so that we might live and why didn't she understand that? She knew what it felt like. James knew. Vanessa understood.

And then the sea grew calm, and I looked down over the rail and saw the submerged faces of my father and brother, nodding their assent from the murk. *Good boy. You're a Boy Scout. A Marine! Finally, the pansy has come home.* I shook my head and turned away as Vacher began issuing his orders, and we snapped into action, bending on and hoisting sails as the Rogue Jet seemed to submerge into the distance.

For the next few hours, I diverted my attention away from the suffocating guilt and worked to become one with the ketch. There was great beauty in her lines and rigging. She would keep us alive, so I wanted to know everything I could about her and become an expert sailor. We soon learned that she, like the sea itself, was full of surprises. She offered up a favorable one when

Vacher found the operating manual for a desalinator unit. He told me that the ketch had to be equipped with this freshwater maker, but he wasn't sure where it had been installed.

The hunt began for any and all deck access hatches and ended in little Trina's hiding place under the cockpit deck, where we found the bulkhead-mounted desalinator and two large freshwater tanks. According to the manual, the unit yielded sixty-liters per hour and operated on 24V-DC.

"You know what this means, Charles? We'll be turning the wind into drinking water," Vacher said, the news powerful enough to dust off the old man's smile.

I returned the grin. "Do you want to tell them?"

"No. That's your job."

"Okay. We really needed some good news, huh?"

"Yes, we did—because the chef's gone, and that's about as depressing as it gets."

I gave a little snort, then headed down into the berthing area to tell some of the others.

WE celebrated our discovery at dinnertime by opening one of only two bottles of wine we had left, and everyone, including Trina, had a small glass. I made a toast. "To living."

Afterward, I slipped off alone to the aft deck. The shadows grew long as I stood there, a bedraggled savage beneath the fiery sky. I closed my eyes and listened to the sea, praying for a whisper of forgiveness.